Irresponsible Puckboy

Also by Eden Finley and Saxon James

Puckboys

Egotistical Puckboy
Irresponsible Puckboy
Shameless Puckboy
Foolish Puckboy
Clueless Puckboy
Bromantic Puckboy
Forbidden Puckboy
Possessive Puckboy
Stubborn Puckboy

IRRESPONSIBLE PUCKBOY

EDEN FINLEY & SAXON JAMES

First published in the United Kingdom in 2022 by Eden Finley and Saxon James

This edition published in the United Kingdom in 2026 by

Canelo, an imprint of
Canelo Digital Publishing Limited,
20 Vauxhall Bridge Road,
London SW1V 2SA
United Kingdom

A Penguin Random House Company
The authorised representative in the EEA is Dorling Kindersley Verlag GmbH.
Arnulfstr. 124, 80636 Munich, Germany

Copyright © Eden Finley and Saxon James 2022

The moral right of Eden Finley and Saxon James to be identified as the creator of this work has been asserted in accordance with the Copyright, Designs and Patents Act, 1988.
All rights reserved. No part of this publication may be reproduced or transmitted in any form or by any means, electronic or mechanical, including photocopy, recording, or any information storage and retrieval system, without permission in writing from the publisher.
No part of this book may be used or reproduced in any manner for the purpose of training artificial intelligence technologies or systems. In accordance with Article 4(3) of the DSM Directive 2019/790, Canelo expressly reserves this work from the text and data mining exception.

A CIP catalogue record for this book is available from the British Library.

ISBN 9 781 83598 486 4

This book is a work of fiction. Names, characters, businesses, organizations, places and events are either the product of the author's imagination or are used fictitiously. Any resemblance to actual persons, living or dead, events or locales is entirely coincidental.

Printed and bound in Great Britain by Clays Ltd, Elcograf S.p.A.

Look for more great books at
www.canelo.co | www.dk.com

This series is about the PR Nightmares of the NHL. These characters are flawed on purpose. Please don't expect perfection because it does not exist here. They're hockey players. The only guarantee is missing teeth.

The use of the NHL and any of its teams is a work of fiction. It in no way reflects the policies or opinions of the actual organization.

Names, characters, businesses, places, events, and incidents are either the products of the authors' imaginations or used in a fictitious manner. Any resemblance to actual persons, living or dead, or actual events is purely coincidental.

CHAPTER ONE

DEX

I'm an eternally happy person.

It's my thing.

Everyone has a thing. My best friend, Tripp, he's the sweet one off the ice but has a razor edge when he's being the best goaltender in the NHL.

I'm the one with bricks for brains who's always smiling.

Well, I'm not smiling today.

Losing the Stanley Cup to Boston last night stung like a bitch, especially when it was followed up by yet another fight with my girlfriend, but then instead of drowning my sorrows with my best friend, he ditched me for half the night. I spent most of it drinking with the team before they headed home and I holed up in an all-night diner and ate my weight in pie.

My gut is hating me for it, but not as much as my head is hating me for all that whiskey I consumed.

All I want is to go to bed and sleep it off, but she will be there. She's always there. I don't even remember when she moved in. Tripp came over one day and asked if Jessica lived with me. When I said no, he pointed out she'd redecorated and all her stuff was there. I'd never lived with someone before, but it didn't take long for me to realize the worst part of sharing your space with someone. When you fight, you can't get away. Hence the all-nighter of whiskey and pie.

Hmm. Sounds like a country song.

She called me *irresponsible*. Again. I want to be offended, but then the waitress asks if I want another slice of pie, and my stomach lets me know it regrets all of my life choices up to this point.

The thing is, I *can* be responsible. Sometimes. When it's important. I just don't see why people choose maturity when the alternative is having fun. She resents my away games, my celebrating and commiserating with the team, and my friendship with Tripp.

Jessica wants to be my whole world, and yeah, I want a relationship, a person I can spend my life with, but that can't be all I have. I need hockey, my mom, my baby sister I adore, and then there's Tripp. Tripp's my bro, and he owns a good chunk of me.

Other women have tried to come between us, and it's never worked. Without him around, everything is ... claustrophobic. Suffocating.

She doesn't understand.

Jessica mentioned a ring. *Again*. When I told her I wasn't ready for that, she got pissed, and then when I said I was going to go out with the team, that was unreasonable. She said she was leaving and to call her when I grow up, but she's threatened to leave countless times, and I don't know what to do anymore.

Would she be more forgiving of me staying out all night if we got married? I doubt it. If anything, my teammates' marriages have shown getting hitched weighs you down even more. I don't want to stand at the other end of an aisle and promise forever when everyone knows forever doesn't mean shit these days. Not for normal people, let alone NHL players.

Marriage isn't something I want, and as much as I want to blame hockey for that, I was anti-marriage even before making it into the NHL.

After my parents' divorce, Dad took off, and Phoebe and I didn't have much to do with him anymore. Mom was distraught, and we had to pick up the pieces. But then she became a serial bride, and every breakup was worse than the last. Lawyers, alimony, fighting …

Phoebe and I love our mother, but she's a disaster when it comes to love. Growing up and seeing what divorce does, both my sister and I vowed we'd never put ourselves through that.

I don't understand why it's so important to Jessica. Bragging rights? My money?

We already live together, so how would a piece of paper change anything?

Maybe I should do it and get it over with. It's important to her, but it's not to me. But then the thought of being married sends a shiver through me. How could I commit when I'm not even sure I could say "I do" without running from the church or setting myself on fire to get out of it?

I need advice, and there's only one person I trust to have my best interests at heart. I'm sure he won't mind me interrupting his hookup now. I've given them all damn night.

I leave the diner and take a car to Tripp's penthouse apartment just off the Strip.

He'll still be in bed since it's officially off-season, and it's where I'd be if not for the shitshow of a night, so I let myself in with my key.

Tripp's apartment overlooks the Wynn golf course, where we'll be spending a lot of time together this summer, and the whole living area is flooded with morning sunlight. His bedroom door is closed, so before I go barging through it, I knock loudly and shout, "Cover up, I'm coming in."

I give them a minute, then push inside.

Apparently, I wasn't loud enough, because Tripp is still fast asleep, and his hookup is staring at the door through weary eyes.

"Move over," I tell him before crawling along the middle of the bed and flopping down between them.

Tripp barely stirs, so I lean right into his face, then shout his name.

His hazel eyes fly wide as he shoots upright. "What the fuck, Dex?"

I crack up laughing even as Tripp stares at me in shock. Then his gaze slides across to the other guy.

"Fucking hell." He turns to face-plant into his pillow. All I can see is the top of his messy red hair.

"Ah, should I go?" the guy asks.

"Actually, maybe you could help." It doesn't look like Tripp is planning to resurface anytime soon, so I settle back into the pillows and tuck my hands behind my head. "I think my girlfriend broke up with me."

The guy's gaze flicks over my head toward Tripp, looking like he isn't sure what to do.

"It's fine," I tell him. "Dex Mitchale, Tripp's bestie. This is nothing I haven't seen before."

"Okay …" He adjusts the sheets around his waist and gets comfortable again. "Austin."

"You were our server last night, right?"

"Yup. So, this girlfriend. Why do you only *think* she broke up with you? Isn't that kind of thing obvious?"

"She said to call her when I grow up or whatever. So does that mean it's over for now? Or we're still together and she wants me to fix my shit before she comes back?"

He cringes. "That sounds like a breakup."

"Damn." I rub my hand over my face, thinking. "She said I was irresponsible, so if I fixed that, do you think she'd come back?"

"Why are you irresponsible?"

"How am I supposed to know?"

Tripp snorts behind me.

I turn my head to grin at him, but his face is still firmly buried. "Feel free to contribute to this conversation."

Nothing. Fine. Back to Austin, then.

Austin is staring at the window. "Look, talking emotions isn't something I thought I'd be doing the day after a hookup, so I'm a bit rusty on advice, but if you have to change for someone, it's probably not worth it."

"I think she wants to get married."

"Is that something *you* want?" he asks.

"Umm ... yes? Well, no, not really, but I could want it. If it made her stop acting like a ..." I cut my words off. My momma taught me to only speak nicely of women, and if I can't say nothing nice, I shouldn't talk at all.

Tripp starts to chuckle behind me and finally reappears. "There is no way you're marrying her when you can't even give a straight answer."

"You're alive!" I cheer.

He gives me a dry look, and I glance back at Austin.

"He loves me. I swear he does."

"I'd love you more if you didn't wake me at the butt crack of dawn to talk about ... *her*."

"You two need to start getting along if you're going to be my best man, Trippy," I say.

"I guess I won't be your best man, then."

I gasp. "You'd let me go through that alone?"

"If you're desperate enough to force yourself to get married when you've never wanted that, then yeah. You can go through it alone."

"You're breaking my heart here."

Tripp lets out a disbelieving noise. "Go home and let us sleep, Dex."

I yawn. "That's a good idea. I'm beat. Let's all sleep and talk about this when we wake up."

Austin doesn't look ready to sleep. "Actually, as fun as this is, I'm going to head out."

"You don't have to," Tripp hurries to say.

"*Sure*," I say, trying not to be offended. "He can stay, but you're ready to kick me out. I'm feeling very unloved this morning."

Tripp's jaw tightens. "Well, I'd like my dick sucked, so if you're planning to do that, by all means, stay."

My eyebrows shoot up.

"Yeah. That's what I thought."

"You two are cute," Austin says, which dissolves my shock as I glow under the praise.

We *are* cute.

Everyone says so.

Tripp and Dex.

Dex and Tripp.

The Mitchell Brothers.

Not that we're brothers. We're closer than that.

"Thanks for last night," Austin says, his voice taking on a husky quality.

"I think I should be thanking you."

I look from one to the other. I'm no stranger to Tripp's hookups, but the way they're looking at each other, like they've got a shared secret—that I guess involves the other's dick—makes me squirm.

Then Austin leans over me and gives Tripp a soft, way-too-slow-to-be-comfortable-for-me kiss, and my eyes narrow.

"Bye." He climbs out of bed, dresses, and leaves.

I'm still staring after him when I say, "He was hot. At least, objectively. Though, he's prettier than a lot of the guys you've been with. Going to call him again?"

When Tripp doesn't answer, I turn my attention to him and find him wearing the odd look he gives me sometimes that I can never figure out.

"You're unbelievable," he says.

"Thank you."

Tripp sighs and gets comfortable again. "You okay?"

"I dunno."

"Go to sleep." His eyes drift closed. "We'll talk later."

"Tripp?"

"Yeah?"

"Can you hold me?" I wriggle closer to him.

"Fuck's sake, I'm naked under here."

"And? It's nothing I haven't seen before. Besides, the blanket is between us, so it's not like it's gay."

"Right. Because being gay would be terrible."

"You know that's not what I mean. It's just platonic snuggles."

Finally, the tension starts to leave him. "Yeah, I know."

When he finally pulls me to him, his arms are warm and comfortable. More dudes really should do this. People joke about us having a bromance all the time, but it's the best way to describe us. I love him. More than Jessica.

Tripp's my ride or die.
No one can come between a friendship like ours.
"Hey, Tripp?"
He acknowledges me with a sleepy grunt.
"It smells like sex in here."

CHAPTER TWO

TRIPP

Waking up wrapped around my best friend isn't a new experience, but for a while now, it's been a painful one. Because as much as I like having Dex around and appreciate that he's not one of those straight guys who automatically think affection from a gay man means they're in love with them, in this case, it's actually true.

Oops.

I don't know when I fell in love with Dex Mitchale, only that I have. And I'm a fucking dumbass for it.

Because while he's talking about marriage to someone who doesn't appreciate him, I'm trying my best to hide my feelings for him. I've been trying for a long time. So long, in fact, that I think I have pretty much accepted the inevitable.

I will be in love with my best friend until the day I die.

My friends tell me I need to get over it, and even though they're right, I've decided to take a new approach: pretend my feelings don't exist.

I've never seen a therapist in my life, but I'm sure they'd tell me I'm making a wise and healthy decision.

I've been trying to put space between us, to try to get over him that way, but I haven't come right out and said I need it. Dex is a sensitive soul. It's one of the first things that ever drew me to him as a friend, but as time has gone on, that need to protect him has only grown. I want to protect his heart, even if it's at the detriment of my own.

If I told Dex I needed time apart, he would think he did something wrong and then spend the next month doing sweet things to make up for it, which would only make me fall for him more.

Telling him I'm in love with him is out of the question, because then he really will give me space, but not the kind I need. He'd apologize profusely about unknowingly hurting me, and then the space and the guilt over asking for it would eat at me. We'd both grow resentful, and it would ruin everything we have.

Wah, wah, wah, tragic gay boy stereotype in love with his straight best friend. I don't want to live without him, but seeing him every day makes it harder and harder to keep my shit under control.

Which is how I've ended up here. Again. Instead of having phenomenal sex with one of our servers at the Stanley Cup celebrations—or commiserations in our case—I'm in bed with Dex.

His dark blond hair tickles my nose and smells like the soap in the locker room with a hint of sweat. I'd rather the scent of his cedar-and-spice shampoo, but this is still good. Hockey arena and sweat. My happy place.

I breathe him in and then realize sniffing the top of my best friend's head is crossing boundaries into creepy territory, so I slip out of bed, throw on some sweats, and head out to my kitchen to make a hangover cure of bacon, eggs, and hash browns.

It's past lunchtime, but I don't care. I need protein, carbs, and salt. It doesn't take long for the smell of cooking pig fat to wake the predictably always hungry Dex.

"Is this a commiseration breakfast or a hungover one?"

"Can't it be both?"

Dex takes a seat on a stool in my kitchen and lowers his head to the marble counter. "I can't believe we lost last night."

As a goalie, it's really hard for me not to take the blame for a loss. It's a team sport, and I know it's not my fault, but I'm the one who let those goals in last night.

"I can't believe I let Anton score in the last two minutes," I say. "We could've gone into overtime and won it."

Dex leans in and whispers, "Don't tell the rest of the team, but I'm kinda happy for Anton and Ezra."

"Of course you are." And I am too. Dex and I won the Stanley Cup three years ago, and even though the competitive side of me is crushed, I can't deny I'm happy for Ezra's first-ever win. I'd still prefer it to be me, but hey, if I had to lose to someone, I'm glad it was to a team that has queer players.

Anton and Ezra are the first-ever couple to take home the Cup.

There's only a handful of us out in the league, so we have our own clique outside of our teams. It's good to have people to talk to who understand what it's like to be a hockey player with all the extra crap we have to deal with as out athletes.

Dex has been there for a lot of the stuff I went through—like derogatory remarks, the media focusing more on my sexuality than playing—but he still doesn't understand. Not completely.

The only ones who do are the guys in the Collective. It's why we stick together.

I plate up the food and slide Dex's share over to him with a coffee and then put mine next to it while I round the counter and take the seat beside him.

He digs right in, but I'm slower in my approach. I watch him for any signs of the melancholy he wore this morning when he climbed into my bed and kicked out … I want to say Boston? Austin? The guy I hooked up with last night. He was very pretty and not very bright. He was exactly what I needed to get a break from pining after Dex, but here I am, a few hours later, in a place I desperately want to belong but know I never will. Because being next to Dex will always come with that dreaded *P* word: platonically.

"Are we going to talk about why you needed cuddles this morning?" I ask and sip my coffee.

"I was kinda hoping we wouldn't have to."

"You know you don't have to do anything when it comes to me, but if you want to talk, I'm here." *Even if I hate your girlfriend and think you could do way better.*

It probably wouldn't get to me so much if Dex was with someone worthy of him, but then again, I doubt anyone would meet that criteria. Jessica loves the lifestyle of being a WAG, but she doesn't actually care about hockey. Some of the other guys' girlfriends and wives are at every game, cheering their men on. Jessica sees it as a socialite hour where she can be in the spotlight because of who she's dating.

I don't want to make her out to be some sort of gold-digging villain, and I've taken it upon myself to tell myself something positive about her every single day to try to change my point of view of her, but it's hard when she acts the way she does. My usual go-to is "She makes Dex happy." Sitting next to him right now, he doesn't look happy.

He's had a few not-so-serious girlfriends in the last three years, and while I hated them all, in the sense they got to have Dex and I didn't, they were genuinely nice women, and they treated Dex right. I have no clue why he's gotten serious with this one, who is all about the drama and attention. Maybe Dex was bored with the *nice* girls.

"I know you don't like her," Dex says. "And maybe I shouldn't have come here this morning to complain about her, but ... I had nowhere else to go."

"You could have gone to Phoebe," I point out.

"Fine, anywhere else I *wanted* to go." He pouts. "Last time I told my sister something about my love life, she ran to Sienna, who told you anyway."

When Dex and I first started hanging out after I joined the team here in Vegas, we made the mistake of introducing our sisters. Now they're the best of friends, just like us. They're also our biggest supporters, and I don't point out that maybe he didn't want to run to his sister because Phoebe feels the exact same way I do about Jessica.

"Well, if you don't want to talk about it, do you want to go play golf?"

"Yes, please. Anything to not think about the breakup. Or not breakup? Do you think we're broken up?"

"Have you been home at all? Was her stuff still there?"

Dex glances away. "I didn't want to go home. If she was there, we'd fight more. If she wasn't ..."

"You would've had your answer. Why don't you message her and ask?"

He takes out his phone and stares at the screen.

I place my hand on his shoulder. "You're scared of what she'll say, aren't you?"

"Yes, but ... is it because I want the answer to be yes or no?"

I want to yell at him to wake up and realize how toxic his relationship is, but I can't. Not again, at least. Dex knows how I feel about her.

"Send her a message," I say.

"Okay." He breathes in deep and taps away, pauses, then closes his eyes as he hits Send.

"Good boy. Now, while you wait for her to respond, let's go play some golf."

—

On our way across the road to Wynn Golf Club, Dex stops suddenly and stares at a random sign above him.

"Why'd you stop?"

He points upward. "Wedding chapel."

Wow, he is not letting this go today. Sure, over the past six months, he's talked about marrying Jessica, but more in the sense that he doesn't know how to avoid it. I guess ultimatums must really work if he's finally seriously considering making the dumbest decision of his life.

"What about it?" I ask, staring at the sign with him.

He grabs my hand and pulls me in the direction of the chapel instead of toward the golf club.

"You're not going to call her to come meet you right now, are you?"

Dex Mitchale, officially off the market? This poor gay man needs some warning to deal with that kind of disappointment.

"No. I just want to see it."

"We live in Vegas. You've seen a million of them."

"Yeah, but I've never been in one."

"Sober, anyway," I add. "Remember when Porter married that chick he met while we were a week deep into our Stanley Cup win celebrations?"

"Nope."

"Exactly."

Dex stops on the sidewalk, like he's even too scared to stand in the parking lot. "It doesn't look too intimidating from out here."

"You sure about that? What if I dared you to go inside?"

"You wouldn't do that to me."

"Wouldn't I? Isn't a big step toward getting over your fear, facing it?"

He purses his lips. "Maybe we *should* go inside and check it out."

"What?" I expected him to turn and walk the other way. "*Why*?"

"Because if Jessica wants to get married, I should see if I can walk in there without breaking out in hives."

"Again, you've been to weddings before," I point out. "Even if you don't remember Porter's wedding, you've been to all the other guys'."

"But I went to those with the mindset of open bar and an excuse to get hammered. I've never sat at any of their weddings and thought, hmm, I can see me doing this one day."

"That's because you've never wanted to get married." I somehow keep my voice patient.

"Well, maybe it's time I change that view."

"Just for her?"

15

Dex slumps. "Even if she does text back and tells me it's over, don't you think the next one will be the same? I might not want to tie the knot, but I don't want to be alone forever. Women want to get married. End of story."

"Lucky I'm gay, then."

Dex's brown eyes narrow, and I roll mine.

"Not all women want to get married. Phoebe doesn't." *For the exact same reason you don't.* I hold off pointing that out.

"Yes, but I don't want to be with my sister. Thanks. I might be fucked-up when it comes to this marriage stuff, but I'm not *that* fucked-up."

"Good to know."

He grabs the hem of my sleeve. "Let's go in there and look around."

"Fine," I relent and trail after him, because I know there's no way this will make him change his mind about marriage. If anything, a seedy wedding chapel will only cement the tackiness of the whole stupid ritual.

Dex isn't the only one who's anti-marriage. I never plan to take that leap myself. I doubt anyone would ever be happy marrying someone who's in love with someone else. But even before all the stupid feelings that are unrequited and *stupid*, I'm one of those gay guys who didn't fight for marriage equality. The way I see it, hetero couples are screwing it up on their own. They didn't need to bring us into it.

I mean, of course it's great that those of us who *do* want to get married are now able to, but it's never been for me.

Dex continues to drag me until we get to a reception area, but before we can speak, the woman behind the desk smiles. "Here for the Johnson-Pike wedding?"

I say, "No," at the same time Dex says, "Yes."

Her gaze darts between us with her brow furrowed. "It's, uh, just through those doors." She points.

"Thank you so much." Dex heads straight for them.

I glance between him and the woman and then swear under my breath as I scramble after him. "I thought we were checking the place out, not crashing a wedding."

"We'll sneak in the back," he reassures me. "It'll be fine."

It's not fine. The receptionist neglected to tell us the wedding is already underway, and when we open the doors, the ten or so people inside turn and stare at us. Including the two standing at the altar. The man is in a camo-patterned suit, and the woman is in a tight, white dress that barely covers her ass. Her veil is longer, reaching the floor.

The room is small and decorated with tacky fake flowers and zigzag-patterned carpet that no doubt hides vomit stains from wasted brides and grooms.

I can't believe I'm giving up a game of golf for this.

"Carry on." Dex waves everyone off.

"Tripp and Dex Mitchell?" the groom says.

The back of my neck heats.

"Surprise," Dex declares. "Your wonderful soon-to-be wife invited us knowing you're a huge fan."

I hang my head in my hand.

"This is so cool!" the groom says.

When I glance up, the bride's mouth is hanging open.

"Umm, sure," she says. "I didn't say anything because I didn't know if they could make it."

"The game last night was brutally close," the groom says.

"We're just going to sit down now and be quiet. Pretend we're not here. We shouldn't be stealing thunder from the happy couple. Right, Dex?"

"Right." He leans in closer. "Is that a thing?"

"Yes, it's a thing." I push him to the empty bench seat at the back and slide in after him.

The whole time we sit there watching these random people get married, I try to imagine Dex and Jessica up there, but I can't see it. Then again, I can't imagine Dex and me up there either.

Dex isn't the marrying kind. End of story. It's no secret his parents' divorce was messy and every divorce his mom went through after that. It's obvious both he and Phoebe were affected by it. They're not against commitment, just promising to love and obey until they die.

Beside me, Dex's knee bounces.

Yeah, he's definitely not the marrying kind.

When the bride and groom are told they can kiss, their guests break out into applause, but Dex turns to me.

"I have an idea."

"Uh-oh."

I don't know what I'm expecting him to say—that we blow off golf and party with these lovely white trashy people, that he's realized he could never marry Jessica; hell, it could even be that he's quitting hockey to become a minister, for all I know—but what does come out of his mouth is so out of left field, I can't be sure I hear it correctly.

"We should get married."

CHAPTER THREE

DEX

Tripp doesn't immediately respond, and I worry I've broken him. He's just ... staring. A lot. I wriggle my fingers in front of his face.

"Did you hear me?"

"Did I?" He finally unfreezes and rubs his jaw. "I thought I heard something about marriage, but that can't be right."

I lower my voice so we don't interrupt the people up front. "Come on, it's the perfect idea."

"*Perfect?*"

"Yes. Remember how pathetic I was at scoring from the left side of the net? How did I get over that? We *practiced*. This will be just like that."

His whole face contorts. "This is ... nothing like that."

I try my best for the puppy dog eyes that have never failed me before. He immediately covers them.

"Nuh-uh. Not the face."

"What face?"

"You *know* what face." Slowly, he removes his hand, revealing his expression that I *think* is supposed to be exasperated but doesn't hide his urge to smile. "Dex, are you following what's happening here?"

19

"Yes." Dumbass Dexter might be an accurate nickname from the media that I don't let get to me, but while I might be a bit clueless, I *can* follow a perfectly reasonable conversation. "I'm asking you to help me like you did then."

"*No.* You're asking me to marry you."

"*Pretend* to marry me."

"You do know that weddings in Las Vegas are legal, right?"

I brush his concern away. "We'll get up there and do the big fancy thing, confess our undying love for each other, and then walk away. If we don't take the paperwork and file it at the county clerk's office, then we're not actually married."

Tripp's face pulls into a frown. "That's true ..."

"And it's not like it will be hard to fake it. I mean, if those two"—I gesture to where they're signing their paperwork—"can convince people they mean forever, we'll have no issues."

We both look toward the front. The couple is borderline trashy, sure, but *aww*, they're so in love. He's looking at her like she's a cinnamon roll, and ... it makes me sorta uncomfortable. I've never been looked at like that.

Which is fine, because not all relationships can be the same, but it would be nice for someone to see me in that way. That, despite my faults and my habit of saying dumb shit without thinking it through, someone could love me so strongly it's obvious to everyone around us just by the way they look at me.

I lean toward Tripp. "Think we can sneak out without them noticing?"

"I wish. But you got us into this mess, and I'm not disappointing this guy on his wedding day."

"Aw, you're such a softie. Photos, then bail?" I turn to him only to find him already watching me. He looks especially freckly today, which might have to do with the lighting in here. It makes his pale skin stand out against the reddish-brown flecks.

"Sounds good."

"And *then* wedding later?" I grin angelically, and Tripp starts to laugh.

"Fine. Yes. You can have your *fake wedding*. I swear you're like a dog with a bone."

I slump into the seat. "I don't want to be alone forever, and if that means tying my life to someone else's, I'm going to need to find a way to do it."

Tripp's quiet for a moment, and it's just as the couple up front are done signing and officially pronounced married that he nudges my side. "You'll always have me. I don't even need the piece of paper."

That makes me warm inside. "What about a ring?"

"The only ring I need is the one that says Stanley Cup Champions on it."

"A-fucking-men."

Tripp and I stick around for some photos and to sign the groom's shirt and the bride's wedding dress. Then we make excuses to leave.

We've barely hit the foyer before I make a beeline for the woman behind the desk.

"Umm, hey. Can we get married?"

"Of course. Did you have a particular date in mind?"

"Yeah. Today."

She turns from her computer to fix me with a look. "We're an *official* wedding venue, sir. We don't do ... those kinds."

Tripp snickers from behind me. The wedding we witnessed says otherwise, but okay, lady. If you want to tell me that shitshow in there was actually planned, I'll believe you.

"Can you point me in the direction of a place that does? I wanna lock this sexy beast up."

She eyes me, then pulls a business card out of her top drawer. "This chapel offers same-day ceremonies. Congratulations on your upcoming nuptials."

I take the card. "Yeah, thanks."

We leave before she can judge us any harder.

"Dex, maybe we should—"

I hold up my finger while I dial the number on the card.

"Tiny chapel, big dreams," comes the chipper voice.

"Ah, yeah, hey. I want to get married."

She giggles. "This is the place to do it."

"Awesome. And we can come in today, yeah?"

"Of course. We're a little busy at the moment and will pick up again tonight, but usually late afternoon is when there isn't much of a wait." She goes over some more details—what we need to bring in terms of ID, the marriage license we need to get from the official marriage license place first—and then we set a time for four o'clock.

"Perfect, see you then!"

I hang up, feeling really good about this plan. If it's that straightforward and easy, it's clearly meant to be.

Tripp sighs. "I guess we're doing this."

"Come on, you have to admit it'll be a fun story."

"Except we're not going to tell a single person about this."

"What?" I pretend to be shocked. "Should I be offended that it's this hard to get you to marry me and you're obviously embarrassed by it?"

"No, you should be flattered that I'm agreeing. This will be the one and only wedding I'll ever have."

"Naw." I bump his jaw with my knuckles. "And you'll always be my first."

"Right." He shifts, suddenly uncomfortable. The change in expression makes me frown, but I try not to draw attention to it. Tripp has always been there for whatever harebrained idea I come up with, and I'm the same for him. No hesitation, no questions asked. But over the last couple of months, I've been picking up on *something*. I don't even know what. Tripp is the same as he's ever been, but there's a pushback coming from him lately, and I don't even know if he's aware he's doing it. I could be reading into things too much, and maybe I'm feeling sore about yet another girlfriend pointing out I'm not the type to stick around for, but I know Tripp. He jumps in with both feet.

Recently, it's been more like a controlled fall.

He comes with me to get the marriage license, but even after that process, there are still a few hours until we can go in.

I clap, hit with an idea. "If this is going to help me get over my fear, we need to go all out. Get into the theme. How about we go and get ready and then meet there at four?"

"Sure, Dex."

"Don't leave me standing at the altar," I warn as he starts to walk away.

"Wouldn't dream of it."

"Love you, bye!" I say, like always.

"Yeah, you too."

—

When it's ten minutes past our meeting time and Tripp still hasn't shown, I'm worried he's going to leave me hanging. I'm anxious enough just being here with the thought that I'm about to promise myself to someone for life—real or not—that every passing minute stretches out forever. I shoot the girl behind the desk *another* reassuring smile and am about to pull out my phone to text him when he barrels through the door.

"Sorry, I'm here."

I crane my neck to look around the guy standing in front of me. The one who looks suspiciously like my best friend, but there's no way Tripp would be dressed like that.

"Whatcha doing?" he asks.

"Looking for the dude I'm marrying today. He must be around here somewhere."

Tripp bats at my head. "You don't think I look good?"

"I think you look … umm, about as put together as the two people we saw get married earlier today."

He hums. "Just what every man wants to hear on his wedding day."

"What's with the outfit?"

"What? You said to dress in theme."

I gesture to my suit. "Yeah, *wedding* theme."

He doesn't look the slightest bit apologetic. "Exactly. Weddings are stupid, so I dressed the part."

I take in his "I'm with stupid" T-shirt, the water wings, and his kilt.

"In that case, you nailed the brief."

"Don't you wanna know what it all means?" he asks innocently.

"I think you're going to tell me anyway."

"The kilt was as close to a dress as I'll go, even for you, and it's my *family* kilt. Only worn on special occasions. The T-shirt, because, duh. I think this whole wedding idea is stupid."

"And the water wings?"

"I thought you'd never ask." He looks proud of himself. "They're to stop me from drowning in all this commitment."

Okay, that's pretty funny, but I'm not going to let him know that. Not when he already looks so smug. "Thank you so much for being supportive."

"I'm here, aren't I?"

I step closer and wrap my arm around his shoulders. "You always are."

We approach the desk, and then it's like a whirlwind as we sign some shit and I hand over my credit card. Even though this is all fake, I'm starting to sweat in my suit.

I still don't know how getting married would somehow cure me of my irresponsibility, but I guess we're about to find out.

My sister is proof that not all women want marriage, but all the ones I've ever dated do. It's like they think that a ring on their finger is an ironclad contract, when my mother is proof that it's not.

So if I want a woman of my own, I need to suck up all my issues and get over myself.

I've never been more grateful for Tripp. There's no one I'd rather be doing this with.

We walk into the room where the actual ceremony will take place, and the sight of the short aisle makes my head spin. I tug at the collar of my shirt because it suddenly feels too tight.

Tripp's hand finds mine. "You good?"

Am I? "I think so."

"We can still back out."

I clear my throat. "Nope. We're here now. Let's go."

And even though my hand is clammy, he doesn't drop it until we reach the front and things get started.

My knowledge of weddings is that they're long and boring, which comes from sitting through all those enormous weddings my teammates have had. But in what seems like no time at all, the officiant is asking for the rings.

I reach for the pocket inside my jacket and pull out my Stanley Cup ring, just as Tripp holds up his own. He did say it was the only one he'd ever need.

The officiant says something ridiculous and mushy, and then he turns to me.

"Dexter, repeat after me."

I hurry to put my game face on and take Tripp's hand.

"I, Dexter James Mitchale, take you, Tripp Alexander Mitchell …"

"I, Dexter James Mitchale, take you, Tripp Alexander Mitchell …" The words feel so foreign.

"To be my husband, through the good times and bad. Through successes and struggles …"

I swallow hard. "To be my husband, through the good times and bad. Through successes and struggles …" At least that part is true. For us. Whatever we've been through in the past three years, we've been through it together.

"Through richer and poorer, and in sickness and health, I will treasure you for as long as we both shall live."

And as I recite the words, the anxiousness inside me settles. Because everything I'm saying … well, it's technically true. Rich or poor? He's my guy. If he's healthy, we'll cause shit together, and if he's sick, I'll distract him until he's better. I *do* treasure him, because I honestly believe there's no one on earth who gets me like he does.

The idea of choosing one person to spend my whole life with is scary.

But as long as Tripp is always there, I know I can get through anything.

CHAPTER FOUR

TRIPP

When Dex suggested getting married, I didn't know whether to laugh or cry. So instead, I blinked at him like he was crazy.

Because this is crazy.

I didn't think he'd actually go through with it. Yet here we are, exchanging *vows*, and it figures that when I finally get everything that I want, it's one hundred percent fake.

He's doing this to try to convince himself he could get married if he was forced to, and I should've put a stop to it before now.

But there's that part of me that wants this so much, I'm letting myself pretend. If only for a while.

The thing about falling in love with your best friend is that it doesn't happen in an instant. And if someone asked me why I loved him, I'm not sure I could come up with any one answer.

He's fiercely loyal. He cares about people, even if he doesn't know them. His outlook on life might be naive, but fuck, everyone could use some naivety—to see the world through the eyes of someone who only sees the good in people.

From the moment I walked into the Vegas locker room, Dex was my best friend. He was the first to welcome me, the first to offer to hang out, and he's been constantly by my side ever since. Somewhere along the way, my feelings just happened. One day we were on the ice for our warm-up skate before a game, and after I did my usual stretching and talking to my goal bar asking for cooperation, Dex skated up to me and held out his fist for me to bump.

It was our own pregame ritual, just between us. Fist bump, chest bump, hug, then a fake-out high five. In that order. Juvenile maybe, but the crowd who's there early enough for warm-ups love it. It wasn't supposed to become a thing, but it did.

And it was in that moment, doing something we had done together thousands of times, that I realized I was in love with him.

We lost that game in a shutout where I let in seven goals before Coach pulled me off and replaced me with Reeves, our backup goalie, who was a rookie at the time and couldn't stop a bullet to save his life. I lost my game because I knew, without a doubt, I was already in too deep with Dex.

There was no falling out of love with him, and I hated myself for it.

"Tripp?" Dex's brown eyes hold the kind of insecurity they usually do when a reporter asks about goal percentages, and he stands there with his lips parted and an "uhhhh" sound coming out his mouth. I swear some of them ask simply to make him look dumb.

"Right. Sorry. Vows." The urge to run out of here is overwhelming, but I can't do that to Dex. He's too precious, and even though this feels real to me, like I've been transported into an alternate dimension and Dex is somehow in love with me too, none of it is.

We're not even going to file the paperwork.

This is an experiment.

A goof.

It's not real.

But as I say the words "I, Tripp Alexander Mitchell, take you, Dexter James Mitchale, to be my husband, through the good times and bad. Through successes and struggles …" I realize that I mean it all.

This might be fake, but my vows are very real.

And as much as this memory will crush me for years to come, adding layers and layers to the unrequited love suffocating my heart, I can't walk out on him.

We try to exchange rings and then quickly realize we shouldn't swap but wear our own. Dex is taller and leaner than I am, so I can barely get his Stanley Cup ring on my fat finger.

I'm bulked out with enough muscle to fill the net but am still toned and flexible enough to move swiftly and protect the goal. Dex is built for speed.

"I now pronounce you married," our officiant, who's about eighty years old, says. Hey, at least he's not an Elvis impersonator. "You may now kiss your husband."

There's an awkward pause where Dex's gaze ping-pongs between the officiant and me. "Only I would've forgotten about this part."

I lean forward and press my lips to his cheek softly. It's not like we've never done that before.

Hell, one time after Dex scored a goal, he skated all the way down the other end to me and planted a kiss on my cheek while I lifted my helmet to get a drink of water.

This kind of affection is normal for us.

I break my lips from him, but Dex doesn't let me get far. He wraps his arms around my back, and he pulls me against him.

"It's our wedding, boo. You have to do better than that." The next minute, his lips are on mine.

A squeak comes from the back of my throat, but then I lean into it.

If this is the only chance I'll ever get to kiss Dex Mitchale, I'm going to take it.

I expect him to pull away, to keep it short and sweet, but surprising me again, his tongue parts my lips and dives into my mouth. My hands grip his suit jacket as I kiss him back. He kisses me like I'm breakable. It's slow, sweet, consuming.

I hate it.

It's the worst thing he's ever unknowingly done.

Because as we stand at an altar, promising ourselves to each other and sealing it with a kiss, my heart has never experienced such pain.

As soon as our mouths break apart, this will be over, and I will be crushed.

I try to burn the final seconds into my mind, and then with what little self-control I have left, I step back, keeping my head low so he can't see my glassy eyes.

"Are you ... crying?" Dex asks.

Well, fuck. I wipe at my face. "I always cry at weddings."

"Because they're so beautiful?"

"No, because every time a couple gets married, a manwhore fairy dies. We just killed someone, and you don't even care." I finally risk looking at his face, because I know he'll be smiling and not so concerned that my eyes are involuntarily leaking.

"A ... manwhore fairy." His brow furrows. "Umm, what exactly is a manwhore fairy?"

"Whenever you have a random hookup, a gay manwhore fairy gets its wings. It's legend, passed on to all of the baby gays."

The officiant clears his throat. "Congratulations. Uh, I don't mean to rush you out, but we do have a 4:30 ceremony, and you still need to sign the certificate."

We quickly get that out of the way, and then he hands me the piece of paper we're never going to file. I hand it off to Dex, because the last thing I need is a reminder that today happened.

Then Dex holds out his hand. "Ready, husband?"

I link my arm with his. "Ready."

"So," Dex says. "Are you going to take my last name? Or should I take yours?"

I laugh. "We've been over this. My spelling is correct, and yours is an abomination. Why do you think everyone uses my spelling when they call us the Mitchell brothers? You should be so lucky to be Mr. Dex Mitchell."

"No arguments from me."

Dear God.

We exit the small chapel, where another couple is waiting. They do a double take at Dex in his suit, and me in my ... uh, wedding attire. I just act like I'm drunk.

Like I want to be.

It was only a short ceremony, but I'd like to erase the memory with as much alcohol as my body can possibly handle.

—

I wake with a groan. Back-to-back nights of drinking was not a good idea. Neither was getting wasted to try to forget everything about that ceremony. I still remember every detail.

Every word.

Every vow.

And that stupid kiss that took my breath away.

TV shows and movies lie! When you get married in Vegas, you're supposed to wake up with no recollection of how it happened.

Dex is sprawled across my bed, still in his suit. His buttons and tie are undone, showing off his impressive and smooth chest, so at least his inability to even undress on his wedding night is on par with the drunken marriage in Vegas shtick.

Maybe that was our problem. We did this all wrong. We were supposed to get drunk before the ceremony, not after. The wedding is clear as day, but the night is a bit of a blur.

I remember laughing. A lot. And then when we came back to my apartment on unsteady feet, Dex climbed into bed next to me and asked me to spoon him like he always does, and I went with it.

Because I'm used to it now.

I'm used to him asking me for affection without realizing the consequences of his request. And why would he question it? It's not like I've ever told him to stop.

I crave his attention, and I like cuddling with him. Even to the detriment of my own heart.

The guys from the Collective keep telling me to set boundaries, and I know I should, but what can I say? I'm a sucker for punishment, apparently.

Dex isn't the one to blame here—I am.

Dex stirs and stretches sleepily, then turns his head toward me with a wide smile on his face. "Hey, hubby."

I groan again. "Why did we drink so much?"

"It's not a wedding if someone isn't getting shitfaced."

"I don't think it's supposed to be the grooms though," I point out.

"Remember when Noszka married ... what was her name? I dunno. The one he divorced not long later. And he got so wasted that he threw up on her wedding dress?"

"And he wonders why that marriage failed."

"At least we didn't puke on each other."

I close my eyes because I want to go back to sleep. "Mm, marriage goals right there."

"You made breakfast yesterday, so I'm going to run out to bring us back some food, seeing as you'd probably prefer the vomiting to eating anything I can cook."

"Can we please stop talking about vomit?"

"Fine. I'll be back soon." Dex jumps out of bed, and I stay, trying to go back to sleep, but I can't.

Flashes of yesterday keep running through my mind.

Drinking, joking around ... Dex dragging me out to the dance floor in some random bar and declaring whatever song came on next would be our wedding song. Then he facepalmed because it was "Baby Got Back."

Didn't stop him from serenading me with it though.

Considering how much he hated the idea of marriage and weddings, last night was a fuck ton of fun. I shouldn't be surprised though. Everything is with Dex.

And now it's over.

He gets back from picking up some coffee and bagels, and just like last night when he climbed into bed with me, him bringing me breakfast feels too ... domestic. The *honey, I'm home* that he calls out doesn't help.

It's like a real marriage. Minus the sex.

Although, from all the countless jokes there are about marriage meaning sex stops, maybe this is the real deal.

I drag my ass out of bed and sit at my kitchen counter. The coffee disappears down my throat almost as fast as the food, but it doesn't make me feel less hungover and gross.

"Well, I did it," Dex says.

"What, you want me to grovel at your feet for getting me breakfast?"

"I mean I got married. I did it. And it wasn't a big deal."

"Maybe it wasn't a big deal because you knew it wasn't real." Of all the details I do remember from last night, one is hazy. "Fuck, where's the certificate thing we signed?"

"Calm down. It's in my jacket pocket."

"Good. The last thing we'd want is for it to be lost in a random Vegas bar. Could you imagine if someone found it? The media would be all over us."

"Yeah, that wouldn't be a fun PR day." Dex slowly sips his coffee, and I get the sense he wants to say something else.

And I don't know if I'm ready to hear it. But I need to. "You going to call Jessica, then?"

"I … uh …"

Time to put on a brave face. "I know you hate that Jessica and I don't like each other, but if you want to marry her, I'm not going to stand in your way."

Dex slides over his phone. "I'm not going to marry her. She finally replied to my text."

> What do you think, genius? Why do you always need everything spelled out for you?

I grit my teeth. This is what makes me so angry when it comes to her.

"All I asked for was clarification." He sounds so dejected.

I rub his shoulder. "I know."

"Eh, it's better this way anyway. Now I can spend all summer with you and not have to deal with her whining about you being my first priority."

My stomach flip-flops, and I know what I should do—tell him I'm busy. Tell him I need some time away from him for a while. But what kind of asshole would do that to him when his girlfriend has just broken up with him? "Want to come on the Collective vacation to Lake Tahoe?"

His face lights up. "Can I?"

"I mean, I'll have to ask the guys, but I'm sure they'll be okay with it." And they will be. Right after they call me an idiot and mention again how I won't get over Dex if I don't put some distance between us. But I know what I'm doing.

I'm going to get over him by not getting over him.

It's completely logical and makes total sense.

"Who's going on the trip?" Dex asks.

"It's only Ezra, Anton, and Oskar this year. The others couldn't make it, so there's plenty of room."

"Please take me away from all the shitty breakup thoughts. Please, please, please, please, please."

"I'll make a call."

CHAPTER FIVE

DEX

Two weeks with the boys.

This is exactly what I need after a long season that ended in a spectacularly disappointing way. I know Ezra a lot better than Anton and Oskar, but they've always been cool, and with Tripp here, I wouldn't give a shit if they were all strangers. We always manage to have a fun time wherever we are.

We drive down a long dirt driveway surrounded by thick tree coverage, and I'm hanging out the window, breathing in the smell of nature, which isn't something we have a whole lot of in Las Vegas.

After another deep lungful, I drop back into my seat.

"Did you bring a leash for your dog, Tripp?" Ezra snarks from the passenger's seat.

I ignore it. It's not my fault it feels good to have the air on my face.

Tripp's in the middle seat between me and Oskar, and I pat his thigh in my excitement.

"This is going to be great."

The others don't match my enthusiasm.

In fact, ever since I shoved my bag in the trunk, there's been a vibe hanging over the group that I can't put my finger on.

Like now. Tripp and Oskar exchange a weird look, and when I glance up front, Anton is watching me in the rearview mirror. Which wouldn't be an issue if he wasn't meant to be concentrating on, you know, the *road*.

"Ah. Tough crowd," I say, trying to lighten the mood.

Ezra laughs, at least. "We can't all be an overexcitable puppy like you. We're pacing our excitement to last the full two weeks."

"Maybe you need better stamina, big guy."

Tripp snorts, and we trade amused looks. It goes a long way to settle the feelings of not being wanted here. Clearly, I'm being paranoid.

Anton slows as we reach the cabin and pulls into a covered parking bay. The place is huge. All stone and wood. Single story but taking up most of the clearing. In front of the house is a large fire pit area and then a fuckton of water between us and the distant mountains.

Anton whistles. "Welcome to Lake Tahoe."

We climb out and stretch. It was about forty-five minutes from Reno airport to here, but Tripp, Oskar, and I aren't exactly small, and even the back seat of a Jeep Grand Cherokee has its limits.

"Anton and I call the main bedroom," Ezra says, grabbing his bag and slinging it over his shoulder.

"Why do you guys get to claim that?"

"Because, *Plus-One*, we'll need the en suite for quick cleanup."

I scowl at the nickname. I know they're only joking, but I can't shake the feeling I'm intruding. Ezra and Anton are being more or less the same, but Oskar has barely acknowledged me at all. He gives me this long look before turning to Tripp. He has the same sort of piercing blue eyes as Ezra, but where Ezra's eyes always seem like they're laughing, Oskar's feel like they're looking for trouble. His full-body tats add to that impression. His left arm is the only thing bare of ink.

"Come on." Tripp hands me my bag. "Let's go pick our rooms."

The stone-and-wood theme continues inside to a living area with a massive fireplace, a timber kitchen, and hardwood floors.

Anton and Ezra take the first bedroom, Oskar ducks into the second, and I follow Tripp down to the third. He walks inside and does a double take when I follow.

"What are you doing?"

I dump my bag on the bed. "What do you mean?"

"Dude, there are five bedrooms. Get your own."

I blink at him. "We're not sharing?"

Tripp looks like he doesn't know what to say. "Are you kidding?"

"I thought … Ezra and Anton are."

"Yeah, because they're planning on banging all night." He takes my bag and hands it to me. "Dex, I love you, but I'm not going two weeks without jerking off. Find your own room."

I almost, *almost* say we can do that shit together—it's not like we're subtle in our rooms at away games. I mean, we don't talk about it, but that's the rule on the road. You always pretend you don't know when the dude in the bed next to you is rubbing one out. But the sharing a bed thing is probably where it crosses a line.

I act like it's no big deal and take my bag before heading down to the next room, wondering if this is one of those things that should have been obvious.

It hadn't occurred to me that we'd have separate rooms.

It's not a big deal, though, because we won't be spending much time in them anyway.

I get changed into some swim shorts and grab my towel because the lake is calling my name. The others must still be unpacking or whatever, because there's no one else around as I head down to the short dock and jump in.

The water is heaven. I dive deep and swim across the murky bottom, killing time until Tripp comes out to join me. And even though the day has started out with awkwardness, I know it won't take long for everyone to loosen up. There's no way any gross lingering feelings can hang around out here.

I have no idea how long I swim for, but when my skin starts to feel more hot than warm, I grab my towel and head in. Anton's sitting on the huge front deck, wearing swim shorts and a T-shirt, black hair parted as neatly as ever, while he sips a glass of scotch or bourbon or something. Even just hanging out casually, he intimidates me a bit. Where Tripp's *thing* is being the sweet one, and I'm the dumbass one, Anton is the one who has his shit together.

"Good swim?"

"Yeah, it was nice." I nod at his swim trunks. "You going in?"

"Maybe when Ezra gets back. I'm relaxing for the moment. Winning the Stanley Cup *really* takes it out of you."

"Is that how it's going to be for two weeks? Constant ribbing by you and Ezra on how you kicked our asses?"

"When you go away with two of the most egotistical guys in the league, you really should be expecting it."

I grin because he's not wrong about that. Hockey players all have a healthy amount of ego, but Anton and Ezra take it to the next level.

"So where'd he go?"

"For a walk somewhere with Oskar and Tripp."

"Tripp?" I turn to look toward the tree line like he's going to pop out at any moment. "He, umm, he didn't say he was leaving." Huh. Well, I guess we never actually talked about going for a swim first; I just assumed he'd join me.

When Anton doesn't reply, I turn to find him watching me. "Maybe he wanted time with his other friends."

"Nah." I immediately dismiss the idea. "We do everything together."

"You don't do ... *everything* together."

My face heats. "Do you ... are you meaning, like, sex stuff?"

Anton shrugs.

"Well, no. We don't do that. Obviously."

Anton eyes me. "Because you're straight, right?"

"Exactly."

He hums. "Don't you ..."

"What?"

"I don't think it's my place."

"Why? We're all friends. I don't know you as well as the others, but we've got two whole weeks to fix that. You're important to Ezra, Ezra's important to Tripp, and Tripp's important to me. That's six degrees of best friend shit."

He rubs his jaw, which is darkened by a day's growth. "Look, I know you and Tripp are close. And you have a great relationship, but don't you ever think you spend *too* much time with him?"

"Have you met Tripp? There's no such thing as too much time with him." And people think *I'm* dumb.

"Look at it this way. Ezra and I are actually dating. We're partners in crime. We're each other's number one. And yet, I chose to stay here while he went off with his friends. I can be his priority without having to be with him all the time."

"To be fair, everyone needs a break from Ezra now and then. He's exhausting."

Anton rubs at the smirk he's trying to push down. "True. But ... the same goes for everyone, don't you think? It's good to have space sometimes."

"What are you saying?"

"He won't forget you just because you're out of sight for a minute." His tone has taken on a tinge of sympathy I don't like.

"It sounds like you're telling me I need to spend less time with Tripp, and I don't."

"How do you know you won't burn out on each other?"

Is that even possible? "Tripp's the sweetest dude ever. It'd be like you asking if I'd ever burn out on chocolate cake. Or those yellow cocktails with that creamy stuff in them. I know you don't know us well, but we've been inseparable since we met. It's how we like it, and I'd never upset him by saying we need time apart."

Anton takes a small sip of his drink. "You know what, I give up."

"Give up on what? Why do I feel like you're trying to tell me something without actually saying it? If the countless articles digging at my intelligence haven't clued you in, I need to be told things straight up or they go right over my head."

He gives me a look that seems too close to pity to be comfortable. It's like I can hear him thinking, *Poor, dumb*

Dex doesn't get it. "You know what? Forget I said anything. It's a queer thing, so you won't understand even if I did explain it to you."

That feeling of not being wanted starts to creep up, but then … Realization dawns on me. "Oh … *Oh*. Is this like an orgy thing? I didn't know you all … *got together* like that. Tripp never said. Is it like a 'what happens on va-gay-tion stays on va-gay-tion'? Because you guys can totally get your rocks off. I'm good at pretending I know nothing."

Anton stares at me, and I'm not sure if he wants to yell at me or laugh. "I don't share Ezra. Ever. Like I said. Forget we even had this conversation."

I want to try to, but I don't think that's possible now.

If they're all not fucking … why is it weird that I'm here?

CHAPTER SIX

TRIPP

As soon as we pass the entrance to the hiking trail, I get whacked on the back of the head. Twice.

"I knew this hike was a ruse." I rub where Oskar and Ezra both hit me.

We stop where we are, blocking the path for anyone else coming either way, but we're the only ones out here that I've seen.

"Duuude," Oskar says.

I look at Ezra to help.

He just shakes his head. "*Dude*."

I throw up my hands. "Dex and Jessica broke up. What was I supposed to do? Say sorry you're going through a rough time, but I'm going to leave you here alone while I go on vacation with my friends? You know that would hurt him."

"And bringing him here hurts you," Ezra counters.

"You're *in love* with him," Oskar exclaims. "A straight guy."

They're not saying anything I don't already know.

"How are you supposed to get over it if you don't have space from him?" Ezra asks softly.

"I'm working on it. Eventually I'll become desensitized to the way he touches me, the adorable smiles he sends my way, and then it'll be easy to ignore the stupid feelings that have no right to live inside me." I don't know how to be without Dex. I've been trying to put distance between us for months, but it doesn't work, so I need a new tactic.

"Look, we love the guy," Ezra says, and Oskar agrees. "But he's never going to pick up on your feelings for him, and by not saying anything, you're not giving him the chance to choose not to hurt you. If he knew how much his affection gets to you, he'd stop doing it."

"Exactly." I throw up my hands. Then I wouldn't have any part of him.

Ezra drags a hand back through his hair. "You're both great people who will do anything for the other, but watching from the outside, you're pucking disasters."

"*Fucking* disasters," Oskar says. "They're so bad they require actual cursing."

I want to argue, but I really can't. Well, except in one aspect. "Just because you're in a relationship now, Ez, that doesn't mean you know everything."

"Of course it doesn't," he says. "I knew everything *before* Anton fell head over heels in love with me. It's probably why he fell hard and fast."

"Weren't you guys sleeping together for months before he'd even admit he liked you as a friend?" Oskar asks.

Ezra waves him off. "Meh, technicalities. He was in love with me before he knew he was in love with me."

I rub my chin. "Hmm, would he say the same thing?"

"Yup. Just ... don't ask him though or anything. Because ... uh ... he's a very private person?"

Oskar turns to me. "He's lying through his teeth."

"Oh, I got that."

Oskar puts his arm around my shoulders. "Okay, here's how we're going to play it. Ezra, you and Anton run interference by inviting Dex whenever you leave the house."

"What if we plan to fuck in the woods?" Ezra asks.

"Keep it in your pants for once," Oskar says. "This is important."

"Wow. What a great … vacation. Where's the fun in hiking if you don't get orgasms out of it?"

"I think I've been hiking wrong," I mumble.

"When we're in the house, I'll be all over Tripp." Oskar turns to me. "Dex will leave you alone if he thinks you've got a boyfriend, won't he?"

I don't tell him how just last week Dex climbed into bed in between me and a hookup. "That won't work."

"Why not?"

"Because you're you. And I'm me. And you and me …" I shudder.

"Whatever. I'm the hottest man you've ever been with."

"Except I've never been with you, and it's going to stay that way."

"I'm sure there's an insult in there somewhere."

"Not at all. I'm not insinuating you're too much of a manwhore for me, or you no doubt have kinks I don't want to know about. At all."

"I'm not *that* kinky. A thing for public sex isn't kinky. And if you think it is, I feel really sorry for your sex life. Maybe we *should* hook up so I could teach you a few things."

I hang my head. "Are we hiking or what?"

Ezra whines. "It's the off-season. Can't we lie and say we did it?"

"Ooh, wager," I say. "If I beat you guys to the end of this trail and back, we'll play the next two weeks how I want to—by supporting our friend who's going through a breakup. If one of you win, we can do it Oskar's way. By trying to keep Dex away from me. Ready, set, go."

I don't give them a chance to object before I take off running. I'm not above cheating to get my way. I do, however, forget to take into account that it's two against one, and those fuckers will stop at nothing when it comes to winning.

So when we're on the second half of the trail, heading back to where we entered, it shouldn't catch me by surprise when Oskar grabs me from behind and holds me back while Ezra sprints to the end.

"Cheaters!" I yell.

"You never set any ground rules," Oskar says, but he doesn't release me. "Come on, boyfriend. Let's tell your bestie that you're my one true love."

Hmm, how to tell my fake husband that I have a fake boyfriend …

I'm starting to regret going on this trip.

—

After I shower the hike off me, I throw myself down on the couch, and then suddenly I'm being sandwiched in between Oskar and Dex.

"Did you have a good walk?" Dex asks.

Oskar pulls me to his side and wraps his arm around my shoulder. "We sure did."

I close my eyes and pray for an alien spaceship to arrive and get me out of here. I wouldn't even hesitate to jump up and down and yell, "Take me! I don't want to be on Earth anymore!"

Dex frowns at Oskar's arm wrapped around me but doesn't mention it. "Want to go for a swim?"

"We were going to do that later tonight after all you kids are in bed." Oskar waggles his eyebrows. "If you get what I mean."

Dex's frown deepens. "Uh, Tripp? Is there something you want to tell me?"

"Nope." Because I can't lie to him. At least, not about this. I apparently have no problem telling him I'm fine when I'm really, really not, but this is where I draw the line.

"Tripp and I are hooking up," Oskar says.

Dex glances at Anton. "That's what you were trying to tell me earlier?"

Wait, what?

"Uh, nope. This is new information. Startling information," Anton says.

"He's lying." Ezra steps up beside his boyfriend. "We've known all along."

Anton leans in close and whispers, "We have?"

I hang my head in my hand.

"My boyfriend forgets these things easily," Ezra says. "We fuck each other so hard every night that our short-term memory is affected from hitting our frontal lobes against the headboard."

Dex cocks his head. "Why don't you have sex facing the other way?"

"I think we've found where your genius lies—in sexual positions." Ezra nudges Anton. "I think we might need to give that one a try."

"Right now?" Anton squeaks and then glances between us.

"Don't worry," Dex says. "Whatever happens on va-gay-tion, stays on va-gay-tion, remember? We will ignore the porn-like soundtrack if you guys need to fuck it out." Then he turns to us. "That goes for you two as well." He runs a hand through his dark blond hair. "I get why you didn't want to share a room now, but you could've *told me*. Pretend I'm not here. I'll hang out in my room, go for a swim, and catch up with you guys when you aren't having couple time."

And there's the Dex I love. So trusting he doesn't pick out the glaring holes in our story, because he doesn't think for a second that his friends would lie to him. I can tell he's not impressed by me not telling him, but he goes straight into supportive best friend mode anyway.

"Great. We can start now," Oskar says and stands, taking me with him.

"Where are we going?"

"Bed." He drags me to the hall.

Before we're out of earshot, I hear Dex mutter, "Love you, bye," in that confused tone of his.

I go along with it, ignoring my guilt, but as soon as the door is closed to Oskar's room, I shove him away from me.

"Mmm, like it rough, huh?"

"*Oskar.*"

"Yeah, baby, call me by my name."

"While you continue with …" I gesture in his general direction. "That. I'm gonna duck into my room and grab my phone, seeing as you have banished us to this room for at least half an hour. Thanks for that."

"Half an hour? I can go all afternoon."

"I've never wanted to punch you more," I say.

"Oh, I've never tried being punched during sex before, but hey, I'm up for anything. Do it."

"We're not actually having sex in here."

"Yes, we are. Or, at least, we have to make it sound like we are. Hmm, how long is a suitable amount of time for foreplay? Like, if we start banging the bed into the wall now, they'll think I haven't prepped you enough." He rubs his chin as if trying to work out a really difficult math problem.

"Why would you be the one to top me in this scenario?"

He waves me off. "Please. You're a total bottom."

I open my mouth to correct him that I go any which way, but that will only encourage him. I can see him now, yelling out, "Flip fuck! It's like a plot twist for sex," so loud everyone in this damn house could hear him.

It's bad enough when he climbs on the bed and starts jumping up and down while making obscene noises.

I love my friends, I really do, and I might possibly be closest with Oskar out of all the Collective guys because he's only an hour-and-a-half plane ride away. But this is a new development in our friendship ... the urge to murder him.

If he makes it the next two weeks still breathing, I'll be surprised. Relieved I won't have to go to prison but surprised.

"I don't think I want to do this," I tell him.

"You're the one who made the bet."

"I know, but I thought I'd *win*."

"Dex will be fine," Oskar says, still jumping. "We might tease him a lot, but that man is resilient. Besides, look at it this way. By putting space between you two, we're stopping him from hurting you, which we both know he'd want. I like Dex, but you're my boy. If that means that I have to be the asshole here, then so be it."

He offers me a pitying smile. "I'm doing this because I care."

I know he does. I can't be mad at him when he really does think he's doing the right thing. It hurts to be in love with Dex, and if I'm honest, I *do* want to get over it, but not at the expense of separating myself from him. I just want the feelings to magically turn off so we can be best friends. This is why I agreed to the stupid plan. If I can get over these feelings, that's all our problems solved.

"Are you done yet?" I ask.

"Just what every guy wants to hear during sex," Oskar says. He jumps higher, the bed creaking with every move. "Come help me. Bang your head against the wall."

I take it serious time is over. "You're ridiculous."

"It's why you love me."

"I can say with no uncertainty that is not true. It might be your worst trait."

He continues to jump, and the bedsprings protest under his weight. "You're wrong. My worst trait is my penis."

I cock my head at him.

"Which is damn near perfect. Just like the rest of me."

"Careful, you're sounding a hell of a lot like Ezra right now."

Finally, he stops, but then he looks at me like I said the worst thing I could ever say. "Take that back."

"Umm, no."

Oskar springs off the bed and tackles me to the ground. We hit with a hard thud, and I grunt in pain. "Yeah, baby, I'm coming so hard." He yells so loud I think they can hear him in Spain.

Then something presses against my thigh. "What the— are you actually hard?"

"Relax. It's nothing to do with you and everything to do with the thought of them listening to us have sex."

I shove him off me. "Are we done *now*?"

"Wait, we need recovery time. Ooh!" He stands and strips off all his clothes and then wraps a towel around his waist. "Be right back."

"Where are you going?"

He opens the door and says loudly, "I'm thirsty from all that fucking."

His footsteps retreat down the hall but stop abruptly.

"He left as soon as you started making sex noises," Ezra says.

"And you couldn't have come and told us?" Oskar exclaims.

"Nope. It was very entertaining. Over with a bit soon though, don't you think?"

I drop my head back against the floor, tempted to check if there's a flight home to Vegas later tonight.

CHAPTER SEVEN

DEX

When I said for them to do their couple stuff and that I'd hang out in between, I didn't realize how much couple stuff there would be.

Ezra and Anton invite me on a whole bunch of things with them, but every time Oskar and Tripp leave to do something, Oskar makes it very clear he wants Tripp all to himself.

After a few days here, I'm beginning to feel a lot like a fifth wheel, and I'm starting to suspect this is worse than sitting around at home whining over a breakup.

Actually, no, it is worse.

Jessica pissed me off because of the things she said, but I don't miss her. Tripp is literally *right there*, sitting across the table from me, and I miss him more than I ever have.

But he's my best friend. And if my best friend is happy, that means more to me than some sulky feelings I'll get over soon enough.

"What are we doing today?" I ask him, and of course Oskar takes that moment to pop up out of nowhere.

"*We're* going up to that drop-off."

"Can I come?" Maybe I can push Oskar off it?

The leer Oskar gives me makes it clear what he's thinking. "You don't want to see what we'll be doing up there."

He's right about that. I really, really don't. And not because of all the gay sex but because anytime Oskar gives Tripp any amount of affection, it makes me ... on edge. Tripp doesn't look like he enjoys it, and maybe that's because he's never been big on full-blown PDAs or because Oskar is so nonstop about it. Oskar isn't acting all that differently toward me, but every time he touches Tripp, this little voice in my head insists he's staking his claim.

On *my* Tripp.

I cross my arms and slump down in my seat. "You can kiss your ... whatever he is. It's not like I've never seen that before." My words come out sulkier than they should.

"Come on, baby," Oskar says, hauling Tripp to his feet. "Let's go get dressed."

Code for sex. I swear they go at it more than Ezra and Anton.

I leave before they can get started, determined not to let Tripp see my disappointment at having to spend another day without him. It's fair. I get Tripp all the time, and he barely sees Oskar. This is the way it *should* be. It's fine. Normal. Nothing to be upset over.

I flee the house so quickly, I almost run into the other happy couple outside.

"Where are you rushing off to?" Ezra asks.

"If I'd known this place was going to be a fuckfest, I would have at least brought noise-canceling headphones."

Anton goes to say something, but Ezra elbows him and says, "We're taking one of the boats out. Want to come?"

"It depends."

"On?" Ezra asks.

"Can you drown me while we're out there?"

"I'm sure it can be arranged. Just don't struggle, okay? Then I'll feel bad."

"Wow." So desperate to spend time with me, he's considering murder. "If Anton hadn't already said he didn't share, I'd think you two were coming onto me."

Ezra laughs, but Anton's still watching me.

"Are you okay, Dex?"

Oh no. He had to go and ask that, didn't he? I'm fine, totally fine, but the second he hits me with that question, my throat gets thick and my eyes start to get all wet. I try to push it all down and remind myself that I'm *happy* for Tripp. If he's happy, I'm happy. That's how we work.

"Yes," I squeak.

"Well, I'm convinced," Ezra says. "Anton, help me get the life vests?"

I hang my head back on a groan. "No. You two aren't leaving me to go and fuck too. Doesn't anyone want to spend time with me on this trip?"

"We've done nothing but spend time with you," Ezra points out. "Gotta be honest here, Dex, I'm having a whole lot less sex than I thought I'd be."

And I'm spending a lot less time with my best friend than I thought I'd be. As that thought crosses my mind though, I push it away. There I go being selfish again. I wasn't supposed to be here, so I can't expect them to change their vacation plans to fit me into them. But … is it so bad that I want them to?

I cross my arms. "Fine. Go."

"Score." He grabs Anton's hand and tries to drag him toward the house, but Anton stands firm.

"Go and get the life vests."

"Is that a euphemism?" Ezra's face scrunches up because that one is a stretch, even for him.

"Dex is feeling left out."

"Well, he came on a trip with two couples," Ezra throws back, but there's something in his voice that sounds … I dunno, guilty maybe?

"I didn't know," I say. "Tripp didn't tell me he was with Oskar, and I don't understand it. Why did he invite me if he wanted to spend all this time with his … boyfriend? Did he think I wouldn't find out? And are they actually boyfriends or just fucking? Tripp's never mentioned it before."

They exchange another one of their looks, and Anton holds up his hands, taking a step back. "You know what, *I'm* getting the life vests. I can't look at this anymore."

He leaves, and Ezra glares after him.

"Can't look at what? Why's he leaving?"

"Nothing, Dex. Come help me get this death trap ready." He starts walking toward a tiny motorboat, and I stall behind him.

"Ah, Ez? You know I was joking about the drowning thing, right?"

"But who says I was?"

Aaand I'm out. "You guys have fun."

I walk around the property for a while, something I've done a few times this week, debating over whether it would be better to cut this trip short and head home. Phoebe can keep me company away from all these couples, and I won't spoil the vacation for Tripp.

I want to be annoyed that he didn't tell me about Oskar, but Tripp's too sweet to rub in that he's in a relationship just as mine ended. And sure, it's weird that he hooked up with that guy after the Stanley Cup, but Tripp would never cheat, so they've clearly got some kind of arrangement for when they're not together. Or maybe it's new. I don't know, and that's what's killing me. I didn't think Tripp kept secrets from me.

I wish they weren't together.

Almost as soon as I think that, guilt takes over. I should want Tripp to be happy. And if the noises I've been hearing coming from Oskar's bedroom are any indication, Tripp is very happy.

Which is good.

Even if it's not with me.

When I'm sure that the sex should be wrapped up, I make my way back to the house, thinking I might as well take a nap until everyone gets back tonight, but on my way in, I pass Oskar walking out.

"Tripp's, ah, having a post-sex nap. Leave him. He hasn't been getting much sleep lately, if you get what I mean." He winks like somehow the innuendo wasn't clear.

"Right." I walk down the hall to the bedrooms, and right before I reach Tripp's door, I glance back over my shoulder to find Oskar watching me. "I'm going," I say, stalking to my room and slamming the door behind me.

It's almost like Oskar doesn't want me around Tripp, which is so damn stupid because we can *both* make him happy.

That's it. I don't care what they're doing this afternoon, I'll be doing it with them. If they're having sex, I'll … I dunno, cheer from the sidelines or something. We can go for a walk, or a hike, or … anything. I don't want to stop them from spending time together, but Oskar can't stop me from spending time with Tripp as well.

I give it five minutes before I creep back out again, and thankfully, Tripp's watchdog is gone.

I have no idea where he is, so feeling like a ninja, I dart to Tripp's door and duck inside, holding my breath that Oskar isn't in there.

And judging by the lump under Tripp's covers, it's only him.

Finally.

I cross to the bed, lift the covers, and climb in, snuggling into his side.

Tripp shoves me. "Oskar, I said don't touch me."

"Oskar?"

His eyes snap open. "Dex, ah ... yeah. Umm, couple rule. He, umm, overheats and is sweaty, and it's gross sleeping against him. He also farts like crazy."

"Aw ... you save your snuggles for me?" It makes me insanely happy. I wriggle in closer until my face is buried in his chest.

"Oskar isn't going to like this."

"Do we care what Oskar likes?"

Tripp doesn't answer me.

"I've missed you," I complain.

"Sorry."

"And you missed me too, right?"

His chest moves with his soft laugh. "Have you been feeling neglected?"

"Very. All you've done is kiss Oskar and have sex with Oskar. Stupid, dumb Oskar."

He hums. "First, I haven't kissed him in front of you, and secondly, I thought you liked him?"

"I did. Now I'm suddenly having doubts. Murderous doubts."

"Remember how you didn't like me saying things about Jessica?"

"What about it?"

"I think this is our problem," he says.

"What?"

"Look at us. I hated when Jessica would get time with you, and now you hate Oskar having time with me."

"Because we're best friends."

"I don't know any best friends like us."

"And?" I try to burrow deeper into his chest so I don't have to look him in the eye, but Tripp pulls me back.

"I think ... I think we need to start looking at us from the outside. If we're ever going to make our relationships work, maybe we need to"—he takes a breath—"stop being so possessive of each other."

"I'm not possessive!"

"Who do I belong to?"

"Me, but—"

He grins.

"Shut up."

Tripp chuckles. "I know it's hard to believe, but when people start a relationship, they want to be that person's world. Not their whole world, because that's unhealthy, but the most important part. I think Jessica could sense she wasn't that for you, which is why she always got so panicked about you spending time with me."

"And Oskar?"

"Is making sure you're *not* that for me. It's ... time we start ... I start ..." He puffs out a breath. "I think I want a proper relationship, and I can't do that—neither of us can do that—when we're in each other's way."

But he's not in my way. I was with Jessica for eighteen months. Which means ... Is he saying I'm in his way? "I've been giving you guys space. I thought we were having this vacation together, and then I get here and you drop a boyfriend on me. What, because Oskar is here I don't get you at all?"

He sighs. "What am I supposed to say to that?"

"Fine. Oskar is so much better than me. Oskar can be your new best friend." I roll onto my back.

Tripp's smirking face appears hovering over me a second later. "Are you sulking?"

"My best friend doesn't love me anymore. Of course I'm sulking."

"I didn't say that."

"Sure you did. A second ago. And I quote, *Dex, you're a stupidhead who is stupid and I hate you*."

He jostles me. "Call yourself a stupidhead again."

"*I* didn't. That was all you."

"Uh-huh."

"I can't believe you would say that about me."

Tripp flicks my nose, and I slap his hand away. He lifts his hand, and I raise mine, ready to block him.

"Oh, it's on." I tackle Tripp, but he gets me in a headlock and flips me onto my back. We wrestle back and forth, slapping and biting, and the bastard even pulls my hair as he shoves me back into the mattress.

We're gasping around heavy breaths when Tripp pins me. "You really suck at—"

A throat clears, and we both freeze.

Tripp quickly scrambles off me at the sight of Oskar standing in the doorway, and I let out a loud groan and cover my face with my arms.

"Should I be jealous?" he asks.

The bastard could at least have the decency to sound threatened.

"Maybe you should be."

Judging by his laugh, he probably isn't though.

"Come on, *boyfriend*, let's take that hike."

I can't take it anymore.

"No." I sit up and glare at him. "It's *my* turn."

"Dex …" Tripp starts, but I don't want to hear it.

I turn to him. "I get it. He has to be your priority now, but I'm still *a* priority, aren't I? When do I get to have you?"

"You don't, Dex; that's the point." Oskar's voice has a warning edge to it.

"Pretty sure I didn't ask you."

"You don't have to ask me to have an opinion on my friend."

"Don't you mean *boyfriend*?" I raise an eyebrow.

"Does it matter what he is to me?" Oskar crosses his arms. "At the end of the day, I can give him things you can't. And if you care about him as much as you say you do, you should be happy to step aside and let Tripp be happy."

"But he can't be happy without me."

Oskar's eyes widen. "Are you hearing yourself?"

And here it comes, the Dex-is-an-idiot tone. "So sorry *you* don't know what it's like to have a best friend."

"I'm beginning to think you don't either."

Tripp climbs out of bed to pull some shorts on. "Can you both shut up?"

"Nope." I stand firm.

"Come on, Tripp. Dex needs to calm down."

"No, I don't." I climb out of bed too because I don't want to be the only one not standing. I'm tempted to take my shirt off as well so that I'm not the only one fully dressed, but that would probably be weird. I think. Yeah, definitely weird.

"Well, you don't exactly seem calm, do you?" Oskar points out.

"Because you're stealing my best friend."

He shrugs. "Sorry, boyfriend trumps best friend."

"Well, *husband* trumps boyfriend! Ha!" I point my finger in his face to really drive the point home.

Then Tripp curses, and I realize I've just messed up.

Oskar's eyes flash. "What the fuck does *that* mean?"

"It was a joke," Tripp quickly says, right as I reply with, "*Fake* husband. I mean. Obviously."

"What are you talking about?"

"Sorry, Tripp." I rub the back of my neck. "I … I didn't mean …"

Oskar pinches the bridge of his nose. "Please tell me you didn't actually get married."

"The whole wedding was a joke," Tripp says. "It's not even legal."

"You're *married*?" His deep voice echoes off the damn walls, he's so loud.

"No," Tripp says, sounding a thousand times more patient than I would. "Dex didn't think he could get married, so we were proving that he could. It was all fake. Calm your tits. Dex suggested it, and I—"

Oskar whirls on me. "I like you, Dex, but Jesus Christ you would have to be the world's biggest dumbass. What is wrong with you? How could you make him do that?" Does Oskar sound … hurt?

I can't even answer him. My annoyance from earlier dries up because yeah, I've been called dumb a lot in my life, but never like that. "I … I …"

"I can't with you two." Oskar throws up his hands and leaves.

"Shit." Tripp shoots a look at me. "What happened to it being a secret?" he hisses before chasing after his boyfriend.

Well, I did what I wanted.

I got one over on Oskar.

It just doesn't feel as good as I thought it was going to, especially when I'm left standing here alone.

CHAPTER EIGHT

TRIPP

"Oskar, wait."

He was so fast to run out of there, he's already storming down the beach by the time I get outside, and I have to run after him. Though I shouldn't have to explain myself.

Oskar isn't actually my boyfriend.

I'm just about to reach him when he whirls around on me.

"You let him talk you into marrying him?"

"No. Not exactly. I didn't think he'd go through with it. I was there as a supportive friend."

"How …" Oskar can't seem to get his words out.

"How, what?"

"How do you do it to yourself, man? I've never loved someone before, but I've been interested in guys who haven't been interested in me, and that was bad enough. How do you put up with him being so insensitive to you?"

"He's not insensitive. He legitimately thinks we feel the same way about each other."

"Then why do I seem to fight for your heart more than you do?"

"It's complicated."

A voice sounds behind me. "What's complicated?"

I don't need to turn to know it's Ezra, and probably Anton too.

"Tripp here got married," Oskar says. "Did either of you know that?"

"Uh, Oskar, I think getting fake married to Tripp is taking your ridiculous charade too far," Ezra says.

"No, no. Not to me." Oskar levels me with a serious stare—one I rarely see from the manwhore playboy that he is. "You want to tell them, or should I?"

"You're making this out to be a bigger deal than it really is."

"Why don't we see what they think?" Oskar nods behind me.

I take a deep breath and slowly turn. "Okay, here's the deal. Dex was contemplating marrying Jessica, but—"

"Somehow Tripp and Dex ended up getting married," Oskar finishes. "Maybe Dex is so dumb he mistook him for her? I mean, they both have boobs, so maybe?"

I turn back to him. "I do not have *boobs*. My chest is pure muscle. And also, quit with the dumb Dex jokes, okay? He really hates it, and he doesn't deserve it."

"Doesn't he?" Anton asks.

I put my back to the water so I can see Oskar and Anton at the same time. "You're joining in on it too? Look, it's one thing to joke about it, and hell, most of the time Dex is in on the joke because he knows when it comes to the media and talking stats that he gets tongue-tied, but he's not actually dumb. The jokes are getting too …"

"Real?" Oskar asks. "Do you think I like being mean to Dex? Every time I've had to point out this week that you and I need alone time to be a couple and he's given me those puppy dog eyes, it's felt like I just kicked Bambi repeatedly. He doesn't see how much he hurts you because you don't let him. We're trying to protect you."

"You don't need to protect me from Dex!" I yell. Myself, sure, but not from him. "He's done nothing wrong. And the way you guys have been treating him ... I want it to stop."

Ezra and Oskar hang their heads like scolded schoolboys, but Anton's gaze ping-pongs between us all. "Have you guys ever gotten the impression Dex is in love with Tripp as much as Tripp is in love with him, but he just doesn't realize?"

There's an echo of scoffs from us all.

"Hear me out," Anton says. "I had a talk with him when we first got here and you three went for a hike. He seemed *lost* without Tripp. And I tried to get him to see why he might feel that way without actually coming out and saying it, but he wasn't getting it."

We all blink at him.

"He practically has hearts in his eyes when he looks at him," Anton pushes.

Ezra's the first to break. "He's always been like that though."

"And that doesn't tell you something?"

"Nah. No way. No offense, Trippy, but Dex is straight. He's so comfortable in his heterosexuality that all your gayness doesn't faze him. That's super straight."

Anton tilts his head. "Maybe he's pan. Maybe if Tripp and Dex had the perfect circumstance in which to explore something, Dex could realize he's fluid."

"Dex is always all over Tripp," Oskar points out. "I know he's, uh, *oblivious*, but if there were feelings there, even he would have picked up on it by now."

"No, I mean—"

"You mean, like, a prison situation?" Ezra asks. "That kind of fluid? Where guys can't fuck women, but they'd rather have sex with their cellmate than their fist?"

"Or *maybe*," I interject before they can keep going, "Dex and I are really close, and even if it's painful for me to have him in all the ways I want except sexually, I know it would hurt more to live without him at all." I look over at Oskar. "And that's how I do it to myself. If you guys had ever experienced a fraction of what I feel for Dex, you'd understand. You do things that are hard for the people you love because your life is so much better with them in it."

Ezra leans in closer to Anton and mutters, "Just so you know, I love you, I will love you forever, but if Henry Cavill comes knocking, you're on your own. Apparently, I don't love you as much as Tripp loves Dex."

"Hey, if Henry Cavill comes knocking, I'll ask him to join us."

"Aww, this is why you're perfect. But also, I don't want to become like Tripp and Dex. There's spending time together, and then there's smothering each other."

Anton pats his cheek. "It's cute you think you'd be the first one to ask for a break. Jesus, it's only been a week on this trip, and I'm ready to not see your face."

Ezra turns his back on him. "Is this better?"

"Much. Thank you." He loops an arm around Ezra's waist and plants a kiss on his head.

"See, I don't understand your relationship entirely, but that's my point," I say. "Don't get me wrong, alone time is sometimes needed, but I can't think of a time where I've ever *wanted* to be away from Dex. Even when I've needed a time-out from him. You two work because you're the same. Dex and I work because—"

"But you're *not* working," Oskar says. "Because you're not together."

"I'm getting tired of trying to explain myself to you guys. I appreciate you being there for me and wanting to protect me. I really, really do. But I've got this handled, okay? So, maybe, can you all back off?"

They glance at each other, as if waiting to come to a group decision before relenting and murmuring half-assed apologies. I know they mean them, and I know they think I'm making a big mistake by maintaining my friendship with Dex and pretend marrying him and I'm only hurting myself, blah, blah, blah, but I don't need it from them too. I'm already hard enough on myself about it.

Oskar approaches me and wraps me in a big hug. "I'm sorry if it seems like I'm pushing. I thought maybe that's what you needed, seeing as you're determined to continue to live in an unhealthy amount of pining. I'll back off. I am officially breaking up with you. I think we're better off as friends. It's not you, it's me. I'm running away to join the circus—"

"Aww, I'm so upset," I deadpan. "To think, who will have all the imaginary sex with me now?"

Both Anton and Ezra say at the same time, "Not it."

"I really am sorry," Oskar says. "And I'll apologize to Dex too if that's what you want me to do."

"It is."

"Okay. Let's go back inside," Oskar says. He keeps his arm around my shoulders all the way into the house, and I finally feel like I might be able to enjoy this vacation without all the pressure of lying to Dex while pretending to be with Oskar while also being fake married to Dex.

All the deceit hurts my brain.

I need Zen and peace.

We get back inside the house to find Dex pacing back and forth in the large living room.

"Are you guys cool now? Did you fix it? I'm so sorry. So, so, so, so sorry," he chants. "I fucked up again because of my stupid mouth, and—"

Oskar approaches him, but Dex flinches as Oskar clasps his shoulder. "We're cool. Tripp and I decided we'd be better off as friends, so go have your vacation with him."

Dex's mouth gapes while he looks at me. "Tripp?"

What's the best way to cover a big fat lie? With another lie ... apparently.

Tripp Mitchell's self-help book, coming soon.

"I told you. Oskar farts like crazy. Not relationship material right there."

"I do not," Oskar says. "Maybe you're smelling your own ass because you're full of shit."

"Ah, friend Oskar is back. Yay," I say.

"And friend Tripp is back," Dex says. "Right?"

"Right."

Dex smiles, but then it quickly drops. "You guys didn't really break up because of me, did you?"

Oskar and I share a look.

"Nah," Oskar says. "It just wasn't right."

"Agreed. We're better as friends."

Dex's grin is back. "In that case, race you to the lake for a swim?"

It's one of Dex's best and worst traits. He's so quick to trust in what he's told, which is great for when I want him to let something go. Not so great when he sees clickbait on the internet about official alien sightings confirmed by NASA.

I push him out of the way to run to my room for my trunks. "You're on."

The second half of the vacation is a million times better than the first. When the guys aren't interfering and being jackasses, worrying about my heart and my feelings, the tension level drops dramatically. And I think the whole boyfriend situation might have finally clued Dex in about giving me space. Maybe. He hasn't once tried to sleep next to me, so that's something. Though it doesn't stop him from slipping in next to me to wake me up. An elbow to the gut usually helps to make him go away, but today, he's relentless.

"It's the last day," he says. "We need to get one more swim in before we leave."

"I can't. My trunks are all packed. Shame." I reach blindly behind me and pat Dex's cheek. "Have fun. I'm going to keep sleeping."

"Nope. Swim. Even if I have to carry you out there myself."

"I'd like to see you try."

"You say that like you think I can't pick you up."

"You *can't*."

"Oh, hell no." Dex jumps up and rounds the bed.

I turn to dead weight as he tries to get his arms under me—one under my knees and one under my neck.

All he manages to do is drag me and drop me on the floor.

"Ow," I complain.

"Then *help* me."

"Nope. You said you could do it."

"I'm getting you in that water. End of story."

"Okay." I continue to lie on the carpet, refusing to move, and when Dex gives up trying to lift me, he resorts to dragging me by my ankles.

He grunts while I laugh, even if the carpet stings my back as he pulls me all the way down the hall.

"What are you guys doing?" Oskar asks from the living room.

"I'm throwing Tripp in the lake in his underwear."

"Ooh, I'm in."

Next thing I know, Oskar joins Dex and grabs my arms.

"No!" I yell.

Between them both, they carry me outside and don't let me go no matter how much I struggle. I'm probably stronger than both of them but not combined.

"You two should go back to all the hostility from last week. Be mean to each other, not to me. I'm loveable, damn it."

They ignore me and carry me down to the single dock at the back of our rental property and throw me off the end.

"I hate you both!" I yell before making a splash and getting a ton of water in my mouth.

"What?" Oskar holds his hand up to his ear. "Can't hear you."

I throw up both my middle fingers.

While Oskar goes back inside the house, Dex comes running for me. He dives off the end of the dock, and I suddenly become a shark victim in a horror movie, moving in a circle, trying to see where he is.

Something grabs my foot and yanks me down.

Dex and I fight and struggle, but it's hard not to take in water when you're laughing through it all.

This is the epitome of Dex and me. This is us. Everything is fun with him. We goof around. And his carefree attitude is one of the many reasons I fell in love with him.

The NHL pressure can be intense, especially if you're having a really good season or a really bad one. When you're on a winning streak, the need to maintain it could make any player choke, and as a goalie, the pressure is only tenfold. Dex takes me away from all that, and I think it's why we became fast friends.

He's my escape.

We swim for a bit until we must lose track of time because Oskar, who we're sharing a ride with to the airport later, comes back outside and waves us in, holding out two towels.

"Shit, are we running late?" I ask as we reach him on the dock.

I pull myself up and dry off.

"Nope. Both of your phones have been going off for the last five minutes." Oskar holds up my phone.

"It's the team PR department." I'm still wet, but I take the phone anyway and answer. "Tripp Mitchell."

"We need a meeting," Graham Thompson says.

"Uh, okay? When? Dex and I fly back into Vegas later today."

"Good. Both of you. Head office. What time can you get here?"

"Uh, we land at three, and then we'll drop our bags off—"

"Nope. See you here at three thirty."

"Wait, what do you—"

Graham ends the call, and my gut sinks.

Something's wrong.

We rush to finish packing, and then we say goodbye to Ezra and Anton, who are flying back to Boston on the red-eye tonight.

We get to the airport early, which was probably a waste of time because the plane isn't ever going to take off *early*, but I can't help stressing about why Graham would want to see me. No, not just me, but Dex as well.

Zen and peace. Zen and peace.

Dex thinks it has something to do with a promo opportunity in the off-season, but he didn't hear Graham's voice. It was like a parent telling their child to come home because the kid accidentally burned down the house.

I don't tell Dex that though. I don't want him to freak out like I am.

A quick Google search doesn't show anything about our nuptials—the first couple of pages of results are all about our friendship and hockey stats—but I can't shake the feeling that's what this is about.

I'm so nervous the entire flight home that my leg bounces the whole way, and Dex finally catches on that something's not right.

"Why do you look so worried? What do you think it is?" He pales. "A trade?"

"No. They wouldn't need us both for that. Unless we're both being traded, but after our season and making it to the finals, thanks in large part to us, I doubt it. The most logical conclusion is that they found out about the fake wedding."

"Oh, fuck. How?"

"Who knows? I couldn't find anything online. But ... what else would it be?"

"Like I said, promo opportunity."

"Why not tell me that on the phone? Why not get my agent to call me?"

"Shit. What if it is about the wedding?"

This is the last thing I wanted—for Dex to worry. I guess I suck at trying to hide my concern. "Let's try not to completely freak out yet." Even if I'm already way past that. "We don't know what it's about."

We totally know what it's about. I just don't know how Graham found out.

And the second we walk through the doors at our practice arena in Summerlin, Graham's there to meet us. "Follow me."

We wheel our suitcases with us, and every time mine makes a clicking noise on the cracks between the tiled floor, I swear the sound is mocking me. It rolls along to the sound of "You're fired, you're fired, you're fired."

They won't terminate our contracts over a harmless joke ... will they?

Graham leads us to one of the small conference rooms, giving away nothing in his expression.

"What's going on?" I ask as we take our seats at the round table.

Graham's gray eyes hold the kind of disappointment I've seen from each and every one of my coaches at some point in my career, and that's when I know for sure ...

He slides his tablet over to us. "Marriage licenses are public record, boys."

Okay, *now* we can officially freak out.

I look at the screen, but it doesn't make sense. "We didn't file it," I murmur.

"What I want to know is what you two are doing getting married in the first place," Graham says. "Without telling us. We were blindsided by this, but it's lucky that we caught it first."

"How? How did you catch it?" I ask.

Dex sits next to me, either stunned into silence or not quite understanding what's going on.

"You don't think we keep tabs on every single one of our players?" Graham asks. "If something new pops up about any of you on the internet, we know about it first. So, married, huh?"

"It's not supposed to be legally. We did it as a goof," I say.

Graham's lips purse. "A goof."

"We didn't file the certificate we signed." I turn to Dex. "Did we?"

Dex takes out his wallet and pulls out a folded piece of paper.

He ... kept it on him?

"It's right here. We didn't file it with the registrar." Dex hands it over to Graham.

Where we're expecting more confusion, Graham stares at us how the media looks at Dex a lot. Like we're the biggest dumbasses to ever dumb.

"What do you two know about weddings? I can't assume much considering neither of you have been married before."

"Uh, that would be a correct assumption," I say.

"Well, when two people love each other very much," he says dryly, "and they want to get married in Vegas, they sign two things. The official marriage license from the license bureau and then the certificate." He places the certificate next to the tablet and taps the paper. "Decorative certificate." Now he points to the license. "Official marriage record. Congratulations. You're now husband and husband."

We're … legally married?

Fucking, fuck fuck.

CHAPTER NINE

DEX

"But ... we didn't file it ..." It's only been pointed out seventy-two times already, but I can't move past it. Even if there were two things we had to sign, the article I skimmed said we were the ones who had to register the marriage, and we didn't do it.

I *told* Tripp it would be fine.

And I've messed up again.

As I stare at the two certificates, it finally starts to sink in.

I'm *married*.

I have a *husband*.

I swing around to Tripp. "I'm sorry. I'll fix it." I turn to Graham. "I *am* going to fix it." This fuckup is on me. I stand, ready to head out and do whatever needs to be done. Divorces are a thing people do. Hell, a lot of our teammates have already been through one, so this isn't anything new.

I'll just—

"Sit down, Dex," Graham says.

I'm stiff as I lower myself back into the seat next to Tripp. He hasn't looked at me once since the news, and I'm itching to comfort him with affection, but the energy comes out as uncontrolled fidgeting instead.

"Given this was a *goof*," Graham levels us with a stare, "I take it you're not planning to stay married?"

Tripp answers too quickly for me to even give the question thought. "Of course not."

"That's what I was worried about. Best friends turned husbands we could work with, but two idiots making a mockery of marriage is more difficult. The media will have a field day."

I'm used to being called an idiot, but Tripp's neck turns red, and then his cheeks follow.

"It wasn't a mockery. It was …" Well, an experiment doesn't sound much better. "This was all my fault."

Graham points to the tablet *again*. "That's not Tripp's signature?"

"It is," Tripp answers. "We were both there. This is on both of us."

"I told him it wouldn't count. It was supposed to be a bit of fun."

"Did it occur to you for a second, Dex, that same-sex couples fought hard for marriage equality? They faced pushback from people saying the divorce rate would increase because queer couples couldn't be committed."

"It's not entirely Dex's fault," Tripp says. "I didn't have to agree to it."

"And yet you got married anyway. I thought you of all people, Tripp, would know to take something like this seriously." Graham slides the marriage certificate back toward me, and I numbly take it and put it carefully back in my wallet.

"So what are you saying?" Tripp asks. "You want us to pretend to be married for real?"

"What aren't you getting? You *are* married 'for real.' But, no. We're your representatives, not your owners. All we're asking for is some time to figure out how to spin this, because the media *will* get wind of it sooner or later, and we need to be ahead of the story. A quickie wedding and a snap divorce will not look good for either of you or the team."

Tripp glances at me and then away again. "What are our options?"

"You can't get divorced. Not yet. Divorces are also public record, and news sites scour those for celebrity gossip. Hell, they probably do it for marriages too, which means we're on borrowed time. We'll look into getting you two an annulment, which means it never happened in the first place, but that might take a while. In the meantime, all we want from you is to lie low. If worse comes to worst, we tell everyone the marriage is real, we trade one of you, and then when you file for divorce, you can tell the media the distance was too hard—"

My gut bottoms out. "No. No, you can't trade us. We're the Mitchell brothers, people come to see us together, we're two of the strongest players on the team—"

Tripp squeezes my arm, which cuts off my panic. But instead of reassuring me, it only reminds me that I could lose this.

Luckily, he's the more levelheaded of us. "Dex is right that the fans won't like it if you trade one of us."

"It's not my favorite option," Graham admits. "But it *is* an option. Can you give us time to come up with alternatives?"

"If you don't end up deciding on a trade, then of course," Tripp says.

And the fact Tripp doesn't want to be separated even after this mess has me reaching for his hand. "We'll lie low," I agree.

"Thank you." Graham rubs his forehead. "But when I say lie low, I mean it. No going out with the guys, no drawing attention. We don't need to give the media a reason to be looking, because if it gets out before we've made a decision"—he pins us with a look—"we'll be forced to go with whatever's on the table."

We're finally released, and as I leave the room, it's like I'm walking out of the principal's office. I've been spoken to before about dumb things I've done, things I've said to the media that I shouldn't have, but nothing like that. Nothing with the threat of a trade hanging over our heads.

If one of us *is* traded, it'll probably be me. There's no way Vegas would trade the goalie who got them to the Stanley Cup game last season. That would be moronic on their part. The fans would be pissed. I'm just another replaceable forward. Moving away, living without Tripp, it would mess with my head.But I'll do it if it's our only option.

We get out into the parking lot, and before I can stop myself, I start to laugh. Not a fun kind of laugh. An oh-fuckstick-did-I-screw-up type of laugh that has a hysterical hitch to it.

Tripp eyes me. "You okay there?"

"Dumbass Dex strikes again." I cover my face with both hands as I let out a long, frustrated sound. "You know, I think this tops the list."

"You keep a list?"

"Dex's finest moments. You should subscribe."

"Why, when I now have a front-row seat to the action?"

I plant my hands on my hips and let out something between a sob and an exhale. "This can't be true. It can't. It has to be one of those Photoshop thingies."

"Uh-huh."

"Clearly someone is pranking us. They have to be."

"Seemed pretty legit to me."

A noise catches in my throat. "How are you so calm?"

"Maybe I just don't see being married to you as the worst thing that could happen."

"But they're talking about a trade. A *trade*. I couldn't even get a fake marriage right, how the hell am I supposed to manage a real one?"

The familiar panic of being the world's biggest screwup starts to claw at my throat again. There has to be an explanation for this. There has to be. "We need to figure out what happened."

"I know we got drunk straight after, but surely you haven't forgotten what got us here. It's obvious what happened. The chapel filed the paperwork."

"But they weren't supposed to. The website I read said *we* had to file it."

"Dex." Tripp squeezes my shoulder, and I immediately cover his hand with mine. "Will going to the chapel to confirm what happened help with … whatever this freak-out is?"

"Yes."

"Okay." He grabs his luggage and nods at me to grab mine. "Then let's get a ride, drop this stuff at home, and head over there."

Before he can take a step, I haul him into a hug. "Thank you for being so cool about this."

"Duh. We're the Mitchell Brothers. We'll chalk it up to being two halves of a whole idiot."

I try not to cringe as I pull away. "That might be the truthiest truth to ever truth about us. Though, I think I'm a whole idiot on my own, so together, we're one and a half of one."

"That's not how math works."

I shrug. "What's that word for when something that's supposed to happen doesn't happen?"

"What?" Tripp screws up his face in confusion.

"You know, there was that old song written about it. It goes like …" I clear my pipes and sing. "*And isn't it moronic? It's like paaaaain—*"

"They're … not the words."

"It was something like that. For us, marriage might be the thing that tears us apart when it's supposed to bring people closer." I couldn't stand it if that happened.

"Real marriages are supposed to bring people closer together. Fake ones are fair game. And I think the word you're looking for is ironic."

I snap my fingers. "That's the word. Anyway, yeah, that's us. Ironic."

"That's not …" Tripp closes his mouth. "You're right. Totally us."

And now I'm going to have to think up a way to fix this, when I'm not so great with the thinking of things.

Thank fuck it's not a long drive to drop our luggage off and head to the chapel.

When we get there, I hand one of the ball caps I grabbed from home over to Tripp. They won't do anything against a hockey fan, but on the off chance someone tries to take a photo, they'll give us some coverage.

There's one couple waiting in reception when we walk in, and I tilt my face away from them as I approach the desk.

"Good morning," the receptionist says. "Here to get married?"

I sling my arm around Tripp's shoulders. "We already are, but it occurred to me that we signed the license but forgot to take it with us so we could register the, umm, marriage." My heart is beating loud enough to be aware of it while I wait for her answer, hoping with everything I have that she'll confirm our mistake and send us on our way.

My hopes are all on the shoulders of this woman with the pale pink lipstick and giant Dolly hair.

"Did you get your certificate?"

I pull out the one from my wallet and show her.

"That's it. All you had to do was obtain the marriage license and sign it. We file all the paperwork."

"Everything is done, then?" I clarify. It's what Tripp said happened, but it still punches me in the gut. Because this is the one thing I was sure of. If we didn't file, we weren't married.

"You should be able to look it up on the register, but there's nothing further for you to take care of."

"Thank you," Tripp says quickly. "Come on, husband."

I hold my panic in until we get back at the car. "I'll fix it."

"Would you stop saying that?"

"But I will. Oskar's right—I'm a dumbass, and I never should have made you do this."

"You didn't—"

"Leave it up to me." I don't need him to tell me this isn't my fault when I'm the one who came up with the idea. "You won't have to do anything. I'll drop you home, and we'll both do whatever we need to in order to stay in Vegas, and then when we get the okay, I'll do the paperwork and you'll be free of me."

"Did I say I wanted to be free of you?"

"Free of this *marriage*. It was a mistake, but we'll put it behind us, and everything will go back to normal."

"Everything?"

"We'll be making ex-husband jokes before you know it." My voice goes its squeakiest yet, but I force myself to give him an easygoing smile. "See? We've got this."

CHAPTER TEN

TRIPP

We've got this, Dex said. He's a liar. Unless by this he means a PR nightmare, an awkward friendship, and a clusterfuck of emotions I don't want to deal with, then yes. We've totally got this.

Dex is adamant about setting things right, so even though he keeps telling me he'll fix it, that I won't be married to him for long, the constant reminder that us being husbands is ridiculous and needs to be "fixed" doesn't sit right in my gut.

I never wanted to get married. Marriage, to me—and to Dex—has never meant anything. But there's something in the way he says it that's like nails on a chalkboard.

I could never be married to you.

I don't want you.

He has never said those words, but when I hear, "This was a huge mistake," I can't help but take it that way.

My head knows it's because he's straight, but my heart likes to pretend logic doesn't exist.

We're not supposed to go out or draw attention to ourselves, but Dex is not himself. He's kind of avoiding me, and I get the impression it's because he feels guilty about the marriage being real. He wouldn't let me take any of the blame, so now we're in this weird place where we're supposed to lie low, but he isn't staying at my place or wanting to even see me. He claims he's busy finding out how to get an annulment.

I don't know what's worse. Spending time with Dex and drowning in unrequited feelings or not seeing him at all. And this was my point to the other guys in the Collective.

I'm bored without Dex. And lonely. And this is why I've never told him about my feelings. Because it will drive him away. I have plenty of friends I can hang out with, but it's different with him. No matter how many people are around, without him, that loneliness is constant.

Normally, when Dex stuff is getting me down, I go out and hook up, but I can't do that. Not when I'm *married*. If it gets out and there're photos of me and some guy or he speaks out saying he was with me, that will be even worse for PR.

When the buzzer for the building sounds, I run to my monitor, hoping it's Dex coming to see me.

I'm mildly disappointed when I see Dex's and my sisters on the screen, but I could do with the distraction. I let them in and then go to my front door, waiting for them to arrive on the elevator.

In our family, I got the recessive red hair gene from our Scottish ancestors from way back when. My sister, Sienna, has strawberry blonde hair, and Phoebe's blonde hair is a shade lighter than Dex's.

Our sisters look more related than Dex or I do to either of them. They even have matching sympathetic stares when the elevator doors open and they catch sight of me.

"My brother is an idiot." Phoebe's welcoming words make me laugh.

"No, he's not." I step aside to let them in.

Sienna hugs me on her way past. "Are you okay?"

I glance at Phoebe. "He told you we got married, didn't he?"

Phoebe gasps. "You whaaaat?"

"I don't believe your fake shock for a second."

"Okay, fine. He did. And then I told Sienna. And that's why we're here."

"To offer some really helpful advice and shower me with sisterly love? I mean, technically, Phoebs, you're my sister now too."

They both step toward me, those pitiful looks still across their faces. As they get closer, I anticipate a group hug, but instead, they both slap me upside the head like Oskar and Ezra did on vacation.

"Ow. Why do people keep doing that?"

"Because you might be as big of an idiot as Dex," Sienna says.

"Bigger," Phoebe agrees.

"Why did you put yourself through the torture of a fake wedding with the man you are secretly in love with?" my sister asks.

"Uh, because he asked me to?"

"I love Dex dearly," Phoebe says, "but you just trusted him to get all the details of the fake wedding correct? Now you're actually married, and this somehow went from a joke to a bigger joke? But not a funny ha-ha joke, but a 'hey, isn't it funny how two grown-ass men can be so totally—'"

I hold up my hand. "I get it. We made mistakes. Big ones. But I'm done trying to figure out how we could've been so dumb and trying to come up with solutions. Team management said they want to trade one of us if we can't get out of this situation with as little drama as possible."

"You can't be traded!" Sienna says. "Either of you. What will Phoebe and I do?"

My sister works for a casino here in Vegas—she moved to be close to me—but Phoebe and Dex are really close too. Dex was sent to Vegas in the expansion draft, and as he tells it, Phoebe helped him move and then never left. Other than to get her own apartment. After surviving shitty childhoods together, they have each other's back. If Dex is traded, she'll leave too.

"If one of us has to be traded, I'll volunteer. Then Sienna can stay here, and you three will still be together."

My sister wraps her arms around me. "But I won't have you."

Phoebe joins the hug. "We love you both and don't want to lose either of you. Also, as a side note, I'm glad he married you and not Jessica."

I laugh, but it's half-hearted. "Whatever happens, we'll work it out." They step away from me, and I can't help myself. I ask, "How is he anyway? He's been avoiding me."

"He feels so guilty," Phoebe says. "He's worried if it gets out, you'll hate him."

"I could never hate—"

She holds up her hand. "I know you never could, but no matter how many times I tell him that, he doesn't believe me. He said you didn't want to get married in the first place."

"I mean, in general no. But it wasn't supposed to be real. I was wearing water wings, for fuck's sake."

"You were *what*?" Sienna asks.

"It was a joke. And then we totally forgot about it, went and had fun on vacation, and then we found out we *actually got married*."

"Dex gets so much shit for being the dumb one, but can we all agree that you're also *not* smart?"

"Hey, I am too."

Phoebe taps her chin. "Remind me which of the three of us accidentally married their best friend."

"I'm never going to live this down, am I?"

"What are sisters for?" Sienna says.

"Love? Encouragement? Emotional support?"

They both stare at me.

"At least you got your dream man after all?" Sienna says. I can't tell if she's being helpful or a smartass.

"Yes," I deadpan. "I'm so happy we've been married for three weeks, only been aware of it for a few days, and he already wants a divorce. You're so right. It's all my dreams come true."

Phoebe cocks her head. "Are you saying you don't want a divorce? Or an annulment?"

"No. Of course I do. But ... I dunno. Would it kill him to not be so eager about getting one? Or maybe stop avoiding me? I'm not mad at him, but if he keeps blowing me off, I will be."

"If it makes you feel any better," Phoebe says as she dumps her handbag on my kitchen counter, "Dex is a mess. When I saw him, he was hunched over his computer, doing that thing where his mouth moves with every word he's trying to read as if saying them out loud would help him understand. He wasn't his usual bubbly self."

That's what I was afraid of. "I'll go knock down his door later today and make sure he knows this isn't all his fault."

Phoebe deflates. "Damn it. I don't want you two to get divorced. You treat my brother right, and you love him to bits—"

"Except your brother doesn't love all my bits." I gesture in the general area of my junk.

"I can understand that," Sienna says. "I mean, dicks aren't really all that pretty to look at, are they? They get the job done though."

I screw up my face. "And this conversation is done. I don't need to know anything about my sister's love life."

Phoebe goes to open her mouth, but I point at her.

"That goes for you too."

Her mouth slams shut again.

That's what I thought.

-

After Sienna and Phoebe leave, I get in my car and drive to Dex's place near the practice arena. His house looks like it came out of a fairy tale in the woods. It's all stone and brick, has five bedrooms, and cost him a cool three mil. But it's not ... him. At all. He bought it last year when one of our guys got traded and put it up for sale. It's on the same street as some of the married guys on the team, and I think Dex only bought it because Jessica sold him on the idea.

How Dex didn't realize she was pushing for a ring is beyond me.

This house screams married with 2.5 kids.

I approach and knock on the door, but when he doesn't answer, I use my key and head straight upstairs, bypassing the ugly-ass modern chandelier hanging from the ceiling.

Jessica said it's supposed to look like flower petals raining from the sky.

When I reach Dex's bedroom, the sound of his shower hits my ears, so I throw myself on his bed and wait.

He walks out five minutes later, buck naked, towel over his head as he tries to dry his hair with one hand, and it's obvious he has absolutely no idea I'm here, because with his other hand, he reaches between his legs and gives his semi a hard stroke.

"Don't stop on my account," I say.

Dex jumps so high it's comical, while the towel drops to the floor. "You scared me."

"What are husbands for?"

His face immediately falls, and so does my mood.

"Come on, Dex. You said we'd be joking about it one day. Why not now?"

Dex picks up his towel and sadly wraps it around his waist. "Because I haven't found a solution yet." He looks at the ground. "I actually gave up days ago, but I didn't know how to tell you."

"Leave it up to the team. They have actual specialists on how to deal with athlete drama." As if speaking about it makes it happen, my phone starts ringing with the PR department phone number popping up. "See. This is them now. I bet they have a solution." I answer with as much optimism as I can muster. "Please tell me it's good news."

"I wish I could, but no. The story just broke on TMZ."

"Fuck." I try to school my reaction, but it tumbles out of me before I can think. And when I turn to Dex, I know it's too late to try to cover it up. Dex sits on the end of the bed by my feet with his head in his hands.

"My reaction exactly," Graham says. "I need to meet with you and Dex again, but it can't be here at headquarters. Photographers have already started showing up. Where are you?"

"We're both at Dex's house."

"Good. I'll be there in ten minutes. Don't leave. You're both a target right now."

He ends the call, and like that, panic mode kicks in. One of us is going to be traded.

It's a long-ass twenty minutes before Graham arrives, not ten, and Dex lets him in.

Graham looks like he could murder one of us. Or both.

Just how hard do NHL teams vet their PR staff? This is Vegas. Plenty of desert to stash our bodies. Though, I'd like to see Graham's scrawny fifty-year-old body carry us out to his car.

And now I'm being dramatic.

"Drink?" I ask him since Dex has seemed to have lost his voice.

"Water, thanks," Graham says.

I fill a glass for him and then lead us over to the couches in Dex's formal living room. The couches are more for decoration than comfort, and I can't sit still.

Graham takes a sip. "So. We don't know how the news got out, but there's no putting it back in now."

"So no annulment?" I ask.

Graham shakes his head. "It's too late for that. And you can't get divorced without admitting it was an offensive joke."

"Trade?" I croak.

Both Dex and I say at the same time, "I'll do it."

Graham's gaze flicks between both of us. "There might be another way, but you're probably not going to like it."

"I'll do anything if it means neither of us gets traded," Dex says.

"You pretend for a while that you're in love and the marriage is real."

Whoosh. My heart sinks. On the one hand, pretending to be in love with Dex will be easy—especially since I won't need to pretend. On the other, just how far do they want us to take this charade?

"Will people even believe that?" Dex asks. "According to everyone else, I'm still with Jessica."

"You don't follow her Insta account?" Graham asks.

"I didn't even when we were together," Dex says.

Graham takes out his phone. "It's my job to know everything my players and their partners are doing at all times."

He hits Play on a video of a smiling Jessica. She's in a bikini, wearing sunglasses, and looks like she's at a party on a beach somewhere.

"Well, it looks like the cat is out of the bag. I want everyone to know that Dex and I had an amazing friendship, but that's all it was. He and Tripp are so cute together, and I'm so happy they can finally acknowledge their love publicly. And don't you guys worry about me. I'm perfectly happy." She wraps her arm around a toned male body, but when the guy lowers his head to the camera and smiles, both Dex and I gasp.

"Fensby?" I exclaim. He's a forward on our second line and is always the first one to tease Dex about being dumb.

The video ends with them kissing, just enough to still be tasteful yet getting the point across.

"I'm so sorry, Dex," I say.

He doesn't take his eyes off the frozen screen. "I don't care. I should ... but I don't."

Well, I fucking care. Not only did she move on from Dex to another teammate of ours, she's released a statement on social media confirming things she has no right to.

"She has basically given your marriage clout," Graham says.

"Talk me through this. Our choices are for one of us to be traded so we can still 'appear' to be a couple but don't need PDA or anything because we won't live near each other anymore. Or to stay where we are and pretend this marriage is real," I say.

"I think those are the best options to keep the backlash off of you guys and the team. If you want to tell everyone it was a joke, we can go that route too, but expect shit to blow up. Players have been hated for less. Fans will turn on you. Ticket sales could drop. Management could take it out on both of you."

"Trade me," Dex says. "This was my fault. So I should be punished."

"Just wait," I snap at him. "You said before you'll do anything to keep us both with the team, but we haven't heard all the details yet." I turn back to Graham. "What would pretending to be married entail?"

"Living together. Going to dinners. Charity events. Team events. Not having sex with other people. Everything you see your other married teammates doing."

I don't make the argument that Appleby cheats on his wife at nearly every away game even though I want to.

I look at Dex. "That does sound like what we normally do anyway. We're always at one another's places, we go to team events together, eat … It's us. Apart from the no sex with other people thing."

"How long for?" Dex asks.

"A year?" Graham says. "Then you can both say that you work better as teammates and friends. Or the spotlight on your relationship from the media was too stressful and made it crumble. The longer you're married though, the better."

"Can you give us a minute?" Dex asks Graham.

Graham stands. "No problem. I'll be in the backyard, making some phone calls. You aren't the only two players in hot water."

"Who else?"

"Jaycox went parasailing and broke his ankle on landing. He could be out for the first couple of games of the season. I swear all of you have pucks for brains." He's not wrong.

Dex is always teased for being dumb, but it's not like any of us are much better. We're just more articulate when it comes to explaining our dumbassery.

"It's only one season," I say.

"One season where we have to act like an actual married couple."

"I can deal with that."

Finally, his brown eyes meet mine. "Can you? Are you sure? I've already made your life ten times more difficult than it needs to be, and—"

"I missed you these last couple of days while you were avoiding me. I can't lose you to another team. I'd be too tempted to let you score a goal every time I played against you."

"I'd be the highest scorer in the league. Maybe I should take the trade."

I shove him. "Good to know your points score is more important than I am."

"Nothing is more important than you." Dex runs a hand through his hair. "So ... am I moving in with you, or do you want to move out to Summerlin?"

"I'm not moving into this house. It's got bad juju all over it." And that juju is Jessica's decorating taste.

"All right, hubby. I guess I'm moving into the penthouse. Party time."

"You're in?" I can't help smiling. "Are you sure you'll be able to keep it in your pants for an entire year?"

As if that news just sinks in, Dex's face falls. "Shit. I guess it's time to get reacquainted with my first-ever girlfriend." He holds up his hand.

"Well, hey, if you're ever desperate enough ..." I waggle my eyebrows. "I am your husband."

It's a joke, but I don't think Dex takes it as one.

His eyebrows shoot up. "Really?"

God, say yes. Just ... let the offer linger.

But I can't. Our friendship is already going through too much awkwardness over this marriage thing to add sex to the mix.

So instead of telling him what I want, I play it off instead. "You wish."

My phone starts ringing, and my immediate thought is that it's already reporters trying to get ahold of us for a quote, but when I pull it out, it's even worse than that.

It's the queer collective. And it's a group video call.

"If Graham comes back in, let him know we're doing this for real. I need to put out this fire." I hold up my phone.

I go into one of the spare bedrooms and hit Answer on the call. Great. They're all here.

"It's a fake marriage, huh?" Oskar smirks.

"Wait, so this is actually true? You guys got married?" Foster asks.

I take a deep breath and put on the performance of a lifetime. "I'd … love … chat." I make sure I pause movement in between words too. "Dealing … crisis. Hello? I think … bad … reception." I quickly hit the End button.

Oh no. The call dropped out.

Shame.

Real shame.

I wonder how long I can play that game. Sooner or later, I'm going to have to face the Collective, but today is not that day. I already know what they'll tell me anyway.

You're only hurting yourself.

But the alternative is hurting Dex, and that's something I'm not willing to do. Ever.

CHAPTER ELEVEN

DEX

I barely know what I've actually agreed to when things start to move fast. By the end of the week, my place is up for lease, and I'm moving all my worldly possessions into Tripp's apartment. Our PR team released a statement about us that was in line with what Jessica had already said: we hid our relationship so it wouldn't affect the team, but we couldn't keep the secret any longer.

The story isn't rock solid, and my biggest fear is someone calling us out, but I'm not going to complain.

If it stops one of us from being traded, I don't care what it is, I'll do it.

I have no problem with pretending to be married to Tripp, because showing public affection for him is something I can do in my sleep. In fact, I'm a thousand times better now than when I was avoiding him. He has a way of making me believe everything will be okay and that I'm invincible when I have him.

There's just one thing I can't stop stressing over: the messages.

Graham has someone managing a joint social media account for us, and between that and my own private ones, I've had a flood of messages and notifications. The homophobic dickwads I can brush off easily enough because I know what they have to say is bullshit; it's the supportive ones that are messing with my head.

People congratulating me for coming out and living my truth. Guys across the NHL, some I've met and some I only know in passing, all declaring support for us. Most of our team have posted fun jokes about how unsubtle we were while texting us in private to find out what's actually going on, and the outpouring of love and support ... makes me feel like a horrible person.

It's completely misplaced.

I remember when Anton came out publicly and announced his relationship with Ezra. Tripp and I watched the press conference, and when I noticed Tripp starting to get choked up, I asked what was wrong.

"I still remember the day I came out. It was the most freeing moment of my life."

I'll never relate to that, and the thought of someone getting choked up over this story of two best friends falling in love and getting married makes me feel like a phony.

I'm an idiot.

But I've always been an honest idiot.

I wish I could go back and smack past Dex upside the head, because ever since I suggested that dumb wedding, everything has snowballed.

My first night in Tripp's place is spent tossing and turning. When I stay here, I'm usually in his bed, with him, chilling and hanging out.

In the guest bed, I can't get comfortable, so I'm awake ridiculously early and make my way into Tripp's living room. I'm scrolling through too many messages to keep track of when Tripp stumbles sleepily from his room. He's only wearing sleep shorts, and his entire torso is covered in freckles.

"Morning." I drink in the sight of him eagerly, because just like he did, I missed him during our days apart.

"Hey. You're up early."

"Couldn't sleep."

He moves away toward the kitchen, and I turn on the couch to watch him.

"Why not?" he asks.

"I'm not used to that bed."

He doesn't respond as he switches on the coffee machine. "Sharing a bed isn't a good idea."

"I know." Though, I don't really. I wasn't suggesting sharing, but if Tripp asked, I'd be in there in a heartbeat.

We've done it plenty of times before. And sure, he'd thrown that joke out about us hooking up, but he can't think that's made things awkward between us. In fact, it's probably a better idea than us hooking up with anyone else, and I know Tripp has a high sex drive, so if he can cover for this whole mess for me, I can do that for him. It's not like it would be hard. The memory of our wedding kiss still makes my lips tingle.

My gaze goes unfocused, and I rub my jaw, trying to work out how long it would take for him to get desperate enough to offer for real. If he did, would I go through with it? It's always been so easy to be affectionate with him; would that really be any different? I know I'm straight, but Tripp doesn't count.

I jump at the sound of Tripp setting a coffee mug on the table in front of me and watch as he sits down on the couch opposite.

"You okay?" he asks.

"Yeah, totally."

His expression tells me he doesn't buy it. "You look like you're trying to do math."

I laugh, but it's not like I can tell him what I was really thinking about, so instead, I unlock my phone again. "I'm having an attack of the guilts."

"The guilts?"

"*Yes*. I feel guilty. Look at this." I round the table to sit next to him and start scrolling through my phone. "Look at all these people. Some of them are sharing their life stories with a total stranger all because they think I'm like them. I don't know if I can pull this off."

He pulls back. "You want the trade?"

"*No*." I don't even like those words coming from his mouth. "I'm worried I'm going to say the wrong thing and it'll make us both look worse than if we admit it was all a joke."

"I don't think you need to worry. It's not like we'll be going out much anyway, and when we do, you can follow my lead."

"Hey, that's an idea," I say, hit with a stroke of brilliance.

"What is?"

"You can teach me to be gay. If you teach me to be gay, I'll live up to what these people are saying."

Tripp stares at me for a long moment. "You want me to … *teach* you? To be gay?"

"Yes." It's the perfect plan.

"And how would I do that, exactly?"

"You tell me. You're the gay one."

A spark of amusement fills Tripp's face. "Uh-huh. And that's the only difference between us, gay and straight?"

"Exactly."

"And what makes you straight?"

Is he stroking out? "I like chicks."

"And what makes me gay?"

"You like dudes."

"Right." He pauses, and I wonder if this is one of those moments where there's context I'm missing. "And can you think of *any* other differences?"

My brain is doing that staticky thing that takes over when I'm asked a hard question. What else is different between us? "I ... can't defend a goal to save myself?"

Tripp snorts back a laugh, then leans right over, into my personal space, and my heart does a backflip. "I fuck guys, Dex. That's the only difference. Is that how you want me to teach you?"

He's joking again, but my face starts to heat. "Ah, I mean, if you think it would—"

"Stop." Tripp shoves me. "You can't act all adorably innocent about me suggesting I fuck you."

"Would you prefer I act grossed out? I'm not sure what the etiquette is here."

"It's not about *etiquette*. You're straight, Dex. Straight guys generally don't want to have sex with gay guys."

I bite the inside of my cheek to stop myself from pointing out Tripp isn't "a gay guy" to me. He's just ... Tripp.

He groans and drops his head back against the couch. "Don't look at me like that."

"Like what? There was no look. I'm not looking."

"Dex ..."

"Tripp ..."

"You look upset," he says.

"I'm not. This is my worried face. If it gets out that we're lying, people will hate you. You don't deserve that."

"Well, we have to make sure it doesn't get out."

That's what has me so panicked. We can be as careful as we like, but I'm sure I'm going to do something thoughtless and fuck up. "That's the problem. I know how to be your best friend, not your husband."

"Isn't it the same thing?" Tripp shifts on the couch so he's facing me. "Don't people always say you should marry your best friend?"

"I guess we took that too literally." I'm still nervous though. "I can't shake the feeling people will know."

"All right, look. The good thing is, a lot of queer couples aren't overly affectionate in public anyway, so most people won't question that, but they will expect something. I'm fine with whatever, but how about you tell me what you're comfortable with, and we'll stick to that."

"Like ... hugging and stuff, you mean?"

He cracks a smile. "And *stuff*."

"Okay, where do we start?"

"The hugging is fine, right? We do that all the time."

"Exactly."

"And we've already agreed no sex with other people." He winks. "*Or* each other."

Hmm ... I don't think I actually agreed to that one at all. "I'll try to keep my hands to myself."

"Speaking of hands, holding them in public, yea or nay?"

"Yes, I'd do that anyway." I think about what else. "Can I call you *husband*?"

"Of course. I assume kissing is obviously a no."

"Is it?"

His attention snaps back to me. "*Isn't* it?"

"It seems like something husbands would do. And I kiss your cheek and head all the time; it's not like your mouth is all that different."

"But … you're straight," he says like he's explaining it for the hundredth time.

"And?"

"You're telling me you'd be comfortable kissing me in front of people without fucking it up?"

I shrug. "I managed it once, didn't I?"

"Yeah, but—"

"It's fine. It's not like I didn't like it."

It takes a minute to pick up on the silence that's fallen over the room. My gaze moves to Tripp's widened eyes.

He clears his throat and breaks eye contact. "I think we can manage with that."

"Okay." Relief trickles through me. "We can do this, can't we?"

"Sure we can." He reaches for his coffee then turns to his phone, so I grab mine and settle in beside him.

My notifications are still full. I can't bring myself to delete any of them. All I know is that even though I feel like a phony, I *like* reading these people's stories. They're trying to connect in a way, and some of them are really sweet.

I scroll through a few more until I reach a message that makes me pause.

> Hey Dex Mitchale, good chance you won't even read this but I've seen some nasty comments from people who think you were only 'playing' straight which is bullshit. My boyfriend and I knew each other on and off the ice for years and never felt that spark for each other. I've never thought about any guy that way. If you'd asked me a few years ago if I'd ever have sex with a dude, the answer

would have been 'hell no.' Then one day, we were dared to kiss, and it changed everything. His gender wasn't important to me, just him. I'm not sure I'll ever be attracted to another man, and I haven't worked out yet if I even consider myself queer because I don't care about labels, but he's the guy I'm going to spend my life with. Once you know, you just know. Even aside from the sex (and, dude, I never realized it could be so hot) he's my person and it sounds like you've found yours. So congrats, and I'm beyond happy to see another player representing us queer guys in the league, no matter what the haters say. All the best.

I read it twice, then read it again, mouth hanging open as I try to digest so much information at once.

This guy doesn't think he's queer even though he plans to spend his life with a man? And people call *me* dumb. Though, I'm sure Tripp has said before no one can tell someone else how to identify.

But if he's straight, *how*? I can't wrap my head around it.

He kissed this guy, and he liked it. So he tried more.

I liked kissing Tripp. Does that mean I'd be like this guy and enjoy more? Or did I only enjoy it *because* it was Tripp?

Wait. Maybe that's this guy's point.

My brain hurts.

All I know is these two were friends who kissed and became more. That's exactly like us. In a roundabout way.

For the first time since getting these messages, I don't feel like a complete fraud. Tripp *is* my person. I want him there always. There's nothing better than when he's spooning me, and that kiss was ... confusing. But I *did* like it.

Would I still like it if we did it again?

I've never even considered sex with a man. I wouldn't know what to do with another dick, but when I jerk off, it feels damn good, so if it feels good for my dick, wouldn't it feel good for someone else's?

I glance over at Tripp and try to see him the way I would if I was gay. He's got really broad shoulders, and his arms are huge in a way mine could never be.

Is that attractive?

I'm not sure.

I can picture myself holding on to them while we kiss, but does that actually mean anything? Kissing isn't sex. And when I try to picture kissing his chest, his abs, his—

I clear my throat and shift.

I've seen his dick countless times, but I've never paid it any attention.

And it's not like I can ask him to flop it out so I can check if it does anything for me.

Okay, how is it possible that I'm more confused than ever?

"Great," Tripp mutters, pulling my attention back to his mouth. He has freckles above his top lip that my gaze gets stuck on.

"What is it?"

"Get dressed, *husband*." He stands and stretches, his shorts slipping down so I get the briefest glimpse of his pubes.

Could I touch them? Maybe. I shake that thought off. "For what?"

"Photoshoot and interview. Apparently, someone wants to run our story."

"Okay, we're so not ready for that. We don't have it all worked out."

"We don't have a choice." He flips his phone around to face me. "Graham's orders. We have to meet him and our agents at the practice rink before our interview this afternoon. I'm assuming he'll give us all the notes we need."

"Our agents?" Oh no. "I've been avoiding his calls."

"Me too. Damon is going to kill me."

CHAPTER TWELVE

TRIPP

Once we get to the head office, I figure I'll have Dex and his agent, plus Graham as witnesses, so Damon King can't yell at me.

I underestimated my agent.

"A heads-up would've been nice" is the first thing he says when he sees me. Across the reception area. Where a whole lot of office staff can hear.

I close the distance between us. "Hi, Damon. I'm so happy to see you too."

"You've been avoiding my calls."

"Have I? Or have I just been too busy with my new husband to even hear the phone?"

Damon's green eyes narrow, and I blink at him innocently.

He turns to Graham and Dex's agent, Russel. "Is there somewhere I can have a moment with these two alone?"

"And let you steal my client?" Russel asks. "No way. You may have cornered the market on queer athletes, but Dex is mine."

Damon King doesn't represent *every* single queer athlete out there, but he has the majority. It helps that he's gay and an ex-athlete himself. When he was starting out in the industry, he was the only agent who would give outed-against-his-will NFL player Matt Jackson a chance. From that moment on, he became the go-to agent for queer athletes. He represents the entire queer collective except for Anton Hayes.

"My athlete roster is full," Damon says. "That's not what this is about."

Russel looks skeptical but lets Damon drag us into the conference room without the others.

He closes the door behind us. "Okay, what's the real story here?"

Dex's eyes widen, looking a lot like a little boy in trouble with the principal at school.

Damon's a no-bullshit kind of agent, so I know I have to tell him the truth.

"It's a PR nightmare. There's a reason I've been avoiding your calls." I haven't wanted to disappoint him. "I've kind of been hoping this will all go away."

Damon rubs his chin. "I've heard marriages can magically disappear, but you have to make sure you find the marriage genie lamp, not the one that grants you wishes."

Dex snorts.

"Okay, the real deal is Dex wasn't sure if he would ever be able to commit because a wedding seemed like a huge thing. He wanted to get a practice run out of the way, but we didn't know the chapel filed the paperwork. Dex—uh, *we* thought we had to file it ..."

And with every word of the story, Damon's face morphs from concerned and slightly pissed-off agent to someone who's trying not to laugh.

When I finish, he takes a moment to compose himself.

I turn to Dex. "He takes my career seriously, I swear."

Damon waves me off. "The only reason I'm laughing is because this is easy to deal with. Do the year. Get divorced, don't get divorced … just … play the game, and you'll be fine."

"W-what if I'm not completely comfortable with *the game*?" Dex asks. "I'm a straight guy pretending to be in love with Tripp. It's … disrespectful."

My heart pangs as much as I try to ignore it. Even though it is what it is and he could never love me for real, it doesn't mean hearing it gets any easier.

Damon's focus darts between the two of us, and then he folds his arms. "Question. Do you love Tripp?"

"What?" Dex shrieks.

"Wow. This doesn't feel like grade school or anything."

"I don't mean romantically," Damon says. "I've seen you guys on the ice, the countless articles about your friendship. You at least love him platonically, don't you?"

"Of course. He's …" Dex's puppy dog eyes meet mine. "He's everything to me. One of the most important people in my life."

Urgh. I didn't sign up to be tortured today, thanks.

Damon points. "That. Right there. Tap into that, and you'll be fine. I'm not going to stand here and give you a lecture about what's right and what's wrong, why you did it, or why you can't get a quickie divorce like anyone else because I could go on hour-long tangents about being in the spotlight and getting situations twisted. Being in the public eye is one of the toughest challenges athletes have to face because people tend to forget they're human first and foremost. Mistakes are made all the time. The key is to get on top of something that could blow up your careers, your fan base, and squash it before it becomes problematic. Okay?"

Dex relaxes, just a fraction. "Are you sure your client roster is full? I'm a whole lot more at ease now."

"I'm not here to poach anyone," Damon says. "But if you ever need to talk, I'm here. Or my partner. He thought he was 'straight' until he met me too." He winks at Dex.

Dex's mouth drops, but before he has the chance to say anything, Damon opens the door to the conference room and lets the others in.

"We're ready to go over this."

We all take a seat, and they run over what we're doing here. *Out Magazine* wants to do a feature on us along with a series of photos of us on the ice in our jerseys and jeans, and then afterward, what they call "tasteful skin" shots.

I don't know if they mean we're going to be practically naked, fully naked, or they're going to cover our skin in bacon seasoning.

I can read the subtext that Damon and Graham aren't saying in front of Russel: we need this to look legit. A magazine feature that showcases how real this is will go a long way toward shutting up anyone who doubts us. The problem is Dex and him selling it when he doesn't think he can.

When I side-eye him, trying to assess how he'll handle it all, his expression is closed off. I hate when I can't read him.

I put my hand on his upper arm. "Hey. If this is too much, we won't do it."

"It's not the photoshoot that scares me. It's the interview. I'm known for saying stupid things. What if I mess it up?"

"Russel and I will both be there to make sure they know what they are and are not allowed to print," Damon says. "It's better doing it this way than an on-air interview."

Graham nods. "Precisely why we chose this magazine."

There's a knock on the glass door, and the receptionist pops her head in. "They're here."

"Great," Graham says. "Send them in. Oh, and get my intern to show the photographer where to set up."

We all stand to meet the interviewer, Sid Baez—the guy who always covers sports for *Out*—and his assistant.

Dex has turned mute—not the best time for that to happen, so reflexively, when we sit down, I reach for his hand and give it a reassuring squeeze. When I try to take it back, his other hand seals on top of mine.

Sid's smile is easy as he takes his seat. "How's married life treating you?"

I blanch. "Getting straight into it, huh?"

"That was actually just a conversational question, but hey, if you want it on the record, we can do that."

"Oh." I swallow my tongue. "In that case, it's good."

Sid's still smiling as he says, "Oh, fun. One-word answers look great in articles."

"Sorry. Umm ..." Wow, is this how Dex feels when reporters ask him questions he doesn't know how to answer?

"New tactic," Sid says. "Let's start from the top. When did you two meet?"

Dex beats me to answer, hands tightening painfully around mine. "We'd played against each other a handful of times when Tripp played for Colorado. I remember hearing the news he'd been traded to Vegas, and I was relieved he'd be guarding our net. He wouldn't let me get a shot past him when we went head-to-head."

I remember walking into a new arena, with a new team, and Dex practically crash-tackling me into a hug. "I think I might have fallen in love with him a little the day I first entered the Vegas locker room. He made me feel welcome. Like I was needed."

"That was three years ago," Sid says. "When did everything change for you two?"

"We were immediate best friends." I swallow hard. "And I had feelings for him for a long time, but I never said anything because he'd only dated women before."

"Ah, yes. Up until recently, you were dating Jessica Cox?" Sid locks eyes on Dex.

"I was. She, uh ..."

Uh-oh. His first stumble.

"She helped me through my confusing feelings for Tripp," he says.

"Are you saying she turned you gay?"

Damon cuts in. "Nope. New direction, please."

"Sorry, I'll rephrase. How did she help you?"

Dex is sweating like when he does post-game interviews and they ask him something about scoring stats and he says, "*We had a great game today. Great game. We worked as a team. And we're a great team. And yeah. We had a great team game today.*"

I can just see him blurting that all over Sid. I step up. "She was always wary of our friendship because we're so close. Dex came to me saying Jessica thought he was in love with me." That part is actually true. Whenever they'd fight, he'd turn up on my doorstep and say she yelled at him that we should just fuck and get it over with. She'd constantly joke that Dex loved me more than he loved her, but I could tell it was one of those jokes that held a lot of truth.

"Uh, yeah," Dex says cautiously. "She encouraged me to follow my heart, and my heart led me to Tripp. I think he's owned it from the beginning, but I was too dumb to see it. Maybe no one's told you this, but I'm not exactly known for my smarts."

Everyone in the room snickers except me because I know it hurts him when he feels the need to be self-deprecating like that.

"So it was a short engagement," Sid says. "Uh, how long exactly?"

"We woke up one morning, and the idea came to me. We were married that afternoon." Dex turns to me, pinning me with those big brown eyes. "And when we were standing at the altar, promising our lives to each other, it felt ... easy. Because I want to be by Tripp's side always. He truly is my other half. I think it goes to show you can fall in love with anyone if you're not paying attention."

My skin heats, and this moment feels too real.

"Then we got shitfaced and stumbled home," Dex finishes, breaking the spell.

"Please don't write that last part in the article," Damon says.

Sid laughs. "I won't."

—

We're left to change in the locker room even though we're only putting our jerseys on and lacing our skates.

I'm thankful for the privacy, though, because I get to check in with Dex. "That wasn't so bad."

He shrugs and takes his shirt off, all the contours of his back muscles rippling as he does. "Most of it was true." He throws his jersey over his head.

I break my gaze from his incredible body and wonder which parts exactly. "Like you practically adopting me as soon as I walked in this very room three years ago?"

He goes to say something but cuts himself off with a grin. "One good thing about it is we have been close for so long, it's not too hard to talk you up."

"*Not too hard*." I hold my heart. "The romance is killlllling me."

I finish lacing my skates and then take off my jacket and shirt to put on a jersey. When my head pops through the hole, I find Dex's gaze trailing over me, but I don't understand.

It's nothing he hasn't seen before.

"You all good?" I ask tentatively.

"Totally. Let's get this over with. Ooh, do you want to go to D for dinner tonight? I feel like steak." Somehow he says it without even making the joke about a big D steak like he usually does.

"We'll have to ask if we're allowed out of our cage yet, but if Graham says yes, then sure."

"Do you reckon this is what Ezra feels like all the time? I mean, before Anton. He was always doing these types of photoshoots and getting in trouble by his team's PR for being photographed with a million different people … I don't even know if I'm allowed to go to the bathroom without permission."

"It's okay." I try to reassure him. "We've done the hard part. Now we just have to take some photos. It's no big deal."

"But … affection and stuff."

"They're not going to ask us to do anything we haven't already done. I've spooned you while I was naked before, for fuck's sake. You've never cared before now."

"What if they ask us to kiss?"

"Again. We've been there, done that, but I doubt they will. Kissing photos are tacky."

"They are? Jessica always wanted us to be kissing in videos and photos and stuff."

"Exhibit A," I mumble.

"Huh?"

"Nothing. Let's get out there." I walk past him to head for the exit, but he grabs my arm and pulls me to him.

"I know I said I was okay with kissing you, and I am, but maybe we should get one out of the way. So we know for sure I won't mess it up."

"A-are you asking me to kiss you?" I stammer.

"I'm terrified everyone's going to know this is all fake, and I'm freaking out here, and what if—"

Against my better judgment, I step forward and press my mouth to his.

I ignore the pang of heartache, the longing I've carried around for years, and try to show him I'm still the same Tripp.

I'm his best friend.

He's my heart and soul.

And nothing will ever change that.

Not even his inability to love me back.

CHAPTER THIRTEEN

DEX

Unlike the first time, I'm prepared. And when Tripp's mouth meets mine, the tingles that race through me are a welcome relief. I'd thought maybe our first kiss was a fluke, but nope. This is ... uh, yeah, Tripp can kiss. I grip his biceps the way I'd pictured earlier and part my lips, waiting for him to do the same. It takes a moment, and then, when our tongues slide together—I suck in a breath I almost choke on.

I pull away, trying to get oxygen running back to my brain and, surprisingly, blood too, since it seems determined to head in the opposite direction.

"Right, well, I'm feeling better about things. Let's go." I can't even look Tripp in the eye after that. He reads me too easily, and I don't want him to see that I liked kissing him when I have no clue what's going through my head. I'd never hear the end of it.

I kissed my husband, and I liked it, but to me, it was no different than when he holds me or I kiss his cheek or we stay up all night talking.

It makes me ... *full*. Happy.

And, actually, kinda hard, so I guess that's one new thing.

I lead the way out onto the ice, where we pose in our skates, with and without our sticks, together and solo. It's no different from any of the other photoshoots we've ever done, and I'm able to relax into it, stop thinking, and act on instinct.

Even when Tripp and I are asked to horse around and act playful, that shit is easy too. Maybe Damon was onto something, and this whole marriage is a part I can nail. Other than hockey, there isn't much in my life that comes effortlessly to me, but being Tripp's husband might be one of them.

When the photographer pauses to check through the photos, I speed toward Tripp and pull into a sudden stop, sending shavings of ice at him.

"Oh, someone thinks they're clever."

"Race you to the other side and back?"

Instead of answering, Tripp takes off.

"Cheater!"

His laughter echoes back to me as I break into a sprint. He has the head start, but while all that bulk might be good for guarding our goals, it puts him at a disadvantage. My career is built on speed, and I've got the body to go with it, so by the time we're rounding the goals at the other end, I pass him. Tripp curses, and I blow him a kiss before pushing harder to take the lead. He doesn't take it easy on me, and as I fly up the ice, the sound of his skates not far behind me, I'm lighter than I've been in a long time. Hockey is nonstop during the season to the point I want a break, but in off-season, I always miss it. Being on the ice, with my best friend at my side, is a feeling so indescribable, I know I'll never get it again outside of this.

When we reach the starting point, I pull up sharply, Tripp barely seconds behind. He's still laughing, and getting that sound from him fills me with a pride so deep, I reach for him and kiss the side of his head.

At the sound of a loud click, I glance up to find a camera pointed toward us. I'd almost forgotten about them.

"That was great, guys," Russel calls. "Only the locker room ones to do, then you're free."

Tripp and I follow them down the chute to the locker room, where the photographer starts to set up while we take off our skates. "These are going to be the more intimate shots," Sid says. "Out there was to showcase your friendship. In here is your relationship."

And this is the part I was scared of. I'd almost thought we'd gotten away without having to do the fake thing, but I guess this is happening.

Photos. With my husband. Who I love.

Technically, both of those things are true though.

"Okay, we need you two both in towels—leave your underwear on underneath if you like—but we're going for post-game bliss."

Post-game bliss? Okay. That's a thing I can do. After all, I've been close to Tripp when he's been wearing less. This time, we'll just be doing it in front of an audience.

My whole face heats up.

Well, not *doing it* ... posing. Yes. That.

Fuck, why do I feel like I've just played back-to-back games?

I turn to find Tripp watching me steadily.

"This okay for you?" he asks.

"Yeah, totally, why wouldn't it be?"

He smiles at Sid. "Camera shy."

"He seemed fine out there."

"That was different." Tripp takes my hand. "We'll get changed and be back." He tugs me after him, grabbing two towels on the way into the shower area. As soon as we're behind the dividing wall, he drops his voice and whispers, "If it's too much, I'll play sick."

Of course he would. But, nope. I'm not being scared off over something like bare skin. "It's fine. We can totally convince them of how in love we are."

"Really?" Tripp cocks an eyebrow. "I know *I* can be convincing."

"Well, so can I. I *do* love you, and for the other stuff, I'll follow your lead." I strip off my jersey and move to unbutton my jeans, but something makes me glance up just as I shove down my fly. Tripp's staring at my hands, slight line between his eyebrows, and the look on his face makes me feel ... *funny*. Hot all over. And now there's no way for me to finish undressing, because if I do, things will get awkward.

Because I'm suddenly rocking a semi.

Just from his eyes on me.

Normally I'd brush it off, but the more I think about that message I read before we left, the more confused I am over whether this means anything.

So I grab one of the towels still slung over his shoulder, wrap it around my waist, and shove my jeans down. It hides the problem enough that Tripp doesn't notice as he starts to undress, and when he's down to his briefs, solid body on display for me, I grab his towel too.

"What are you doing?" he asks, amused.

"Well ... we need to be comfortable with touching each other." I step forward and wrap it around his waist; then, as I tuck it in, the backs of my fingers graze his V and linger.

"Dex …"

I drag my eyes from his body up to meet Tripp's stare. Unasked questions pass between us, and I … I don't know what to say. Literally. My mind is blank. Static. Where words are gone, instinct takes their place, and I have the strongest urge to kiss him again.

So I do.

Only this time, he jerks away.

"I think we're okay with the touching thing," he says, his voice all scratchy. "We should get back out there."

He spins on his heel, and I watch his broad back disappear into the locker room. I'm too … *something* to follow him. Something I can't name or place, but it has my feet glued to the tile and my eyes pinned on the place he disappeared to.

I jump when Damon's face appears around the divide. "Everything okay in here?"

I know I'm supposed to answer, but what the hell do I say?

Maybe I want to kiss Tripp again, and for some reason that thought makes me get hard?

"Need to piss."

"Okay …"

Damon's gaze burns my skin as I pass through to where the urinals are and force myself to go. At least it helps take care of my overeager problem.

My mouth still feels dry after I wash my hands and join them again. Tripp is sitting on a bench, and Sid directs me to put my feet up and sit along it, head on Tripp's shoulder.

It shouldn't be a big deal.

It shouldn't be different from usual.

It is though.

I sit the way he's told me, and even as Tripp's arm wraps around my waist and he pulls me back against him, I can't relax. I can't sink into his hold like I have a thousand times before, because I'm more ... *aware* of him. The flare of heat where his skin touches mine, the rise and fall of each soft breath that I normally count to fall asleep is hitting my neck and shoulder and sending goose bumps over my body.

"Cold, Dex?" the photographer asks.

"'M fine."

"Okay, a few shots like this. Maybe some with your eyes closed, Dex, or smiling. Tripp, I want a couple of you either looking down at him or kissing his hair. Things like that. Basically, I want to feel the love, so if it feels right, do it."

If it feels right? Normally touching Tripp does, but the only thing that feels right is standing up and walking out of here.

There's too much riding on this for me to screw up, so I take a deep breath and remind myself that I can get through anything with him here.

Each photo, each pose, I'm still awkward and not feeling it, but I *try*.

Cuddled together on the bench.

Tripp with me backed into a locker and smiling at him.

With his lips on my neck.

Cradling my head as we laugh.

Fingers linked, foreheads together.

"There's one more I'd like to try," Sid says, scrolling through the photos. "Lose the towels, and Tripp, I'll have you sitting on the bench; Dex, you'll straddle his lap. These photos are sweet but still friendly. They're missing the sexual connection I'm looking for."

This is what I was worried about. I look at Tripp, waiting for him to put an end to it, but his expression is closed off, and no one else speaks up. I can feel the attention of everyone in the room on us.

Tripp drops his towel and takes position.

If Tripp can do this, so can I, confusion be damned. I'm not doing a great job to hide it, but if I care about Tripp, I have to.

I snap off my towel and cross toward him with a confidence I don't feel. His eyes are on me, and I can tell he's looking without seeing, but that doesn't stop my heartbeat going berserk anyway.

I climb into his lap, knees either side of his thick thighs, and link my hands behind his neck.

Tripp's gaze sharpens on me.

His lips part on a breath, and then, almost like he's scared to, his hands close over my sides.

"Good. Much better," Sid says.

I'm barely aware of the camera.

The only thing in the room is Tripp. His long eyelashes, intense hazel eyes, a crooked nose that usually leads to an equally crooked smile, but there's nothing amused about his expression right now.

My hands find their way into his hair, and I hold back a shiver as his dip lower. Along my ribs, over my waist, coming to a rest on my hips.

He squeezes.

Tight.

So fucking secure.

It grounds me.

And then his thumb ducks under the elastic waistband of my Calvin Kleins.

Oh, shit.

My hands tighten in his hair as I try to stop the rush of desire hitting my groin, try, desperately, to think of anything—*anything*—else other than the way my cock is thickening.

It's no use.

And when it grazes his abs, I shoot back off his lap, cheeks blazing. I rush for the showers where I left my clothes, hands planting firmly in front of my dick.

"Wait, Dexter, that's a perfectly normal—" Sid starts.

"We're done here," I call back over my shoulder. There's no way I can keep going, because I'm not even sure which part is fake anymore.

And that scares me.

I've always loved Tripp. I've always loved being close to him.

But the only boners I've ever cracked around him are the morning wood we both wake up with.

This was more than that.

This boner was one hundred percent linked to Tripp.

But having another man's hands on him shouldn't make a straight dude hard, no matter how much he loves his friend.

So now I'm entering freak-out mode, because I'm too dumb to deal with this by myself. Tripp is the one I go to about sex things or advice on relationships, but how can I begin to explain this one to him?

I'm scared.

But when I think about why, it's not the answer I'm expecting.

I'm not scared of the thought of being with a guy like that.

I'm scared of being dumb again.

Of confusing these feelings for something they're not.

Of doing something to lose Tripp for good.

But most of all, I'm scared that these feelings for Tripp might go away, and I really, really don't want them to.

CHAPTER FOURTEEN

TRIPP

I'm left in the locker room with all eyes on me and no idea how to excuse why Dex would run out of here like that. *Way to throw me under the bus, dude.*

"He's, uh, still shy when it comes to all this ... stuff." Then I realize that might sound weird considering we're supposed to be married for real, not just on paper. "I mean, he's comfortable with me at home, obviously. But yeah, maybe the audience was too much for him."

That sounds legit. I think. I glance at Damon to see if I pulled it off. His tentative and forced smile tells me no. Especially when we're always so affectionate in public.

But that's different. It's never been *sexual*.

And from what I could feel against my stomach, that was definitely sexual. It's not like I've never felt his hard-on before. We've shared a bed countless times because of Dex's craving for affection. I've always dismissed it, because you can't help what your dick does at times, and he has never freaked out like that before.

I tell myself not to read into it, because there has to be a simple explanation. Like the stress of the photoshoot had a weird reaction on his body. It wasn't me he was turned on by; it was ... biology.

Or maybe he really was self-conscious about it because there were cameras and people about.

Though, that thought doesn't fill me with warmth if he's so worried that people might actually believe he could be into me. Or guys in general.

Dex has never once given me any indication he has issues with me being gay, but maybe it's different when it comes to other people thinking *he is*.

"I'm pretty sure we got the shot," Sid says.

"Then I can get dressed and head out?"

"Yep. We have everything we need."

I hurry to get changed so I can get to the car to meet Dex, but when I get there, he's nowhere to be found. Dammit. He should have known I'd come straight after him, which means if he's not embarrassed or feeling stupid, he's back to guilty again.

I'm about to turn around and check out the rest of the building when my phone chimes in my pocket.

> I caught an Uber home. I'm so sorry. This is all my fault.

I hate that he's laying the blame firmly on his own shoulders when he really doesn't need to. This is my mistake as much as it is his, but with everything in overdrive—it breaking in the press, us suddenly having to pretend we're a real couple—it's like we're constantly bombarded with the reminder that we made a mistake, and Dex is adamant about taking responsibility.

I didn't have to say yes to fake marrying him.

We keep dancing around what it really means to be married in the public eye, what we're going to have to endure, and this was only our first taste of it.

I get home, and as soon as I walk through the door, Dex glances up at me from his spot on the couch. His deep brown eyes are glossy, he looks so distraught, and I don't give a shit about anything else we have going on. All I want is to make him feel better. I march over to Dex, and without warning, I tackle him on the couch.

"What are you—"

I blow a huge raspberry on his neck, and he squirms to get away from me while laughing uncontrollably. He laughs so hard he can't breathe, and the sound is like coming home.

"There's my Dex," I say and lift up but stay on top of him.

His happiness fades. "What do you mean?"

"This whole situation is fucking with us, and it's a mess, and I hate it, but we need to find a way to make it work."

Dex shifts so he's sitting up again, and I move to do the same, planting my ass next to him on the couch.

He runs a hand through his hair. "I don't know how to make it work. And I didn't know I'd ..." He sucks in a sharp breath.

"Get hard while straddling me? It was a physical reaction, that's all. It's fine."

"I want to say this is really hard, but I know what your response will be."

"It *is* hard. *So* hard. We can't cock it up." I joke, but it's true. I was managing my feelings for Dex, and now he's being thrust at me more than ever. "But every time you blame yourself for this situation, I can't help thinking that's your way of wanting to give up. I'm expecting you to change your mind and take the trade any minute. And that would be worse than if it got out."

Dex turns to me. "I don't want to take the trade. But I can't stand the thought of you being dragged into whatever backlash if it happens. I'm an asshole."

"Yes. You're a complete monster. How dare you agonize over the possibility of hurting my feelings! You're the worst!"

He hangs his head. "It would kill me if this hurt you, because I'm not lying when I say you're the most important person in my life."

"I know. And that's why I think we need to let this go. I don't blame you, and you can't either. Husbands face things together, and that's what we're going to do."

"Move on," Dex murmurs.

"Yep. Starting with a night off from being married."

"Uh, I don't think that's how marriages work."

"Well, the thing about marriage is we get to choose what we're allowed and not allowed to do in ours. And I say, instead of being *husbands* tonight, we need to go back to being best friends. We should focus on that instead of our 'marriage.'"

"You don't mean to hook up …"

"Fuck no." As much as I love sex, I also hate knowing Dex is having sex with someone who isn't me.

"Then how do we do that?"

"Margarita Mondays at that horribly decorated Mexican hole-in-the-wall that has amazing food."

Dex finally gets some of his usual spark back. "Oh, I am in."

While Dex scarfs his sixth taco for the night, I sit across from him, buzzing from all the margaritas.

This is exactly what we needed.

For the first time since this whole mess started, we actually feel like *us* again.

As long as I pretend not to notice the strange looks he occasionally throws my way.

"Okay, I have a question for you," Dex says around a mouthful of food. "Would you rather have a one-night stand with a woman or have sex with the entire queer collective at the same time?"

I lift my drink. "I would rather drink this and not answer that question."

"Is it because you've already done the second one?"

I choke on my drink. "I most certainly have not, fuck-youverymuch. I have standards."

"I dunno. You're married to me, so that doesn't exactly back your theory."

Hey, at least we're joking about it now. "True. Let me ask you something, then. Would you rather a one-night stand with a guy or fuck the entire … oh, wait, having sex with multiple girls at once would be your dream. Ooh, I've got it. One-night stand with a guy or have sex with Sienna?"

Dex screws up his face. "One night with a guy. Hands down. Having sex with Sienna would be like having sex with Phoebe, and oh shit, I think I'm going to throw up all the tacos I just ate. You're evil. At least my options weren't mean."

"Just because we're all queer, that doesn't mean we actually want to fuck each other. I have never, ever, ever had sex with any of them."

"Wait. Not even Oskar?"

"Not even Oskar. We … we were never dating."

Dex puts the rest of his taco back on his plate. "So that was … all an act?"

"Yes."

"But the sex … I heard you."

I down the rest of my drink. "Oskar always takes things too far. I'm sorry I didn't put a stop to it."

"You went along with it though. I don't … I don't understand."

I pick my words carefully. "They were concerned that we spend too much time together."

"What?" Dex has never sounded more confused. "That's not possible."

"Well, this funny thing can happen with little gay boys called the Straight Best Friend, and they wanted to make sure I didn't, uh, fall for you. They wanted to make sure I wasn't getting things confused between us."

He gives a hollow laugh. "And now we're married."

"No. Nope. We're moving on, remember? No guilty tone. Now, can we please forget how it got started?" And I must sound convincing enough, because he grins.

"Lucky for you, my brain doesn't like to retain information, so it's already gone. You're sorry, I'm sorry, we're all sorry."

"Good. Now." I tap my chin. "This one-night stand with a guy thing. Would you rather fuck Coach Roland or Graham?"

"Now you're being pure fucking evil," he grumbles.

"Wait until you see where I'm dragging you next. There'll be endless possibilities for your choice to actually happen."

Dex's face lights up. "You're finally going to take me to Rump?"

Rump is my favorite gay bar in Vegas, and Dex has asked to come with me before, but once I tell him I won't be there long, just long enough to find a hookup, he leaves me to myself.

I love it because of the decent hookups and cheap drinks. And by cheap, I mean the cheapest on the Strip, so still really, really expensive. "Yep, you're taking your husband dancing. And seeing as I'm probably not allowed to grind up on other dudes, you're going to have to endure it."

"Grind up on me anytime, baby."

I was right. Taking the night off from our marriage to become best friends is exactly what we needed. And the very thing that always gets me hurt.

But by this point, I hurt when I'm with him. I hurt when I'm without him.

There's nothing else I can possibly do.

CHAPTER FIFTEEN

DEX

It's impossible to be down or confused when you're full of margaritas and tacos. Tripp's suggestion for us to go out was genius, and now, as we wait in line for Rump, I can finally relax. Things this afternoon have almost been back to normal, and I didn't realize exactly how empty I was until now.

The pressure of being married has gone to my head, and it's sad that we're closer and more affectionate as best friends than husbands. But if we have a whole year of this ahead, we're sure as hell going to make it work.

A trade isn't an option.

"Would you rather," I start, "nipple piercing or dick piercing?"

"Nipple for me, dick for the guy I'm with."

Well, that's something I've never considered. "Is that ... does it make a difference?"

"Yes."

"I know with chicks it helps hit the—"

"Same thing for dudes, just different location."

Oh. "Huh. I hadn't thought of that before."

"It also makes giving head more interesting."

"It does?" Okay, when I'd asked that question, I didn't think it all the way through. I'd meant which would Tripp rather get, but now that we're talking about it, I have *way* too much cock on the brain. I can't stop picturing it, and now I'm really curious about how it all works. You'd think having a gay best friend would mean I know a hell of a lot more about gay sex than I actually do.

"What do you like about it?" I ask.

"What?"

"Giving head."

Tripp looks at me funny. "It's a dick, and dicks are hot."

Not the answer I was hoping for, but I have no clue what I wanted to hear. I don't think dicks are hot, so that doesn't help me. But when Tripp looks away and I let myself take him in again, I can't deny the stirring of interest that hits me.

I'm curious.

Probably too curious for a straight guy.

But until I'm faced with a cock, how will I ever know how I'd react? I never thought I'd get hard over having Tripp touch me, and that happened, so maybe I *could* find a dick sexy. Or his, at least.

And I promised myself I wouldn't think about these things tonight. Tonight is about getting back to normal. I wrap my arm around Tripp's neck and haul him closer to press a kiss to his hair.

"You smell like hot sauce," he says, elbowing me.

I breathe hot sauce breath all over his cheek and tighten my hold on him.

"Fuck off," Tripp says, squirming.

"Sharing's caring."

"One bro does not share stank breath with another bro."

"Good thing we're husbands now, then."

We wrestle as the line moves forward and only break apart once we hit the front and the bouncer apologizes to Tripp about making him wait in line instead of being let straight in, as though it's some huge fail on his part.

"I didn't realize you came here that much," I say.

"I don't, but they like it when I do because, you know, publicity of having an NHL player at their venue. I always tell them not to give me VIP treatment, but they don't listen."

Finally, I get my first view of Rump.

It's busy and looks like most clubs I've been to. Dark and moody with flashing lights over the dance floor. The biggest difference here is it's about ninety percent guys.

Tripp's come here plenty of times without me, and I've always thankfully been aware enough that it's his place to hook up, so I've never pushed to come with him even though I'd be an awesome wingman.

But as Tripp takes my hand and pulls me through the crowd, I'm suddenly very glad he said that grinding up on other guys is out of the question, because even in the dark club, he's getting a lot of attention.

I have no idea if these guys recognize him or think he's hot, but I definitely notice the heads turning in our direction.

Tripp pauses, tugging me close to tilt his lips to my ear. "Drinks or dancing?" He pulls back to see my reply, and I use it as a chance to try to see him the way the guys here do. The dark red hair and freckles are adorable, and his hazel eyes are big and round, but that's where the soft qualities end. His jawline is solid, his neck and shoulders are thick, and there's an overpowering masculine quality to him that I've never paid much attention to before.

Tripp has always been Tripp. All of these things put together make up my best friend, but breaking his features down into his nose, his hands, the quiet confidence he has when he's around me ...

"Dex?" His crooked smirk comes out and connects with some sort of hook behind my belly button. It tugs and feels weird and good at the same time.

"Dancing," I shout.

His hand tightens around mine, and he starts walking again.

It wasn't a hard question when the margaritas are still making everything softer around the edges.

Tripp gets attention on the dance floor too, so as soon as he comes to a stop in the crowd of bodies, I immediately pull him against me. I've always been needy for his attention, and it's no different tonight. I want to be the only one Tripp pays attention to.

It's selfish, sure, but *I'm* his husband—technically—and his best friend, and the rest of the guys here are nothing to him.

My hands close over his back until we're chest to chest, and Tripp's breath hits my jaw.

"Last chance to back out of the grinding," he says.

"What, you think I don't have moves?" I let my hands fall to his ass and pull him tighter against me. Having a muscular body pressed against mine isn't as weird as it probably should be, but this is far from the first time I've been close to Tripp. It's just the first time I've done it while grabbing his ass.

"I know you've got moves," he says, voice barely audible over the music. "You forget, I know everything about you." Then after a second of hesitating, Tripp's hands find my sides, slide down to my hips like earlier, and then dip lower to grab my ass as well. "You're playing *my* game now, Dex."

"I like games."

He pumps his eyebrows. "You going to get a boner again?"

I drop my head onto his shoulder. "You just had to remind me. I'm sorry."

"Why?"

I pull back. "I ... I *poked* you with it."

Tripp's head falls back on a laugh. "This may come as a shock to you, but I *like* being poked by dicks."

Before I can stop myself, I picture Tripp bent over and ... "So you bottom? Shit. Can I even ask that?"

"No, you can't." He presses his lips to my ear, and I get a nose full of lime from our margaritas. "The only guys who get to ask that question are the ones I'm about to sleep with."

"I guess no one will find out for a year, then, huh?"

"I guess so." Nose trailing over my cheek, Tripp's hands tighten on my ass. "So would *you* rather ..."

"Yeah?"

"Top or bottom for your hypothetical hookup with Coach?"

I huff. "I'm not answering that."

"But you like games."

"I thought you weren't allowed to ask that question."

"Yes, but this is a hypothetical. Not real life."

Fair point. I'm not sure what my answer would be, but when it comes to Coach, it's a giant hell no to both. Graham too. Hell, maybe every guy in this bar. And if I can't even answer a hypothetical, then where is this curiosity coming from?

I release Tripp's ass to run my hands up and under his shirt. "I'll answer, but only if we take Coach out of the question."

"Ah, so you do want Graham after all."

I shudder. "Not him either."

"Fine ... what about with ..." He pulls back just enough to meet my gaze. "Your husband?"

Flutters break out in my gut. I was hoping he'd ask that. "Are we still talking hypothetically?"

His Adam's apple bounces, and he doesn't answer.

Somehow his hands squeeze even tighter and *fuck*, I swear he's going to give me bruises, but I don't ask him to stop. I can't read body language, and I usually miss a lot when it comes to people not using their words, but this ... right here and now, it's like I can hear what Tripp is saying without him saying anything.

It's hypothetical if I want it to be hypothetical.

I'm certain I don't want it to be.

This is nice. Dancing with him. His thigh between my legs.

I let my fingers trail over his hard abs as I think through his question as if he's actually propositioning me. I'm not entirely sure he is, because he was adamant on keeping this marriage official on paper only, but I can't help thinking about what it would be like. To be with Tripp. In *that* way.

I think ... I think I'd want it. "Maybe I'd try both. But ... well, you know what you're doing, right? Coach wouldn't put me in as goalie for a game because it's not my area of expertise, so ... well, I'd want you—uh, *my husband* to do it to me first. I've never, umm ..."

"Done anal before?" His voice is gravelly, and it makes my cheeks flush.

"Yeah ... but it's different than with a chick, isn't it?"

"Well, yeah, I can think of one big fucking difference."

And when Tripp shifts, I can *feel* one big fucking difference too. One hard, thick difference pressed against my thigh.

He goes to pull back, like his point has been made, but I crush him against me. Torsos flush, foreheads pressed together, his hard-on against my thigh, and my rapidly thickening dick against his.

It's just a physical reaction.

Sure.

Right.

That's what's happening here.

The physical reaction is why my blood feels overheated.

The physical reaction is why I can't move away.

The physical reaction is why I grind myself against him and—actually, that one *is* accurate.

But even if I am the dumbest person on earth, I also know it's not the physical reaction making that urge to kiss him rise up in me again.

This time when I grab his ass with one hand, there's nothing polite about it. I palm one of his round cheeks and twist my free hand through his hair. I'm breathing harder, my heartbeat is drumming so fast I'm sure he can probably feel it, and sweat is breaking out along my skin.

"Turn around," he growls.

It's the last thing I want to do. Turning around means being further from kissing him. Turning around means losing the pressure against my cock. But I do it, because it's Tripp and he asked, and I'd give him anything.

I turn, and Tripp's hands close over my abs, holding me against him and then ... then I'm met with a whole new sensation. His hard cock rests firmly in the crease of my ass, and my cheeks heat to boiling point. My cock is pressed against my fly, begging to be set free, to be touched, and I'd worry about someone noticing my problem if the guys around us weren't all in similar situations.

"Still think you'd want to bottom?" he rasps.

"More than ever."

Tripp's exhales are loud against my ear, and I'm not even aware that I'm grinding back against him until he grabs my hips tightly.

"Fuck, you need to stop that," he warns.

I turn my head until our lips are a breath apart. "Please, Tripp. I've never been so hard in my life."

He curses under his breath. "You can't say those things to me."

"So it's okay for me to rub it against you if I don't talk about it?" I whine. Because, shit. It's *aching*. I'm not going to be able to dance much longer with him wrapped around me like this.

"Exactly," Tripp says.

"Fine." I grab his hand and bring it down over my cock. If I can rub against his leg, why not his hand?

His grip tightens and makes me whimper.

"Yes ..."

"Oh, fuck." He nips at my ear at the same time as he grinds against me again. "I ... I can take care of that. If you want me to." His voice breaks, and the sound is so hot, I almost forget to answer.

"Yes. Please. Now."

He releases me, but before I can ask him what the hell, he takes my hand and drags me through the club. We reach a bathroom that Tripp leads me into, and ignoring the one dude washing his hands, Tripp kicks open a cubicle and shoves me inside.

His jaw is tense, hazel eyes darker than usual, and it occurs to me I've never seen him like this before.

I've been missing out.

Tripp pushes me up against the wall and covers my body with his. He fumbles with my fly, one hand rubbing me through my jeans, and just as he gets them open and is about to pull me out ...

"Wait."

Tripp freezes.

"I want to kiss you."

Our eyes lock, and some of the tension leaves his face. "You do?"

I tug his face to mine.

And like earlier, tingles explode across my skin. His tongue pushes into my mouth, and I relax into the kiss, into knowing it's Tripp, into getting to share this with him. Our friendship has always been perfect, but this, here, *fuck*. If I thought cuddling with him was the most amazing thing, I was wrong.

Kissing Tripp is addictive.

He shoves my jeans and briefs down my thighs and closes his hand around my cock. His fingers are rough and thick, and when he spits into his hand and starts to jerk me off, there's nothing sweet or delicate about it. It's blinding, burning need. It's pure want.

I grab his ass and press my thigh between his legs, and Tripp starts to thrust against me with purpose. It's hot. So fucking hot.

I can barely stop to catch my breath, let alone think. All I know is I should have been doing this with Tripp a lifetime ago, because fucking hell, how does this feel so good?

His hand works me over confidently. Tight but not too tight, paying the tip the perfect amount of attention to drive me crazy. I'm close way too quickly. And I know that's the point of a quickie, but I never want this to end.

I grip his ass, encouraging his thrusts to get harder, faster. He's panting, and I'm swallowing every noise he's making. Taking them from him. Making them mine. I wish we were home and could take this slower. I want to touch him. I want to learn what a cock other than mine feels like in my hand. But too soon, I'm slipping.

My balls start to draw up, pleasure pulling them tighter and tighter. "You need to come."

"Goddamn it, Dex."

I'm about to offer to pull him out when he drives his cock into my leg painfully, and his whole body goes stiff. Seeing the way his head drops back and his eyes fall closed …

I close my hand around his and start to jerk off hard and fast, fucking the fist we've made around my cock until it's too much, too good, too … everything.

"Tripp …" I moan as it hits me. My cock jerks as I spill over our hands, panting hard and closing my eyes as I let the intense waves of pleasure pass over me.

I've never, ever done anything like that.

And when I open my eyes and find Tripp watching me, I give him a lazy smile before tugging him into another slow kiss. I'm still high. Still buzzing. It's going to take a while for me to come down from something so indescribable.

My brain is too scrambled to work out how I'm feeling; all I know is that sex has always been great, but never, ever like that. Maybe it's all the cock. Maybe it's because I was so goddamn horny beforehand, or maybe it's because of Tripp and how much I already love him.

I don't know what to say after that. How to tell him what it meant to me or how happy I am that I got to experience it with him.

I kiss him again. "If someone had told me that's what it was like to have a husband, I would have found me one a long time ago."

CHAPTER SIXTEEN

TRIPP

Fuuuuck, what am I doing?

Do I regret it? Not yet. Do I want a repeat? Right fucking now, before we both sober up and realize we've crossed lines we shouldn't have.

"Let's go home," I say in his ear.

We stumble outside the club, but Dex's hand doesn't leave me the whole walk to a designated Uber pickup area. Whether it's around my shoulder, tugging my shirt, or holding my hand, Dex's affection is back. It more than makes up for the sticky mess in my pants.

The buzz in my veins is worth the possibility of being hurt tomorrow when he blames the alcohol, confusion over being married, and any other excuse a supposed straight guy clings to the morning after.

While we wait for our car, Dex pulls me right up against him. His hands are on my hips, his mouth is just an inch away, and even though every self-preservation instinct is telling me to pull away, I can't step back. My feet won't allow it.

"So," he murmurs. "We've never done that before."

"No, we haven't."

"Why not? We should've been doing that the whole time. You've been holding out on me."

I run my hand down his arm. "Oh, honey, if you've never had a handy before, I really worry about your taste in women. Also, when gay guys offer straight guys shared orgasms, it can get messy, and I'm not talking about all the cum."

"I mean, I get that, but ... this was ... it was ..."

"It was a margarita-and-taco-induced thrill."

"Nah, it was more than that. It was ..." While he tries to think of a word, our car pulls up.

"This is us." I pull him into the car and slide through to give him enough room to get in, but as soon as he does, he closes the gap between us.

He wraps his arm around my shoulders, and even though he is an affectionate guy, he's right. What we did was something else entirely. It wasn't just a hookup. It wasn't just friends.

I'm sure tomorrow we'll have a lot of time to try to figure it out, but right now, I don't want to. I don't want to ruin this.

And if a handjob and frotting in a bathroom stall is all I get, then it's all I get. It's more than I ever thought I would have with Dex.

He leans in and breathes into my ear. "You know what I want to try next? When I get you home, I want to touch you this time."

"Jesus fuck," I hiss.

"What was that?" the Uber driver asks.

"Sorry, that wasn't directed at you. My frie—uh, husband, is being mean to me." I'm thankful my place isn't far because I swear the driver keeps glaring at us in the rearview mirror.

When we pull up to the building, we can't get out of the car fast enough. In the elevator, we paw at each other.

He nips my neck, I grab his ass, and we're all wandering hands and mouths.

Dex works his way up my neck, his kisses alternating between soft and rough, and by the time his lips find mine, I'm so hungry for him, I don't want to part to walk to my apartment door.

I fumble with my keys but manage to get the door unlocked, and we don't stop kissing for a second. My head spins, and if possible, I feel like I'm even more drunk than when I was back at the club, even though we stopped drinking before we got there.

I'm drunk on Dex. On his scent, his body.

My only fear is waking up tomorrow and realizing this is all a dream. A vivid and sexy dream.

But with the simple clearing of a throat from somewhere in my apartment, my dream turns into a nightmare. And that's how I know this is reality and not some sleep-induced fantasy.

Because there is no way in hell a sexy dream would include having my parents watch me hooking up with my dream guy. They're standing there in their pajamas, obviously having made themselves at home. Last time they visited me from Seattle, I gave them a spare key to let themselves in and out while I was at practice or away games. I guess they kept it.

They stare at me with the same looks on their faces as the time they found out I crashed the car when I was a teenager.

It's disappointment and anger all rolled into one.

"Mom? Dad?" I quickly push Dex off me.

"So it's true, then," Mom says. "You got married and didn't even tell us."

Dad folds his arms. "We thought maybe there was some mistake or it was a rumor, because all of Dex's stuff is in the guest bedroom. But …"

I swallow hard. I can't lie to my parents. I just can't.

So no words pass my lips.

"There's no room in Tripp's closet," Dex says. "I'm keeping my stuff there until he throws out all of his ugly clothes."

Ugly clothes? Say what?

I turn to him. "They're *designer*. But you wouldn't know a label if it jumped out at you and bit you on your ass."

"Well, I guess we have a lot to talk about in the morning," Mom says. "But I'm tired from waiting up for you all night."

I shudder. "Whoa, flashback from when I was eighteen. That's creepy."

Mom and Dad head down the hallway to the second guest bed that Sienna crashes in occasionally, and I turn to Dex.

"Well, that wasn't awkward as fuck."

"Not at all. It's not every day you meet your in-laws with a hard-on after putting fresh hickeys all over their son's neck." His fingers trail over my skin, and I gasp.

"You didn't? Also, what are you talking about? You've met my parents countless times."

"Not as your husband." He glances to where my parents disappeared. "Do you think … are they going to hate me after this?"

"No. They will love you because they've always loved you. Hell, they'll probably even want to claim you in our divorce."

Dex winces, and I wonder if this is one of those times it's too real for him.

I tug on his hand. "Come on. Let's go to bed." I lead him to my room, but he stops me outside the door.

"Didn't we say we weren't going to share anymore?"

I lean in and drop my voice. "We also said no sex stuff. Making each other come was against the rules, and we've already broken that one tonight."

Dex pulls me against him. "I guess if we're going to do something wrong, we should make it worth it."

His head dips, moving closer and closer until his breath tickles my skin. I want to kiss him again, but the thought of having sex while my parents sleep down the hall is too teenagery for me.

I step back. "Let's go to sleep."

"Wait, wha?" His voice goes all high-pitched and weird.

I laugh and pull him into the bedroom. "I'm not having straight-guy-experimental-sex with my parents in the other room. Sorry, not happening." And I should get some type of award for saying no to that.

"But … I just found out how good you are at sex stuff. You can't take it away from me now!"

"Did you maybe not want to yell that so loud? It's bad enough I have to lie to my parents. Don't make it worse for me. Please."

"Fine." He takes off his shirt, revealing rippling abs and that lean muscle that makes him fast on the ice.

"And now you're not playing fair."

"Fair?" He undoes his pants. "You're the one who's making me go to bed like this." His jeans drop to the floor, revealing a very large and hard bulge in the front of his boxer briefs.

My mouth waters. "Okay, fuck it. But you have to be silent." I immediately drop to my knees.

Dex's hand lands on my shoulder. "Hey, whoa, hold up a second."

Damn it. My mouth is right in front of his hard dick tenting in his boxers, and now he stops me?

Where I expect him to say he's changed his mind already, all he says is, "I thought it was my turn to do things to you."

"If you let me suck your dick right now, you can do anything you want to me afterward."

Dex's big goofy grin appears, and like it always does, it hits me square in the chest. "In that case, go right ahead. If your hand can do magical things, I can't wait to see what your mouth can do."

Oh, buddy, you have no idea.

I run my hands up his hairy thighs and then around to his ass, giving his firm globes a hard squeeze before dipping my fingers into the waistband of his underwear and tugging them down.

His hard cock springs free, and I don't even know the number of times I've thought about this moment. I never dreamed it would actually happen though.

As much as my brain tells me to take it slow, as soon as my mouth encloses over the head of his dick and salty precum hits my tongue, there's no holding me back.

I suck him greedily, tasting all of him.

His knees buckle, and for a second, I think he might fall, but he reaches behind him for my bedside table to steady himself.

Even if he did fall, we'd keep going, because goddamn, he feels so good in my mouth. I try to bring my A-game, but I'm too distracted by how much I love this to really concentrate.

I need to make him come. I want to swallow all of him.

I'm hard just from blowing him, and when I look up into his hooded eyes as he stares at me working him over, I swear I almost come in my pants for the second time tonight.

He looks so blissed-out, biting his lip while he tries to stay silent. His breathing is rapid, but he doesn't take his eyes off me the whole time.

I take him all the way to the back of my mouth, as far as I can manage until my eyes water and my gag reflex fights me. And when my hand cups his balls and gives a gentle tug, the first trickles of cum start to fill my throat.

He's done a good job of staying silent until now. The cry Dex releases makes me want to slap him, but then his thighs tense and I'm hit with a wave of cum on my tongue, and his orgasm is more important than keeping quiet.

I keep sucking, keep bobbing my head, trying to get every last drop until he pulls out of my mouth.

"I …" He starts but then suddenly turns and lies across my king bed. "Holy fuck. That was … was …"

I wipe my mouth as I stand and give him a smug smile.

Dex leans up on his elbows. "Do you think gay guys give the best head because they have a dick and know what's good?"

"I'll take that as a compliment."

He flops back again. "Fuck. Damn."

I take off my shirt and then undo my pants that are still sticky from the club. Dex eyes me as I undress completely. Having him check me out properly is a foreign concept to me.

In locker rooms, sharing a hotel room on the road, he's never once looked at me the way he is now.

"Just let me recover, and then prepare yourself for the most awkward handjob of your life."

"Can't wait."

And even though we get under the covers and he falls asleep the minute I spoon him, I don't care. What he just gave me was worth more than a handjob.

CHAPTER SEVENTEEN

DEX

I wake to Tripp's arms around me, both of us sweaty under the covers, and I kick them down to the foot of the bed. Tripp shifts, hard cock pressing against my ass and ... wait ...

The night before comes back to me in flashes of tacos and dancing and Tripp on his knees.

I fell a-fucking-sleep!

If it wasn't official before now, I'll take my dumbass crown, because who the hell falls asleep after the blowjob of their life? All I wanted to do was repay him because he deserved it after that.

He grunts and buries his face into my neck as his cock drags over my ass again.

Hmm. I guess now I have my chance.

I roll over carefully, making sure to keep Tripp's arm firmly around my waist. He's still asleep, but his eyelids are twitching like he's on the verge of waking up, and like it always does, his face makes me smile.

It's not his face I want this morning though.

I glance down between us, our twin erections side by side, and have a moment of *holy shit* at what I'm seeing. Hooking up with him last night was easy because it was Tripp. His dick wasn't in the equation. But if I want this sex stuff to continue—and I really, really do—I'm not leaving it all up to him.

When it comes to my partner, I want to do nothing short of blow their mind.

People say chicks fake it all the time, and I've always called bullshit on that theory, but after last night ... I've never been with someone who made it so obviously clear how much they wanted me. And the thing is, it's not even about the sex.

There's a connection between us that runs so deep I swear I need it for my survival. It's always been there, always been intense, but last night that connection finally burst free, and being with Tripp wasn't just right, it was necessary.

So with that thought in mind, I reach for his cock.

Like the rest of him, he's thicker than me. For some reason, that thought *really* turns me on. To be hit with solid proof that the dick I'm holding isn't mine. His is redder, veinier, curves slightly toward his abs, whereas mine stands straight and tall, like a good little soldier.

"Dex ..." His sleep-drunk voice sends shivers through me.

"Good morning, husband."

His eyes crack open, full of lust, and yep. This. No one has ever, *ever* looked at me that way. I tighten my hand around the head of his cock, vowing that I'm going to do everything in my power to be worthy of that look. "I almost thought I dreamed it ..."

"Took me a moment as well."

"And you ... how are you—"

There's a loud knock on the door, and we quickly spring apart.

"Boys? Time to wake up. *Now*." Wow. Mira sounds pissed.

Tripp groans, draping his arm over his face. "*Aaand* there goes my dick. I'll never get hard again, I swear."

"You better." I lean over and kiss his jaw. "Don't be giving me a new toy to play with and then taking it away."

He peers out at me. "You really—"

More banging. "*Now*. I'm not scared to come in there."

"Fucking mothers." Tripp throws his legs over the side of the bed. I guess our morning together is over, and now I'm faced with something more intimidating than giving my first-ever handjob. Making Tripp's parents fall in love with me, not as his friend and teammate, but as his husband.

Damn, I'm nervous.

Tripp pulls on sleep shorts and walks out, but I duck in for the fastest shower ever first. I need to wash the smell of sweat and cum off me, but I'm anxious about keeping them waiting.

So I ignore my cock while I scrub myself with Tripp's bodywash. I'm still not totally dry as I pull on my clothes and rush to meet them.

The three of them are around the table, talking. Tripp's dad, Karl, is built like him with reddish-brown hair, and his mom is strawberry blonde and freckled. They've both passed on Tripp's most dominant characteristics, and somehow he manages to look like them but not. Tripp is ... he's uniquely ... him. And until recently, I didn't think about his appearance in a sexual way. At least, I didn't realize I was looking at him in a sexual way, but maybe I have been. If it's this easy to fall into bed with him, doesn't that mean on some level, I've always found him attractive?

My heart is in my throat as I approach and go for a totally casual greeting. "Morning, everyone."

"It's already midday," Mira replies.

Karl almost grins, I swear he does. "Dexter. How are you?"

"Great. I forget how much I love the downtime in off-season."

Mira hums. "So that's why you married my son? Boredom."

I cringe, and Tripp curses under his breath.

"What?" she asks. "I still can't believe this is real. That you two would actually go and get married without telling anyone."

I fill my cup with coffee and approach the table, trying for an innocent expression. "It wasn't on purpose. We were just walking by the chapel and figured, hey, we're in love, let's do it. Then it just happened."

"It *just* happened?" Karl asks skeptically.

"Yep."

"Is 'in love' code for drunk?" Mira shoots back at me.

"*Mom.*"

"I'm sorry, Tripp, but I'm struggling to figure out how my son could get married without inviting us and then can't even pick up the phone to let us know. Are you mad at us? Is it because we didn't move to Vegas like Sienna to be with you?"

"What? No. It's not …" I can tell Tripp wants to be honest. He's so conflicted, I almost do it myself, but then finding out the wedding was all a sham is a fast way for them not to take me seriously. I have that problem enough.

Maybe I'm straight.

Maybe these feelings for Tripp are only because it's Tripp. I don't know. But I do know, if he wants it, I want to see where this goes. Maybe after the year we end up getting divorced anyway, but it won't be from lack of trying on my end.

And the first part of a successful relationship is getting my in-laws to love me too.

"It's all my fault."

Three stares fly to me.

"I was so wrapped up in it all that I've been taking up every free second Tripp has. You know what the honeymoon period is like."

Tripp closes his eyes, like he wishes he could shove the words back in my mouth, but his lips are pressed suspiciously tight. Win.

Mira at least looks less mad.

"I'm sorry. Don't be mad at Tripp. I love him so much I wanted all his attention."

"Well, that's nothing new," Karl says. "But a phone call is hardly a big ask."

"You're right. We also didn't know how to tell you though, because the whole, ah, eloping thing was a surprise to all of us. A *good* surprise." I direct that last part to Tripp. Because it was. So, so good. I've never been happier to be a dumbass. "Let me make it up to you. You're my family now too."

My winning smile barely cracks Mira's annoyance. But while the change is subtle, I pick up on it. Now she just looks resigned to having me as a son-in-law. Resignation is a step up from irritation, so I'm calling that a win.

"Let's start by taking you to lunch. Somewhere *really* fancy. Tripp, do you think Enzo could get us in at the—"

"You know," Karl says. "I have always wanted to go to that place. You know the hotel. The really tall one with the restaurant and the zip line."

"The Strat?" My voice squeaks. I pretend it didn't happen. The thing most people don't know about me, because they don't need to, is I'm terrified of heights.

Planes aren't great, but I can close the window shade and focus on my phone, and buildings like Tripp's are fine because they're not enormous. We're only twelve stories up here.

It's a world of difference from getting in an elevator, traveling higher and higher only to be spat out in a building that I *swear to God* is constantly swaying and looks on top of the world.

Tripp must pick up on my panic. "Sorry, Dad, I think that one will be booked out."

"Not for us," I manage. If my father-in-law wants Top of the World, he's going to get it. And I will one hundred percent keep my cool and not focus at all on what would happen if the building suddenly collapses. "I'll make the call."

And one unfortunate part of being well-known is that as soon as I say Tripp and Dex Mitchale—the superior spelling—there's a table for four waiting.

Fantastic.

I grab some clothes from the guest room and go to change in Tripp's.

He follows me inside. "Enzo's would have been fine."

"Nope. Not for my in-laws. They get whatever they want."

"We should have told them the truth."

I turn to him, worried I've screwed up again. "Should we?"

He shrugs. "The thing is, I don't really know what the truth is anymore."

"We accidentally got married, and until last night we were still best friends, but then you sucked my dick and I kinda want to try it too?"

He laughs. "Yeah. So telling the truth is out, then."

"Fair enough."

Before he can move toward his bathroom, I grab him and pull him against me. My lips find his neck and the red marks I left there last night. Seeing my marks against Tripp's freckles makes me want to leave more. All over.

"People will see us today," he points out. "You okay with that?"

"The only difference I see is that instead of doing this"—I kiss his cheek—"I'll be doing this." My lips meet his, and we share a soft, slow kiss.

He lets out a shuddery breath as he pulls back. "Okay. I think you'll be fine."

And I am.

With the relationship stuff.

But when we pull up at the Strat, and I tilt my head back to look at the top of the building, I think I'm going to wet myself.

"You all right?" Tripp asks as we climb out of the car.

I grab his hand and squeeze tight. "Don't let me die."

"You have more chance of choking on lunch than falling off the building."

"But you're saying there's still a chance?"

I purposely chose a black button-up to hide the sweat marks, but a quick glance in the elevator mirror shows the black isn't doing a whole lot. Tripp doesn't drop my hand, and the higher we go, the higher those numbers on the display climb, the more unsettled I get.

I can do this.

I can do this.

The elevator doors finally ping open, and we step out into the foyer.

But the second I glimpse the view through the floor-to-ceiling windows, my feet freeze.

I can't do this.

"Dex …" Tripp whispers as his parents approach the concierge.

"I'm good. I'm fine. Could you just carry me, maybe?" Because I really can't get my feet to move.

He forcefully pulls me after him, and I stagger along, my feet feeling like they're filled with lead.

"A seat furthest from the windows," Tripp tells the man behind the counter.

"We reserved you the best view of the city."

"Yeah, look, I'm scared of heights, and Dex forgot to mention it when he booked. Any chance of being moved?"

"We can make it work. And congratulations on your marriage."

That almost makes me feel better. Almost. At least it would if I didn't feel like I was going to hurl all over the floor.

Another server shows up to lead us to our table, and I keep my gaze trained on our joined hands and trust Tripp to lead me. I know the fear will settle the longer we're up here, but I can't stop picturing the glass disappearing and us all tipping out the side.

"Since when are you scared of heights?" Mira asks as the server hands out menus and leaves.

"Not me. My *husband*."

Karl turns to me. "Why didn't you say anything?"

I cringe. "It doesn't matter. I'm fine. This is fine. I just wish they'd make the building stop swaying."

"The building isn't swaying," Tripp points out.

"Then why do I feel like I'm going to fall off my chair?"

Mira finally gives me that indulgent look I'm so used to seeing from her. "You really do get yourself into the worst situations, don't you, Dex?"

"You should have spoken up," Karl says.

Tripp's hand tightens around mine. "When it comes to the people he loves, there's nothing Dex won't do. This is an *extreme* exhibit A."

"Goddamn, Dex." Karl picks up his menu. "You couldn't let us be mad at you about the whole wedding thing for a bit longer?"

"I want you to like me," I say.

"We always have." Mira nods. "But next time you mess up—and we all know you two screw heads will do *something*—just remember you don't need to get yourself close to passing out to make it up to us."

"So we're forgiven?" I ask, ignoring the way my head spins.

"Like we could say otherwise." Mira tilts her head. "Should we go, honey? You're looking pale."

"Please, for the love of Gretzky, do not make me stand up again now." I close my eyes and lean forward to rest my head on the table. And like he can read my mind, Tripp's hand rubs circles on my back.

And if I focus on that, it makes me forget everything else.

Including the very possible, highly likely drop to my death.

"I guess the observation deck is out after this?" Karl mutters.

It takes everything in me not to sob.

CHAPTER EIGHTEEN

TRIPP

"Do you need us to drop you off anywhere on the way home?" I ask my parents while we walk to the car. "CVS? Grocery store … Airport?"

Mom glares at me, but Dad laughs.

"You wouldn't be trying to get rid of us to spend time with your new husband, would you?" Mom asks.

"Maybe." That's exactly what I'm trying to do. Because I hate all this lying. It twists my insides and makes me nauseous. Lying to the public to save our image is one thing—that's necessary sometimes—but lying to my parents? I'm starting to regret letting Dex take the lead and keeping my parents in the dark.

Not only that, but I'm desperate to get Dex alone and find out what he was thinking last night. I know what I was thinking—that Dex, perfect Dexter Mitchale, the man of my dreams, let me touch him and kiss him and suck his amazing dick, so there was no way I was going to turn that down.

But what was he doing? What does it mean? Maybe he's looking down the barrel of twelve months without being able to have sex with someone else. Maybe Anton was right when he said given the circumstances, Dex could realize it's possible to be attracted to me. That theory would work with how Dex has been acting today.

It doesn't fill me with reassurance though. Him only realizing he's attracted to me because he can't have anyone else sounds a hell of a lot like "I'd do you ... if you were the last man on earth."

Dad slaps my back. "You don't need to worry about us. We're out of your hair tonight. I have to work in the morning, and you know your mother doesn't like to fly alone."

Okay. Tonight. I can deal with a couple more hours.

Maybe.

"Your sister finishes work at three and said she'll be by to see us before we leave."

Sienna. Shit. She knows this whole thing is fake.

I get Dex to drive us home while I get my phone out and text Sienna.

> Long story, but don't tell Mom and Dad that Dex's and my marriage is fake. They think it's real.

She's at work, so she won't see it until she's done, but she checks her phone religiously, so she shouldn't miss it. But then I reread my text and again am hit with why did I let this get so out of hand? The deception is really sinking in.

When we get home, I busy myself with washing the coffee cups from this morning and the plates my parents used when they had breakfast at whatever crazy hour they woke up at. It doesn't take long for Mom to join me.

"I could've done that. We're the ones imposing on you and your husband. Wow. Husband. It's surreal to say that aloud."

I don't know where it comes from—the guilt, maybe—but I accidentally blurt, "It's not actually real."

Then I can't look at my mother.

Her delicate hand touches my shoulder. "What do you mean?"

I turn to her. "It was supposed to be a joke, but we're dumbasses and accidentally got married for real, and now the team's PR agent is doing everything they can to try to convince people it is real so it doesn't look bad on the team or us." The words come out in one long rush.

"Oh, honey." Mom steps forward and hugs me. "That must be difficult for you."

"You have no idea," I mumble.

"I think I do. It's obvious how you feel about him."

"To everyone but him evidently."

"I'm not sure that boy even knows his own feelings. I mean, if this is all fake like you say it is, why is he going to such big lengths to impress us and make sure he's always touching you in public?"

"Graham from PR is telling us to act like a couple to cover our asses."

"Hmm." Mom purses her lips.

"What?"

"That doesn't explain why you two came home last night trying to eat each other's faces."

I wince. "Uhh, yeah. About that ... I don't even know what that was."

"Have you talked to him about it?"

"No. Because we were interrupted by unexpected visitors," I say dryly.

"Talk to him. Maybe this marriage isn't so fake to him after all."

I'm reminded of the other part of what Anton said while we were away—that it's possible Dex has feelings for me too but didn't know it.

I haven't stopped to think about it too hard because I don't want to give weight to an idea that could hurt me. Especially when it's so unrealistic.

Dex is an open book, and he hasn't mentioned wanting to give anything more than sex a try. And just because we got off together last night and I gave him a blowjob, that's not going to magically create feelings just because I want it to.

I already know Dex is not the type of guy to associate sex with emotions. Neither am I. Usually.

But with Dex ... everything is jumbled in my head.

"You're overthinking this, honey," Mom says.

"You think so?"

"I can see why it would be confusing, but ... I mean ... you're married now. Even if it started as an accident, why don't you see where it can go?"

Sure, because that's not going to end in heartache or anything. Though I don't think I can avoid it at this point anyway. "You just want to keep Dex, don't you?"

"As far as sons-in-law go, he's a good one."

Before I can tell her exactly why this whole thing is a bad idea, the buzzer for the front of the building sounds, and I go to the intercom to see my sister's face on the security camera.

"Sienna's here." I buzz her up, and then Mom and I go to the front door to meet her.

When she gets off the elevator, she's all smiles. "Where's my favorite brother-in-law? The one who's totally in love with Tripp, and it's very, very real."

"I'm so glad I told Mom the truth because if I hadn't, your act certainly would have."

Mom smiles. "And that's why you never got away with anything as a teenager." She hugs Sienna. "I love you, my dear, but you can't lie to save your life."

"Damn it. I was going to have so much fun."

"Definitely glad I told Mom the truth," I say.

"Truth about what?" Dad asks.

I go to tell him, when my mother cuts me off.

"Nothing you need to worry about. Let's go catch up with our daughter and leave the newlyweds alone for a while." Then she looks at me in the way only a mother can.

Her expression tells me to do the right thing and talk to my husband.

She takes Sienna by the arm and says, "Okay, take me to your apartment so I can clean it."

"Mom," Sienna whines.

As soon as they're out the door, I turn to go find Dex, only to run right into him.

His arms wrap around my back. "I thought they'd never leave."

He doesn't give me a chance to say we need to talk when he kisses me with a needy force.

I stumble back, but he pulls me closer. The protest that we need to talk comes out like a soft moan, which only encourages him.

We fumble our way over to the couch, and we fall with Dex on top of me. He doesn't break from my mouth, only dives deeper with his tongue.

I need to back away. We need to talk. But when I break my lips from his, he kisses my neck instead, and my words die.

Dex's muscular body grinds against mine. My head spins, my aching cock wants more, but we have to set some boundaries or ... fuck, I'm in so much trouble. I need to know what we're doing.

"Dex, wait—"

But then his hand reaches between us and undoes the fly on my jeans, pausing right as he lifts his head. "Wait? For what?"

His warm brown eyes, filled with heat but a touch of vulnerability, make me forget everything.

"I don't fucking know."

"I want to touch you," he begs. "I've wanted to since last night. Please, can I?"

"I'm not going to stop you."

Then the tables are turned. Where last night, I was the one jerking him off while rutting against him, he's now doing the same.

His hand works me over, his touch sends shivers down my spine, and the whole experience is even more surreal sober than it was in a drunken haze last night.

His grip is firm and confident, and he knows how to drive me crazy. His thumb swipes over the tip, collecting precum that he uses to make my cock glide through his fist easier.

Dex feels so good against me, so much better than I ever could have imagined. My fantasies don't live up to this real-life connection.

We're best friends. I've always felt close to him. But this, it's more than close. I'm—

"Holy fuck, I'm gonna come already," I rasp.

He's had his hand on me for all of a couple of minutes, but I can't hold back. I slam my eyes closed as I unleash, riding the wave that even Dex's chuckle can't bring down.

When I can finally catch my breath and the ropes of cum settle on my skin and the bottom of my shirt, Dex lifts up and looks me in the eye.

Where he was wearing his puppy dog eyes before, now he's all smug.

"And I was worried I was going to be bad at that."

I don't want to tell him it had nothing to do with the quality of handjob and everything to do with him being the one giving it to me, so I opt for casual snark instead. "Come on, dude. I know you've had plenty of practice at that. I room with you at away games."

"Mm, true. But being the one who draws out the sound of you coming is so much sexier than hearing you do it."

"Oh, really?"

"Mmhmm." His hand is still around my dick, and he strokes lightly.

"Want me to return the favor?"

"Hmm, nah. We'll call this one even since I fell asleep last night after promising you another orgasm." Dex sits up and wipes the rest of my cum on his shirt. "But today has gotten me thinking, and—"

"Oh God, don't tell me. You've decided it's a good idea for us to adopt a child. As a joke. On a whim."

Dex laughs. "How'd you know?"

"After this marriage, I wouldn't put anything past you."

"About that. Uh ... our marriage. We're stuck in it for at least a year, right?"

"Right."

"Maybe ... we could keep doing what we've been doing? It's not like we're allowed to be with anyone else, so I figure ... why not give it a shot?"

Can I keep this up for a whole year? Pretending to be married to him while actually in love with him? Having sex with him and getting him off because he's not allowed to have sex with his usual type?

"It might be a lot to ask, but I figured it's the most logical thing."

"You? Logical? Since when?"

"Ha ha. You're sooo funny."

The thing is, it *is* logical. We're married, so we may as well get the perks of it.

But how will adding sex to our dynamic—no matter how much I've wanted this for years—affect our friendship?

And as if even contemplating doing this with Dex summons him, my phone starts ringing with Oskar's name on the screen. Again. I hit the Ignore button for the billionth time and wonder how long it will take for him to get sick of me ignoring him and hop a plane to Vegas.

Our summer only has a couple of weeks left, so I'm hoping he's too busy to come yell at me in person. The other guys have tried to contact me, but they're nowhere near as pushy and protective as Oskar is.

Thanks to making it to the Stanley Cup finals last season, our vacation has been short, but I'd go back to practice tomorrow if it meant I could avoid Oskar for longer. But thinking of preseason training also makes me pause. Because if Dex and I do this, it could affect our team too.

"What about the team?" I ask Dex.

"What about them? This has nothing to do with them. This is about you and me. About *us*."

Us.

Dex and Tripp.

The Mitchell brothers.

Best friends.

Husbands.

Fuck buddies?

Then again, can you really be fuck buddies with your husband?

CHAPTER NINETEEN

DEX

When our break started, I never would have believed I'd be in a relationship with my best friend by the end of it. It's a weird dynamic because he's my husband, but we've really only just started dating, so he should be my boyfriend, but on the other hand, it's *Tripp*.

If I'd pulled my head out of my ass years ago and realized how good it is to have sex with him, we probably would be married by now anyway—if we'd ever wanted that—because the only difference between then and now is that I get to make him come at night.

And goddamn, whoever sent me that message was right—it *is* the hottest thing I've ever done.

"So what's on the agenda for today?" Tripp asks, joining me in the kitchen. He's pulled on a pair of sleep shorts, even though we've both been sleeping naked every night. I pull him to me and snap the elastic waistband in protest.

"Can the first thing be banning pants?" I ask.

"Our sisters might stop visiting if we bring that rule in."

"Good," I grumble. "Then we'll stop being interrupted when we want to have sex."

The last few nights this week, our sisters have taken it upon themselves to stop in for dinner or invite us out for drinks. It's nothing unusual to how it normally is during the off-season, but it does mean I haven't been getting anywhere near enough orgasms.

Tripp laughs. "I've had so many handjobs this week my dick is going to get chafed."

"About that …" I shift, rubbing my thumbs over his sides. "Maybe I could, ah, try using my mouth next time."

"You want to suck me off?"

I'm quick to nod, and I can't seem to make myself stop.

Tripp strokes my throat. "Will you swallow?"

"Fuck yeah."

"Think you're man enough to take it all?" I know that's Tripp's teasing voice. I'm just not sure whether it's because he thinks I can't eat cum, or I'm all talk with no follow-through.

"Let's find out." Then I sink to my knees, pulling his shorts down with me.

Eye to eye with his cock, I have a moment's hesitation.

"Problem?" Tripp asks.

"Looks a whole lot different from this angle." He's not fully erect yet, but this close up, I can see his manscaped red pubes, heavy balls, and rapidly thickening length. The scent of sex hits my nose and makes my own cock take interest.

Okay. Time to blow my best friend's mind by blowing his other head first.

I take him in my hand and lean in to lick the swollen tip. Hmm. Okay. Skin. A hint of bodywash. Not bad. I flatten out my tongue and lick him again, then start at the base and work my way up. My tongue traces every vein and dips into the ridge under his head, and when a tiny bead of precum appears, I lean in to taste it.

It tastes a little salty, but ... I think I like it. My lips wrap around the tip, and I suck, trying to draw more out, to get another taste, and when it bursts on my tongue, the taste shoots straight to my cock. Yep. Okay. I definitely, definitely like that.

I press my palm to where my cock is straining against my briefs as my gaze flicks up to check in with Tripp.

His lips are parted, pupils blown, and when our gazes clash, he lets out this strangled noise in his throat and drops back to lean against the counter.

"Shit, Dex." The desperation in his voice spurs me on.

I try to keep eye contact as I draw him in farther, but his cock bumps the top of my mouth, and I gag so hard I almost hurl. I'm coughing as I pull back, and just as I'm about to apologize, his fingers twist through my hair.

"That was hot. Keep going."

Challenge accepted.

I dive on him, and at first, I'm hyperaware of everything I'm doing, probably trying too hard, but every time I glance up, Tripp's stare gets hotter and hotter. He keeps a tight hold on my hair, and between that and the tiny thrusts he's doing into my mouth, I'm starting to get too turned on to care how I'm doing.

My only aim is to make Tripp feel as incredible as he makes me, and every little drop of precum feels like a gift, a sign that I'm on the right track and to keep going. I have no idea if there's too much spit or I'm gagging too much, but I blow him like my life depends on it, and I know from being on the receiving end that even sloppy blowjobs feel amazing. Besides, now we're together, I'll have plenty of time to figure this out.

I moan around his length as I manage to get more than halfway down this time, and there's something about his obvious arousal, about being on my knees for him, that is so goddamn hot I can't control myself. My hand closes around my cock, and I squeeze, trying to get it to calm down, wanting to focus on nothing but Tripp and making him feel good.

"My balls," he says, voice rough.

I pull off long enough to spit in my hand, and then I cup his balls and keep sucking him. His thrusts are getting deeper, and as I roll and squeeze his sac, it draws up tight to his body.

"Touch my hole."

Umm ...

Huh.

All right then.

I've never touched another person's asshole, but hey, we're in this now. And dick is new and I seem to love it, so maybe that'll be a brand-new toy for me too.

I pull back so I can see Tripp's face as I stroke him with one hand, sucking on the tip, and my hand that was playing with his balls dips backward. I feel my way along his taint, then dip my fingers up into the crease of his ass. It only takes a second when—

Bingo.

My slippery fingers stroke over the spot, and Tripp's head drops back, thick neck exposed and straining.

"I'm close."

Oh holy shit, me too. Tripp starts to move his hips, and now my initial hesitation has passed, this is hot as fuck. I rub his hole while I hollow my cheeks and suck with purpose. My knees are getting sore from the tile, but my head is fuzzy with desire, and the harder I work, the more I'm rewarded with Tripp's taste until he grips my head tight enough to make me stop.

"Sure you want to swallow?"

Unable to answer with a mouthful of cock, I lock eyes with him and suck harder. He's not taking it from me now.

"Get ready," he warns, then releases my hair to rest his hand on the back of my head as he starts to fuck my mouth with small, shallow thrusts.

His grunt gives me a split-second warning, and then his cock twitches and I get my first real taste. Then another and another and … shit.

There's more than I prepared for, and when I almost inhale it, I cough so hard I swear it almost shoots from my nose. Cum splatters over Tripp's cock and thighs and ends up all down my chin.

Well, that didn't go as expected.

I glance up, *oops* look firmly planted on my face to find Tripp's widened eyes staring at me.

Then he cracks up laughing. "Dex, that was the single hottest moment of my life … until it wasn't."

I yank up his sleep shorts, wipe my face off on the outside, then push to my feet. At least the embarrassment has helped my cock to settle. Tripp's happy face makes me smile, so hey, maybe I fucked the ending, but we got ninety percent there.

"A for effort?"

"I'd give you more than that if I could." He tugs me into a kiss. "You sure you've never sucked dick before?"

"Well, there was that one time in college …"

He jerks back, mouth hanging open, and wow. I can't believe he bought that.

"Kidding. Before you, it wasn't something I'd ever thought about."

"Well, when faced with the options of celibacy or dick, it's a hard choice."

Maybe some might think so, but the choice isn't hard at all with Tripp. The hugging came naturally. The affection, the kissing, and now this. Being this way with Tripp is the easiest thing I've ever done. I don't need to think, I don't need to work at it, I can be me and love him, and it all makes sense in my brain.

"Thank fuck for getting married, huh? Otherwise this might never have happened." Because I was too stupid to see what was right in front of me. I slap his ass. "ATV time."

"What?"

I move to rinse my dishes from breakfast. "We only have a few days left until training camp; we need to make the most of them."

"And the hiking, golf, poker tournament, and gondola boat ride weren't enough?"

"Did you miss the part where I said *ATVs*?"

"My mistake." Tripp plucks at his sleep shorts. "I guess I better shower ... again."

"Race you."

We fight the whole way there, and then, under the steam, Tripp gets on his knees for me this time.

It's official. I'm putting in a petition for every day to start this way.

"I feel like a tourist," Tripp says after we're dressed and heading out the door.

"You said you've never done any of these things since moving here."

"I moved across the road from the golf course for a reason. I'd planned to spend my entire off-season there."

"And we have. And I can't believe I'm about to say this, but there's more to Las Vegas than a golf course and hockey arena." I pretend to gasp.

"There *is*? You mean golf courses and hockey arenas *aren't* the reason people come to Las Vegas? But what else could there possibly be?"

I palm his face. "Okay, smartass. I guess the casinos are there too. My point is no husband of mine will be walking around having not taken an ATV out into the desert one time." Husband still doesn't feel like the right word for what we are, but I guess it's the most accurate. It's what we are, but it reminds me of the joke that started this and how, as much as I'm fine being married to Tripp forever, the choice wasn't fully ours. If we went back and knew the whole thing was legit, I doubt either of us would have gone there.

This way, we have a get-out-of-jail-free card in a year, but I'm determined for us never to use it. I'm going to be the best ... husband? Boyfriend? Partner? Tripp has ever had.

And as we get to the place to rent out ATVs, I remind myself it doesn't matter. He's my *Tripp*. I don't need another word for it.

We spend the day tearing around the desert tracks, racing and competing on who can get the most air over the jumps. Coach will kill us if either of us gets injured, but that doesn't hold me back. If I'd known this is what married life could be like, I would have been on board a whole lot sooner.

Except I suspect this would never be possible with anyone but Tripp.

Sleepy mornings, and constant orgasms, and ATV racing in the desert.

Somehow, I've hit the jackpot.

I'm so glad this is real.

CHAPTER TWENTY

TRIPP

I wish this could be real. I mean, sure, having a best friend is great, but have you ever had a husband? I thought marriage was supposed to be all fighting and no sex. Dex and I are still us but with orgasms. And, like, mutual orgasms, not just lonely, pining, jerking off by myself orgasms.

But our days of doing an interview here, blowjobs there, public appearances where we amp up the love angle followed by handjobs at home are all coming to a close this morning. Because it's the beginning of training camp, and we have to meet the team at the practice arena at ten.

Every fall after the summer break reminds me of going back to school.

Usually, some guys from the team will get together during the off-season, but because we had a shorter break this time, there were no big gatherings or events to attend.

Either that or Dex and I weren't invited.

We get along with everyone on the team fine, but we've always been in our own little bubble.

I'm nervous about what the guys will say about the wedding and how we're supposed to play this for the team.

Dex said we should lean into the marriage, which turns out didn't need a whole lot of leaning—we've fallen into a pattern naturally. It's like we're an actual couple, even though in a year we'll be signing those divorce papers. So maybe we should just ... run with it.

My only concern with that is getting too attached to the idea that I'm Dex Mitchale's husband and we're actually together.

I don't want that disappointment when our time is up.

Dex's alarm blares. I've been awake for a couple of hours, enjoying Dex's warmth and dreading wake-up time. First day of training camp is usually exciting, and I can't sleep because I'm like a kid on Christmas, but this year, I can't sleep for a whole slew of other reasons.

Like facing the team, the press, the public. We've only had a taste of what's to come.

Dex stirs and blindly reaches for his phone, but instead of turning off his alarm, he throws it across the room.

"I don't think that works," I say.

"Yes, it does, because now I need to get up to turn it off, and I won't be tempted to stay in bed and come all over you when we need to get our asses to practice."

I let out a long sigh. "And so it starts all over again. Another season."

Dex slides out of bed and reaches above him. His lean muscles tighten, and my gaze drops to his ass.

Sleeping naked with him is new, but I'm definitely not complaining about getting that sight every morning.

Never in my wildest dreams did I think I would ever be hooking up with Dex, but in those moments where I wished for it, thought about it, or jerked off to it, there was always a moment of awkwardness. I tried to suppress my feelings because I knew if Dex was to ever be interested in me in real life, it would be difficult to go from friends to lovers.

But just like everything with Dex, being with him is easy. A lot easier than I thought it would be. And today might change everything.

It's not the first time we've gotten ready for practice and gone together, but it's got a different vibe.

Dex doesn't seem to have my hesitance, but why would he? This is Dex. He doesn't get hung up on things; he's not the type of person to overthink every little detail ... Maybe I need to take his lead and ... see what happens.

When we get to the arena, Dex holds my hand from the parking lot to the players' entrance, where I slip out of his hold.

He frowns, but I shrug him off.

"I don't want to freak out the guys with all this PDA stuff. I figure while we're with the team, we don't act any differently to how we usually do."

He hesitates before nodding. "Good idea."

On our way to the locker room, we pass through the rink, where the rookies from last year, some AHL players who are hoping to get called up, and some newly drafted players are on the ice. They had an earlier start time than us so they could go through drills and show the coaches what they've got.

For some of them, this is their only shot. Being drafted doesn't mean they get a contract. From here, they might get sent to the AHL for more training; some of them who are young enough will keep playing for the juniors. Most of them won't make the team this year. Coaches like to wait to sign draftees until they're older and stronger, but occasionally there'll be an outlier. And from what I can see, everyone on the ice right now has the potential to be that outlier. Then again, if they outskate the rookies from last year, it might just mean our rooks will get sent down to the AHL for conditioning and more training.

"Damn. The new kids are fast," Dex says.

"Or are we old and slow now?"

"The first one. Fuck, hopefully the first one."

"Let's go suit up and see which one of these guys might make the team."

As soon as Dex and I walk into the locker room, I've never heard so many hockey players be silent at once.

Reeves, my backup goalie, is the first to say something. "Uh, congratulations?"

Dex smiles wide. "Thanks, man."

"Where were our invites, assholes?" Braylon asks.

"We only invited people we like," I quip.

Dex rolls his eyes. "It was literally us, the officiant, and a witness who worked at the chapel."

"Exactly my point."

The guys all boo me, but they know I'm playing with them. I'm happy it went this way and not—

"Is no one going to ask it?" Fensby cuts in.

Spoke too soon.

Patrick Fensby is the least likable guy on the team. He's a center—same position as Dex—but Fensby is second line to Dex's first. He puts a lot in the basket, but he's not a team player. He always tries to be the one to score and has been called on it a thousand times, but because he's one of the top scorers in the league, the coaches tend to look the other way. Because if a guy can get twice as many shots on goal, he's bound to get some of them in.

He's been gunning for Dex's spot since he joined the team two years ago.

"Ask away, Fensby." I act like I don't care, because I actually don't. I'm just worried on Dex's behalf.

Fensby steps toe to toe with Dex. "How long were you two fucking behind Jessica's back?"

"Here we go." I want to yell the entire reason we got married in the first place was because of her. We're in this mess thanks to the woman he's defending because she happens to be where he parks his dick at night.

"We weren't," Dex says.

"Not what she says."

"Why do you care?" I ask. "You're with her now, and I couldn't be happier for you. You deserve her."

Dex points my way. "What Tripp said. There're no hard feelings on my end, so if you make her happy, I'm happy for her."

Hmm, that's Dex's lying tone, but he's so subtle about it, I doubt anyone else would be able to tell.

"And so you're suddenly gay?" Fensby asks.

"Hey, whoa," Adler says, stepping up behind us. Team captain to the rescue. "We accept everyone here. And if Dex doesn't have an issue with you breaking bro code and dating his ex, you shouldn't worry about how he ident—"

"Sexuality doesn't work like that." I'm wasting my breath, but I can't hold it in.

"I'm ... uh ..." Dex blinks, and oh no. He's pulling that face that he does when reporters ask him hard questions.

"There's something weird about this whole thing," Fensby says, and now I'm worried for my sake as well as Dex's.

"Weird how?" Adler asks. "The whole team has joked about these two being secretly in love for years."

I guess that explains the lack of shock around here.

"Why don't you worry about your own sex life," Dex says. "You're going to need it with some of the freaky shit Jessica's into."

I turn to my best friend ... uh, husband, and try to assess his face, because I couldn't tell if that was his lying tone again or not.

Fensby looks as confused as I am.

We're broken up by Coach's booming voice. "What are we all doing standing around? Get your asses out on the ice."

And like that, another season gets underway.

CHAPTER TWENTY-ONE

DEX

Sweat is pooling on my lower back as I fight tooth and nail for us to get on the board. San Jose has pulled ahead by two, so there's still hope, but as the minutes tick down to the end of the game, that hope is quickly being overridden by frustration.

I intercept a pass from Jarett and head for the blue line, but before I can line up my shot, Oskar flies past, strips the puck, and sends it sailing toward Rosky.

It's a mess of back and forth over possession, so Coach signals for a line change, and as I hit the team box, Fensby sends me a cocky smirk on his way out.

That guy, I swear.

I've always been able to low-key ignore him because while he might have skill, he has a shitty attitude, whereas I can score and still be a team player.

This year? I don't think I can claim either of those things.

Hockey is hard.

Who knew?

Sure, I have to work for it, but there's a level of instinct and intuition that comes with playing that I seem to be missing this year.

This is our fifth preseason game, and if we lose this, it'll be our fourth loss. Thank fuck preseason doesn't count for standings, or we'd be screwed.

I watch as Oskar takes a shot on goal, but Tripp pulls some kind of contortionist move to shut him out. Tripp's been feeling the pressure as much as me, but you wouldn't know it. He's not having the season of his life, but he's still playing well enough to avoid the attention that comes with totally choking.

I've always been in awe of how fast he moves out there. I could never do what he does.

A loud shout goes up, and my attention snaps from Tripp to Fensby, who's on a breakaway. My gut surges into my throat as I watch him cross the blue line and shoot. For one heart-stopping second, the worst thought possible jumps into my mind—*I hope he misses*. But then the lamp lights up, and I remind myself that Fensby or not, we're a team, and I hate myself for forgetting that.

I force a smile and fist pump along with the guys beside me before we're sent back out there.

It's no use though.

The score ends 2-1, and we all trudge down the chute with a black cloud hanging over the team. Maybe I'm more in tune to it this season because it feels like it's mostly my fault, but while my teammates can shake off a loss easy enough, that's never been me.

I know it's part of the game, and I try not to focus on it for long, but there's always that pit in my gut that takes hold until we get our next win.

Last season, I barely had to worry about it because the team was on fire. This year, we have the same players, but we're not the same team. And the only difference I can think of is that Tripp and I are married now.

The Mitchell brothers' magic is missing.

We reach the locker room and strip down to our base layers. Most of the guys head in to cool down, but I drop onto the bench, needing a minute's separation from the team.

Tripp takes the place beside me, and I automatically lean over and press my forehead to his shoulder. Like always, the loss suddenly doesn't seem so bad. Tripp gives me a taste of the bigger picture, and even though I'm disappointed, I can deal with it when he's right next to me. I'm cautious not to be over the top in front of the others, so I don't pull him to me the way I want to, but this is something we've done a million times before.

I assume it won't be a problem.

I'm wrong.

Fensby's loud scoff fills the room. "No one wants to see that."

I pull away, looking up to find him glaring at me. "See what?"

"You know exactly what I'm talking about."

"Do I?" I growl. Fensby's been toeing the line with me, and right now, he's picking the wrong time to say shit. "Maybe you should spell it out for me."

"All I'm saying is we're here to play a game. We don't need to be faced with you two fucking around every day."

I shove to my feet. "Sorry. I must have missed the part where I had my cock out."

He steps up to me. "Problem, Dexter?"

"Yeah, it's called your face," Tripp says. He tries to tug me back down beside him, but I don't go. There's a ringing in my ears that's driving me nuts, and I'd like nothing better than to take my disappointment and frustration out on Fensby.

"I find it funny that you never had an issue with Tripp and me before we got together, and now suddenly, you don't want to see us being close."

"What are you implying?"

"Seems pretty homophobic to me."

He sneers. "Or maybe I think you're both shitty people for dragging a sweet person like Jessica into your life and then betraying her."

"I never cheated."

"You think I'm going to believe that?"

My fist is itching to hit him, but that's a fast way off the team. I wouldn't be surprised if that's exactly what he's hoping for.

So instead, I force a deep breath and go low. "I think I've finally figured out your issue."

His cocky expression slips for a fraction of a second.

"She said my name, didn't she? When you were fucking her?" I shrug. "And now you think that somehow defending her against something that didn't happen is the way to gain bonus points." I cuff him on the shoulder a bit harder than I normally would. "Good luck with that."

"Please. You really think she hasn't filled me in on your mediocre sex life?" He laughs in my face. "She never thought refusing to peg you would send you after the real thing."

What? I never …

I shove him, and he shoves me back, but before I can make a dumb choice, Tripp jumps up and pulls me back.

"No need to worry about us, Fensby. We appreciate your concern, but we've got things covered."

But that's the thing. We talk a big talk, and our sex life is amazing, but the few times I've brought up fucking, somehow we've ended up in handjobs or blowjobs and never got to that.

"You sure?" Fensby asks with mock concern. "Because Dex seems tense this year. He's scored, what, once during preseason?"

"Twice, asshole."

"Ah, my mistake. I stopped counting when you weren't a challenge anymore. Don't get too comfortable on the first line, buddy."

As he walks away, I turn to Tripp and grit through my teeth, "I hate him."

"Yep, me too."

"Hey, one more thing," Fensby calls from the door to the weights room. "How do you guys handle being married and called the Mitchell brothers? Doesn't that gross you out? Or do you use it as some sick kind of role play?"

"You're a dick," Tripp says. "Worry about your own mediocre sex life."

"I'm not the one who needs to worry." He eyes Tripp in a way that makes my skin crawl. "Fifty bucks says Dex goes back to pussy before the season is over."

Adler's leaving the weight room as Fensby says that and nudges him. "Cut it out, man, that's not cool."

"Yeah, say that shit again!" I yell.

He's finally gone too far. Hit me where it hurts and I'll be upset; go after Tripp and I'll fucking end you.

"What the hell is going on in here?" Coach's voice reaches the room before he does, and the four of us freeze. He looks from me and Tripp to Adler and Fensby, jaw getting tense.

"Nothing, Coach," I quickly say.

"Don't lie to me." His raised voice attracts others from the team. "Is there an issue here?"

Three of us answer with "no," but Fensby says, "You've got to tell them to stop with the PDA."

"Oh. So there is a problem?" Coach asks.

"We weren't even PDA ... ing." I screw up my face. Word talk good. "Tripp was consoling me after that mess of a game, just like he would any other teammate."

"I don't go hugging any of my teammates," Fensby says.

"Maybe if you did, the team might like you more," I point out.

"Let me be very clear here." Coach lifts his voice so even those in the weight room will be able to hear. "Preseason has been an embarrassment without bringing this crap into the locker room. Now unless something changes, I won't hesitate to trade any one of you. Act like adults." He turns to Fensby. "Keep your unwanted opinions to yourself." Then his stare snaps to me. "And pick up your game."

He turns and stomps from the room as my gut falls out my ass. I drop back onto the bench, but no one else moves.

A trade is all part of the game, but it's not a part we enjoy. Through the season, we work side by side, seven days a week. Your team becomes your family, and having to leave and join someone else's is a massive hit to your game.

Leaving all that would be hard enough without factoring Tripp into it.

Even before we started dating, I couldn't bear the thought of not having him here, and if Coach's look meant anything, my head is on the chopping block.

I can't be traded.

I can't leave here.

Not while we're exploring this thing between us and finding a way to make it work. I hate the thought of waking up anywhere without Tripp. I might be having a shit time on the ice, but it's barely been two weeks. I can turn things around. And outside of here, at home, I've never been happier.

I need to brush this off.

If I don't want to be traded, there's only one option.

I need to refocus on the game and forget about Fensby and the taunts he sends my way.

I can do it.

I can totally do it.

"Dex, Adler, press conference."

Fuck.

So maybe I can do it *after* I get my ass handed to me.

CHAPTER TWENTY-TWO

TRIPP

"Are you coming to dinner with Oskar?" I ask Dex when he comes out of the showers.

He's in an unusually down mood thanks to Fensby being a dick right before the media pile-on, and I'm not talking about a normal human level of down. Dex is always bright and happy. His disposition is usually annoyingly sunny, which makes moods like this easy to pick.

So when he shakes his head and says he'll see me at home, I know something's really wrong. He doesn't even look at me as he dresses.

"Want me to cancel?" I'm hoping he says yes. I've been conveniently too busy to join the queer collective on any of their video calls or pick up when Oskar has tried to reach me. It finally all caught up to me when tonight on the ice, Oskar skated over and said I have a lot of explaining to do.

Which is true. I haven't spoken to any of the guys since the news got out that Dex and I are legally married, because I've been anticipating many lectures about setting myself up for heartache.

"No, don't do that." Dex pulls on his navy suit jacket. It's my favorite suit of his because it makes his dark eyes brighter, and he deserves to be the brightest thing in a room. "It's a rule you have to catch up with Oskar when he's in town."

"Yeah, only a silly rule, not a law."

"Yet, you guys always manage to make time for each other because you're like family. Seriously, go."

"You're okay?"

Dex's eyes are weary, and he runs a hand through his wet hair. "Just trying to get my head around the game. That's all."

"It doesn't count for standings," I remind him.

"I'm in a slump, and the season hasn't even started yet."

I rub his arm. "Here, you take my car home. I'll order an Uber to take me downtown."

"I'll drop you off and then head home."

"It's out of the way."

Dex grabs my hand and pulls me against him. "And I'm your husband. So I'll drop you off." Then he leans in and kisses me, not caring if Fensby sees and complains again.

It's as easy as that to get me to melt for him and let the issue go.

When he drops me off, I ask again if he wants to come in and eat with us, but he declines.

I'm too busy worrying about Dex to remember to protect myself from Oskar, who likes to slap the back of my head when I've done something boneheaded.

He clips me on my way past him. "Nice game, sweetheart."

"Asshole," I mutter when I sit.

"Now, I can't be sure, you might have to remind me, but I think I remember you telling me that your fake wedding will never get out ... Now suddenly you're married. Oh, and it's legal. I know because I checked."

"Oh, shit, look at the time. I should go home." I stand, but Oskar reaches over and pushes me back down.

"Don't even. You've been avoiding my calls, and I thought you might have bailed on tonight. I was all prepared to show up on your doorstep to hunt you down. Now spill."

I hang my head. "We didn't know it was legal. That's what the call from PR was about while we were on vacation. They found out, and now we're in a media circus where we have to pretend that it's real and that we're in love because people will hate us and the team if it got out that we did it as a joke."

Oskar hums. "How convenient."

"Believe me when I say it's not convenient at all."

"No, I suppose being married to a guy you're in love with can't be easy. At least, not when he doesn't love you back."

"Dex loves me ... in his own way."

"In his own platonic, delusional way, sure."

I bite back the *fuck you* I want to send his way. "Can we not get into this again? You know where I firmly stand when it comes to Dex. You don't need to keep telling me I have to get over him. I know I do. It's ... even more difficult with having to keep up this charade. I'm not allowed to sleep with anyone else."

Oskar cringes. "Celibacy? Screw that."

Right. Sure. Celibacy.

I glance away.

"Wait. Anyone *else*? Oh, Trippy, tell me you didn't."

"Didn't what?"

"Let Dex into your inner sanctum."

"I didn't." Not with his dick, at least. His fingers have been there a few times, but I've always been the one to ask for it, so I haven't pushed him for more. Oskar doesn't need to know any of this though.

Oskar's eyes narrow. "What about your ... outer sanctum?"

"What is my outer sanctum, and why does that sound so dirty?"

"Have you had sex with Dex?"

"Hey, that rhymes! And I'm, uh, thirsty." I reach for the water on the table and pour a glass, but Oskar takes it off me before I can drink it.

"Spill it, Tripp Mitchell."

"It's nothing." I glance around the restaurant, but no one's paying attention to us.

"Don't make me video call the rest of the Collective and see if they think you and Dex fucking is nothing." He takes out his phone, but I quickly grab it off him.

"Don't. I ... okay, fine. We've been fooling around, but it's out of desperation."

Oskar leans back in his seat. "Huh. So Anton was right? Dex would go gay in a prison situation?"

"Apparently," I murmur.

"Think you can really do this without getting hurt?"

"Nope."

"Do I need to lecture you?"

"Double nope."

Oskar nods. "Fair enough. I will reserve my protective instincts for people who actually want it."

"Really?"

"Really."

I'm suspicious. "Why?"

"Why, what?"

"Why aren't you hassling me like you normally would?"

"Like I said when we were at Lake Tahoe, I'm the only one fighting to protect your heart, which made me realize … maybe you don't want to protect it. As one of your very best friends, I need to let you make your own mistakes and be there for you when everything shatters."

I've never heard Oskar seem so sympathetic and serious and—

I slump. "You want the details, don't you? Where we've done it, how we've done it, how adventurous Dex is—"

Oskar laughs. "Well, I wasn't going to come right out and ask, but since you brought it up …"

"No."

"Please? Just a little? Does he bottom? I can totally see that happening. Dex doesn't do things half-assed."

"What happened to me being the total bottom?" I ask, still having no idea where he got that from while we were away.

"Yeah, but you'd do anything for Dex. Once he gets a stupid idea in his head—"

"Sleeping with me is not stupid."

Oskar ignores me. "Damn. In my mind, maybe you sneak into the arena after dark. All those surveillance cameras. Making your own little sex tape for the world to see."

"Seriously, what is your obsession with public sex? It's going to get you into trouble one day."

"I'm counting on it. I'm still waiting for Lane to call me into his office and spank me for being a naughty boy."

"Lane …"

"The new PR rep for San Jose. He makes me want to do bad things so he'll yell at me."

"And you think I'm the fucked-up one for being in love with my *husband*."

Oskar waves me off. "Please. There is nothing more fucked-up than you and Dex. You guys are ... pucked-up."

"Original and oh so funny. Hurry up and eat so I can get home to where Dex is sulking because he's in a slump."

"He's not in a slump. You guys are always that shit. Which reminds me, you could've at least let me have a goal tonight."

"You know that's not how this friendship works. On the ice, you're the enemy. Off the ice, you're like that annoying big brother who's annoying."

"You wouldn't have me any other way."

Well, yeah, he's right.

He's right about a lot of things.

The main one being he'll be the one to pick up my pieces when Dex inevitably wants to stop playing pretend.

We eat in relative silence after that—never come between a hockey player and his food—and then we look up our schedules for the season to see when each of us will be meeting up with the other queer collective guys.

I won't cross paths with another member until mid-November, but one of Oskar's first regular-season games is against New York. He'll be facing Ollie Strömberg, who's already admitted he's retiring this year.

The only OG out hockey player left in the league is retiring. I can't wrap my head around it. The entire reason guys like Oskar and me have a career is because of guys like Strömberg.

It's the end of an era.

I skip dessert with Oskar because I want to get home. There was something not right with Dex's behavior. We've had bad games before. Faced losses.

It makes me concerned it's not the game but Fensby and Jessica that's actually getting to him. I've been trying not to think about that all night because I didn't want to spill my worries all over Oskar. He worries about me enough as it is.

But as I enter my apartment and find Dex on the couch, his head buried in his phone and his dark blond hair falling in his face, it comes flooding back.

I throw myself down next to him and then lean over, putting my head on his shoulder.

He quickly closes whatever app he was looking at, and I missed what was on the screen. My gut sinks. I can't help reading into that too. Was it Jessica's Insta account?

"I need to ask you something," Dex says and refuses to look at me.

"What is it?" I try not to panic yet. It could be anything.

What he does say not only takes me by surprise, I didn't even know he'd been thinking about it.

"Why haven't we had sex yet?"

CHAPTER TWENTY-THREE

DEX

I turn my phone over and over in my hands, waiting for Tripp's answer. The whole time he's been out, the question has been eating at me, worrying me. Doesn't he *want* to have sex with me?

All I know is if he's having second thoughts about our relationship, I'm not sure how I'll handle it.

Is he only following through with this because he feels like he doesn't have another choice? *Urgh.*

"Uh ... Dex? What do you think we've been doing the past few weeks?"

"No, like ..." I make a circle with my forefinger and thumb, then poke my other finger through it.

Tripp cracks up laughing. "Why aren't we fucking, you mean?"

"Exactly."

Hearing him laugh loosens some of that dread I'd worked myself up to, and I finally turn to face him.

He has a weird look on his face as he studies me. "I thought you liked my mouth ..." Tripp reaches for my dick, and I quickly snatch up his hand. If he touches me, I'll get distracted again, and nope. We are having this conversation.

"Tripp, I'm serious. Do you …" I clear my throat. "I mean, I read lots of gay dudes don't do that, so do you just not like it?"

"Nope. I'm pro penetration."

"So it's me, then?"

"It's not …" Tripp presses his lips together, and I think for a second that he's mad. Then he smiles. "I didn't realize what we were doing wasn't enough for you."

"No, it is. I love it all. But that's why I want to try it." And the grossness from today's game finally starts to recede as excitement at doing this takes over. "Can we? Please?"

"Like I'd ever say no to you." He grins, but I don't return it.

"You can though. Always."

"I know. That's not what I—"

"Why are you hesitating? Is it a me thing? You don't want to go there because it's me? Did I do something wrong?"

"I don't want you to ever think I have a problem with you." Tripp turns to face me and grips my hands, which are nervously wringing together. "It's not … you." Tripp blinks up at me, and I believe him, but it makes me want to ask what is it, then? But I have to admit, I think I'm scared to hear the answer. If it's not me, maybe it's us. Maybe it's the pressure of making it feel good—I get that with chicks sometimes. Performance anxiety can be a bitch, so instead of putting that on him, I back down.

"If you don't, it's fine. I'll let you suck me off instead."

"My husband. So generous."

He hasn't denied it though. Ouch.

"Dex …" Tripp tackles me into the couch and grinds his hard cock into my thigh. "Does it feel like I don't want to?"

"Well, mini Tripp seems on board."

"Fuck you. Don't call my cock that."

"Oh yeah? Make me."

He shoves me, and all talk of sex is forgotten as we play fight, trying to knock each other off the couch. I finally get Tripp in a headlock when we both go tumbling to the floor.

"Ah, shit." Tripp laughs, and I roll us so I'm hovering over him.

I peck his freckled nose. "Will you do it?"

He opens his mouth, then quickly closes it again.

"I can ask that now, can't I? You said I can ask if we're fucking, so can I finally know if you top or bottom?"

"I'm versatile."

"Oh, really …" Immediately, I'm thinking of all the ways we can explore this new development. "Tripp flips." I snigger. "Dex has sex with Tripp who flips."

"Yeah, gotta tell you, Dr. Seuss is not a turn-on."

"You don't wanna see my green eggs and ham?"

"Gross. What is it tonight with people and euphemisms that don't even make sense?"

I tilt my head. "Do I want to know?"

"You really don't."

Fair enough. If Oskar's involved, I'll take Tripp's word for it. I lean down and kiss him, a long, satisfied hum leaving me as his tongue meets mine. The worst thing about game nights is it means hours without Tripp's mouth on me.

Tripp's hands close over my ass, and my hips tilt forward into his. "Want me to fuck you?"

"Mhmm. Yes. Definitely. Please."

He smiles against my lips. "You're very ... enthusiastic."

"I've seen how turned on it makes you when I shove my fingers up there, and ... I dunno. There's something really hot about the thought of your cock filling me."

He inhales sharply. "Yes, there really is."

"So you'll do it? Gonna make love to me, Trippy?"

His eyes shoot wide and meet mine.

"Gonna finally show me some butt love?"

"I'll show your butt some pent-up sexual frustration."

"Close enough." I stand, and I haul Tripp to his feet. I'm not nervous, exactly. It's more that I'm worried I won't like it when I really, really want to.

He takes my hand. "Come on, hubby. I'm about to blow your mind."

"I'm holding you to that."

We both strip on our way to the bedroom. I'm only wearing sweats and a T-shirt, so I'm buck naked while Tripp is still unbuttoning his shirt. I reach for his suit pants and make quick work of shoving them off; then he's standing there, erection straining against his boxer briefs, ripped body making my mouth water.

I want to ... ungh. "Do you think it's possible to be a non-cannibal cannibal? Like, I don't want to *actually* eat you, but I'm having the biggest urge to bite you right now."

"Way to make things weird."

"You're about to see my asshole. Can things get weirder?"

"Trust me when I say that will be straight-up sexy."

"Only, not so straight." I flop back on the bed and then spread my legs, planting my feet on the mattress.

Tripp's eyes widen, locked on the sight, and then he shoves his boxer briefs down and kicks them off.

My stare zeroes in on his cock. His big, hard cock. Somehow, that thing is going inside me. I stifle a moan and stroke my suddenly needy erection.

"Like I said," he rasps. "Sexy as fuck."

"I, umm, showered while you were gone."

"Yeah?"

"I watched a video on how to prepare things."

His eyes darken. "You got yourself ready for me?"

"I really wanted it."

Tripp grabs lube and a condom, then tosses them on the bed before climbing up and covering me. "How are you the way that you are?"

"What do you mean?"

"Before we started this, you had never before ... now, you're ... sometimes it feels like you're jumping into this even faster than me."

"Well, yeah. It's *you*. What reason would I have to hold back?"

Tripp drops his forehead to mine and then starts to kiss his way down my face. He rolls his hips, bringing our dicks together, and I melt into the bed. By the time he gets to my lips, I'm aching for the kiss he gives me. My hands can't stop roaming over his broad torso, and when I get to his nipples, I squeeze them, and he hisses.

Tripp retaliates by closing his teeth over my lip. I roll him and pinch his ass, so he pulls my hair as we go back and forth wrestling. We're all soft laughter and deep kisses and rough hands.

Somehow, we end up in the middle of the bed, Tripp on top of me, his delicious, round shoulder hovering over my face. I can't help leaning forward and closing my teeth over it. I bite him, not hard enough to hurt, but enough to sink my teeth in and feel the slight give of his skin. My lips replace my teeth, sucking a bruise into his shoulder, marking him as mine. Only mine.

My husband, my best friend, my *everything*.

He clicks open the lube as he arches his neck, giving me more access, and then he snakes his arm between us and through my legs until his slippery fingers slip into my crease. I immediately spread my thighs, giving him all the room he needs.

Tripp rubs me in a way that's indescribable, and no matter how I try to resist, my body melts into a puddle of want. The entire time he rubs and presses, my nerves come alive.

The first digit he pushes inside me is uncomfortable but not painful, and after a few moments of fucking me with it, it starts to feel so good tingles spread across my skin.

The anxious knot in my gut disappears. If I can adjust from pain to pleasure like this, the thought of him rocking inside me like that makes my head spin.

I've only ever done the fucking before—and yeah, I want a go at Tripp's ass—but having someone else inside me is new and different, and something I never even thought to consider. It feels like a bizarre kind of power move for me to be spreading my legs and begging that he fucks me, and I'm completely down with it.

It makes sense that it's Tripp I'm doing this with.

"Keep relaxed, just like that," he murmurs and works another finger in. His encouragement is so … *Tripp* that I don't even question it. I'm putting all my trust in him, but it's easy. Because he's him.

Like last time, there's the burn, and then it slowly eases away.

I suck another mark onto his skin. "You're good at this."

"I've had lots of experience."

I smirk. "I guess we've got plenty of time for me to get experienced too."

He claims my mouth again, getting more confident as he stretches and rubs at places I've never realized could be so much fun. My ass is buzzing, and the more he works me open, the more it makes my cock throb. Like it's a secret agreement between my ass and my balls. *When one of us is having fun, we're all having fun.* And goddammit, this is fun.

I start rocking my hips back onto his digits, wanting him deeper, feeling all kinds of filthy and horny and desperate.

"I think it's time for you to fuck me now," I say.

"Not yet."

"Trippy," I whine. "You're supposed to love me. Why are you torturing me like this?"

"I haven't even begun, babe. Ready for the showstopper?"

"The w—" Tripp presses deep, and suddenly, my whole ass lights up. "*Ah. Fuck.*" I have no idea why my voice is making that noise, but how can I even start to think about that when he's blowing my brains out?

I'm vaguely aware of a soft chuckle as Tripp pulls his fingers out, and when he goes to move away, I grip him to me.

"No. Do it again." I grind my cock up into his abs, and yes, that's the spot.

"Geez, give me a sec." He reaches for the condom, and I have to wait an unreasonable amount of time for him to tear it open and roll it down his magnificent cock. "You ready?"

I answer by whining and pulling my knees up.

He covers his smile with his hand as he rubs lube over his cock. "You should see how you look."

"Sexy?"

Tripp groans. "You have no idea. You literally have no idea. If I die right here and now and your face is the last thing I see, I will have no regrets."

I preen at his roundabout praise even though he's talking about death. "If you are going to die, can you at least make sure I come first? Thanks."

"Hold on, baby. Things are about to get real."

CHAPTER TWENTY-FOUR

TRIPP

Fuck. Things are getting *too* real, but am I going to stop? No way.

Everything I've ever wanted, everything I've ever dreamed of, is splayed out beneath me, begging for my dick.

The surge of possession courses through me. I want to own Dex. I want him to be mine for real. It's difficult to remind myself of what this is—fun experimenting. Besties being together while not really being together.

A PR stunt gone too far.

My heart giving in.

After this, there will be no other men for me. No one would be able to live up to the pedestal I keep Dex on.

And that's why I've refrained from doing this. From taking this step. Because I know I will fall apart after it's done. This is just another notch on the Tripp Mitchell belt of heartache when it comes to Dex Mitchale.

"Tripp." Dex's needy, gravelly voice gives me new energy. It lifts me up while longing tries to push me down.

I have to get through this. It has to last, and I need to make sure I take note of every sound he makes, every face he pulls. Every and any indication of pleasure, I have to commit to memory. Because I wasn't being dramatic when I said I could die happy. I might even prefer it because I know what comes next.

Sure, we'll keep up this charade for the media, for our team, and for everyone else. But there will never come a time where I can legitimately call Dex mine, and taking this step—being inside him and owning his body—will only make the downfall more painful.

"I need you," Dex whispers.

He's saying all the right things, everything I've only ever dreamed of him saying, and I can't hold back any longer.

I grab one of his strong thighs and wrap it around my waist while I position my cock at his entrance.

As I begin to press inside him, slowly and so fucking carefully, I watch as his face contorts. First at the discomfort and then with determination. His eyes are closed in concentration, but I want him to see me. To know that I'm the one above him. He's taking my cock, and we're doing this. Together.

"Look at me," I say softly.

His deep brown eyes meet mine, and I swear my heart stops.

"Breathe," I coach.

Dex's lips part, and he sucks in a breath. I take advantage of his open mouth and close mine over it. My tongue dives in while I keep easing my cock inside the tightest damn ass I've ever experienced.

Dex grunts, and I quickly break my mouth away and lean up on my elbow.

"You okay?"

He nods.

"Can you talk?"

A shake of his head now.

"I'll let you adjust."

"No. Don't stop. Please don't stop." Dex's desperation almost has me slamming home, but I don't want to hurt him.

"Relax for me."

He does, and I move a little deeper before pausing again.

"Tell me what to do to make this good for you," he says.

My beautiful Dex. "It's already the best sex of my life."

Happiness explodes deep in my gut because I'm not even lying. After years of fighting my need for him, after telling myself this will never happen ... I get to have Dex in a way I never thought I could.

"I never thought this could happen," I say. "Ever. I've thought about it for so long."

Dex cocks his head. "You have?"

I'm dangerously close to word vomiting my feelings for him, and now is not the time. I'm not sure there ever will be a time to tell him the whole truth that I'm so deeply in love with him there's no coming back from it.

"I'm a hot-blooded gay man, and you're gorgeous. Inside and out." I lean down and kiss the tip of his nose.

"I bet if I'd thought about it, I would have tried to make this happen sooner."

I want to believe him, but I'm not sure I do. We're here because of happenstance.

I press a soft kiss to Dex's jaw. "Tell me when you're good."

"I'm good. So good. I don't think I've ever been gooder."

I huff a laugh and close my hand around his cock. I stroke slowly with a soft grip but then get tighter and faster the harder he gets.

"Actually, no. Now. *Now* I'm the goodest." Dex's voice squeaks.

I thrust inside him, trying to hold back the pleasure that rips through me. Being inside him meets all of my expectations and none of them at the same time. Never in my dreams did I have to hold back because, of course, in my dreams, this wasn't Dex's first time, and I could slam inside him with little to no prep. At the same time, holding back makes me appreciate the experience more than I thought I would.

Sex is sex.

It feels good. It's about getting off. It's not intimate or personal.

Sex with someone you're head over heels in love with?

It's not just sex.

It's *everything*.

I slowly pull back out to the tip and move inside him again, not yet going too fast but quicker than before. My cock passes his prostate, and Dex yelps and clings to my shoulders.

"Nope. Changing my answer. It's now. Now is good, so good." He's so fucking adorable.

"Why don't you wait for the end? Then you can tell me your favorite part."

"Like a theme park ride?"

"Exactly like that." I thrust inside again, grinding deep.

Dex whines, but I set an even pace, letting him adjust and giving him time to get used to the new sensations.

He lies there, holding me, lifting his hips to meet my thrusts, and the trust shining in his eyes almost breaks me.

"Stop worrying about hurting me." He gives me an encouraging squeeze. "I'm more than ready. I swear it."

"Hold your knees." It comes out confident and like an order. Maybe that last part of me was holding on to that thread of doubt that he won't change his mind. That halfway through, he'd push me away. But he's not. He's needy for me. Begging. And I've never seen Dex look hotter.

His cheeks are flushed like they get after being on the ice, but this isn't from exhaustion. It's not from a workout. It's from pure lust.

Then, surprising me, Dex hooks his arms around his knees to hold his legs back, and I finally let go.

My hips meet his ass in a punishing rhythm with every thrust. His mouth drops open, heavy breaths loud between us, and when I tear my gaze away from his face and look down ... fucking hell. It's obscene. So gloriously obscene.

His cock is angry and red trapped between us, leaving behind a pool of precum in his happy trail. Every time I move in and out, I get a quick glimpse of my cock before it disappears again, and it's the surreal thought of this actually happening that only makes the experience more intense.

I'm inside Dex Mitchale.

Dex Mitchale is the one who gasps and drops his head back while I pound into him.

And it's Dex Mitchale's neck that I suck on while trying not to come. I don't want this to end, but I know I'm close. I straighten up, gripping onto Dex's narrow hips. Taking in his impressive muscles, his darkened eyes, the way his dampened dark blond hair looks brown from sweat and is plastered to his forehead. His wide jaw clenches, and his eyes meet mine.

"I'm about to come …" I warn. "What do you need to get there?"

"Cock. Touch." Dex's hand desperately searches for his dick, but I swat him away.

"My job." I practically strangle his cock as I pump inside him hard and fast, chasing release for both of us. Dex's whole body flushes, not just his cheeks now, and I know mine would look the same. His gaze is on my freckled chest, and he runs his fingertips over my pecs.

I'm so close.

So. So. Close. The sweet relief I get when Dex beats me to the punch is short-lived because as soon as I see his cum splash all over his abs, my balls tighten, and my orgasm hits. I ride the brain-numbing high until my limbs feel boneless.

I collapse on top of him, our hot and sweaty bodies melting together, and Dex wraps his arms around my back.

"You were right," he says breathlessly. "But I can't pick the best part. That was the goodest sex ever."

That's an understatement.

I roll off him and onto my back, my chest still heaving, and I wait for the regret to come. I wait for that little voice to tell me all of this will end soon enough. But it doesn't.

The power of the almighty orgasm is too strong to wreck this for me.

So far.

Dex leans up on his elbow, and there's the dread I've been waiting for. As he looks down at me with a frown on his face, I hold my breath for what he's about to say.

He doesn't want to do it again.

He can't keep up the charade.

Yeah, he came, but … *meh*.

What he does come out with though ... "Do you think sex will up my game? Ezra and Anton swear by it. They always fuck the night before, and it won them the Cup last year."

The laugh that leaves my mouth is relief and a metaphoric eye roll in one. "Yes, because the entire hockey season is dependent on who got some D and who didn't."

"My game can use all the luck it can get."

"It's still preseason. You have time to turn it around."

"I'm just hoping your dick has Ezra's magic touch."

I screw up my face. "Please don't say Ezra and touch and dick in the same sentence. It does things to my brain that I don't want to imagine."

"Sorry. I ... I really need to do something."

I turn my head, and my heart almost breaks at the sight of Dex's glistening puppy dog eyes. "You're really worried, aren't you?"

"It's the worst preseason I've had since I was a rookie. I have a right to be worried."

"It's still preseason. I promise it'll turn around."

—

It doesn't turn around. Not for Dex, and not for me. If anything, his bad playing has rubbed off on me.

The rest of preseason is a disaster, and we're going into the first game of the regular season with one win. One.

Dex and I aren't the only ones out there, but it's like the team can't get their shit together this year.

We were one goal away from winning the Stanley Cup just months ago, and now we can't find the net. Our opponents can though.

It's why I'm no longer on speaking terms with my goalpost. It's in a time-out.

At least we have a home game up first, which should give us the upper hand, but as we hit the ice for warm-ups and I'm stretching, it's like I can see the black cloud of negativity floating above the team. At the other end, Anaheim—who didn't even make the playoffs last year—looks ready and eager to go. But hey, who wouldn't be when they won six of their preseason games.

As I take my place in front of the net, I suck in a sharp breath. "Okay, postie. We've got this, okay? Can we call a truce? Please? No answer means you agree, and that agreement is legally binding. Let's do this." I kiss the bar and lower my helmet so the guys can fire warm-up shots at me.

Dex avoids eye contact with me the whole time, and I can't say I blame him. Whenever hockey is mentioned, he shuts down. He's been moved to second line, while Fensby has taken his spot on first.

Coach is working with the lines, trying to find a groove, but if you ask me, all he's done is mess up the vibe even more.

I've seen it all from my end of the ice—the sloppy passes, the hesitance.

We're not working as a team.

Before we head back to the locker room so they can resurface the ice and get ready for the pregame festivities, I pull Dex back and then hold out my fist for him to bump.

He sighs but offers it up.

Fist bump. Chest bump. Hug. Fake-out high five.

The crowd who are here early enough to see it all cheer because they love it, but Dex doesn't even crack a smile.

"It's not like it's been helping," he says.

"Don't mess with the system, dude." I slap his back.

"Maybe we should mess with the system. Something's gotta give."

I hate seeing him so down, especially with himself. He gets ridiculed for not being the brightest crayon in the box, but to me, he has always outshone everyone else. Not because of his brains but because of his happy and bubbly personality.

He quietly sulks while the coaches try to pep us up, but none of it matters when we get out there. Because we still suck. From the second the puck drops, I earn my keep. They come at me from all angles. Our defense is broken, our offense doesn't even get a chance at the puck, and Anaheim is on a rampage.

I let two past me in the first ten minutes of the game, but this can't be put all on me.

Adler skates by me in between plays. "Pull it together, man."

"Tell our D men to pull it together," I grit out. "I've let in two out of how many shots? Tell them to maybe help me protect the fucking goal."

He pulls to a stop. "Shake it off, bro. We're still in this."

With the encouragement from our team captain, I manage to keep Anaheim out of my crease. But barely.

By the end of the first period, it feels like the third. And in our short break in the locker room, Coach yells at all of us.

"You can't leave everything up to Mitchell out there. It's a miracle Anaheim only has two on the board with how sloppy you all are."

Thank you, I say in my head because no way am I saying it aloud and bringing his holy wrath down on me.

"Where's the team from last season?"

"I dunno," Fensby says. "But I do know of one big difference." He glares at Dex.

"That was rhetorical, Fensby," Coach says. "How many shots on goal have you taken tonight?"

Fensby goes to open his mouth when Coach cuts him off.

"Also rhetorical," Coach snaps. "Get back out there and turn this around."

Easier said than done.

It's not even close.

And when the final buzzer in the third sounds, we walk away with zero points on the board.

Great start to the season, guys.

We're all doom and gloom as we head down the chute, trying to stay positive for the cameras while we spout bullshit about just needing to find our rhythm and that Anaheim played really well.

They didn't. They didn't even need to. We were disasters out there.

Dex is frustrated. The tension rolls off him. His usual easygoing nature is gone, and as he undresses, he throws his gloves and skates in his cubby with so much force, it makes a resounding *thud*.

"We'll get there," I murmur.

"And if we don't?" He turns to me. "Maybe that trade will happen after all."

At least then we'd have a clean break.

We're so exhausted and mentally drained that when we get home, we both crash out without even a goodnight kiss or handjob. And when I wake, Dex isn't snuggled into me like usual. He's sitting up, his delicious abs on display, but his focus is on his phone in his hands, and the scowl on his face isn't my Dex.

"What are you looking at?" My voice is croaky from sleep.

He flinches. "Fans being brutal."

"Well, yeah, we sucked ass last night, and not in the fun way."

Dex's anger disappears for the briefest moment where his eyebrows shoot up into his hairline. "You do that?"

Oh, honey. "You still don't know half the stuff I do in bed."

He puts his phone down. "Why not?"

"Because I'm trying to ease you into this whole gay sex thing. When you first learn to drive, you don't floor it in a Lamborghini."

Dex eyes me. "And in this situation, you're the Lambo?"

"Mmhmm."

"What if I don't want you to ease me into it? I'm doing all right so far, aren't I?" His face falls. "Fuck. Aren't I?"

I laugh. "You're acing it. But we have an entire year to explore each other." I nod toward his phone on his stomach. "What are the fans saying?"

"That us being married messed with the team dynamics."

"Wait, what?"

He shows me his screen, which is the Twitter feed for the hashtag #mitchellmarriagecurse.

"Stay off Twitter. That's where rationality goes to die."

"How can people be out there saying things like they want us to break up and that I played hockey better before I was gay? And why do they assume I'm gay because I'm married to a man now? Why does being married to you suddenly cancel out all the women I've been with?"

I know exactly what he means. "Welcome to the other side of being in a same-sex relationship."

"This is … normal for you?"

"Haven't you ever wondered why I don't have a Twitter account other than the one the team runs for me? Ever since I was drafted and came out, I've been dealing with this kind of shit. It's all part of the territory."

Dex looks stunned. "Why … why didn't I know? I've seen stuff here and there, but … not like this. This is … everywhere. And constant. There's been a hundred new tweets about us since I woke up this morning."

I take his phone. "Which is why I stay away from it."

"How do you all deal with it? You, Oskar, Ezra, Anton—"

"Maybe you should talk to Anton. He only came out last season. Guys like Ezra and me, we've been out from the beginning, so we haven't known any different. It sucks that with all the progress we've made, there are still people out there who want to blame our sexuality for everything, but at the same time, there are some really great things that come from being an out hockey player too."

"Like what?"

I check the time. It's still early Saturday, which is perfect, and we don't have to be at the practice arena until this afternoon for a skate to keep loose for our away game tomorrow night. "Let me show you."

CHAPTER TWENTY-FIVE

DEX

When Tripp said he was going to take me somewhere to see the upside of his being out, I've gotta say, I expected a gay strip club or something.

So sitting here, staring out the windshield at a small ice center just outside of Spring Valley, has me confused.

"What are we doing here?"

Tripp puts the car into park and turns off the engine. "We're going to talk to some people who might be able to help."

"Like a team psychologist? We have one of those."

Tripp gives me his crooked smile that makes my gut all jittery and unclicks my seat belt. "Get your ass out and you'll see."

He grabs our gear bags out of the trunk, and I follow him across the quiet parking lot and into the center. There aren't many people around, and I worry whether we're supposed to be in here or not. "You sure this is okay?"

"Trust me." He opens the door to the rink and waits for me to pass.

Down on the ice, there's a junior team running drills.

"In here." There are only three rows of seating, and Tripp nudges me into the back one.

I go quietly, and we sit there listening to the familiar sound of skates on ice and the clip of the puck hitting their blades.

"You going to explain yet?" I ask.

"These guys are part of a minor hockey club."

"Cool." Minor hockey teams usually play for sport and fun, not with the drive to get into the big leagues, and if Tripp has brought me here to point out what my future looks like if I don't get my shit together, I'm gonna be pissed. That will only put more pressure on me and my game.

"This team is the Rainbow Raiders. All queer players and allies."

Oh. My eyebrows jump up, and I watch the kids with renewed interest. "But hockey is all about You Can Play. Why do they need a queer team?"

"Because that might be the official stance, but as you've seen this morning and from Fensby, good intentions can't actually bring change to people who don't want it."

Being here isn't making me feel any better. The opposite, actually.

"You're in your head, Dex. That's all this is. We both know you're an incredible player, but you're being hit with negativity from all sides, and you're not used to it. I wanted to give you something positive to try and drown out that noise. To show you the reason people like Ezra and me chose to be out from the start."

I shift, feeling distinctly uncomfortable with the idea. "That's the thing though. I think that's what has been getting me down the most. I'm a fraud. Every time I get a message, every time I see a sign saying *Mitchells married* or *You're my Queeros*, it gets to my head. All these people are *so* focused on us, and I'm terrified they'll find out what

I did and call me out. Then you'll be dragged down and hurt too. This morning was a taste of what that could be. All I keep seeing is these people putting hope in me, and then finding out that I'm not who they think I am, and letting everyone down. Then I'll be traded. And you'll be dealing with the fallout, but I won't be here to get through it with you."

Tripp sighs, then reaches over and links his fingers through mine. "I have a question."

"Yeah?"

"Why aren't you who they think you are?"

"Well … I don't know. I mean, I haven't been through all the nastiness, and can I really claim being queer, when other than with you I'm straight? Do you actually count?"

He's quiet for a moment, and when I finally force myself to look at him, his expression is … strange. "Why don't I count?"

"Because …" Fuck, I don't even know. "You're *you*. You're not … I don't …" I force a long inhale while I try to work out what I'm saying. "You're not a guy to me. You're Tripp."

"But I *am* a guy."

"Yes, but that doesn't matter to me. Everything we're doing, I couldn't do it with someone else. I don't want to." Even having sex with women, while enjoyable, has never felt the way it does with Tripp. Things with us are intense, and I think our connection has something to do with that. I'm worried if our relationship fails that I'll never have that again.

"Do you really still think of yourself as straight?"

His question throws me. "Well, aren't I? It's not like I can suddenly claim gay just because I love getting naked with you."

Tripp starts to laugh. "Actually, that's exactly what it means. Well, kind of. You're not gay, but I don't think you're straight either. Straight guys usually don't like dick, whether that dick is attached to their best friend or not."

"What about brojobs?"

"Some straight guys experiment, sure, but they know deep down it isn't right. Is that what you're telling me? That being with me isn't right?"

"Of course not." I scowl. "I've never ... you're my best friend. I l—" I almost say *I love you*, but for some reason, the words stick in my throat. We've never been shy about saying it to each other—I used to say it all the time when we'd end a call or I'd leave his apartment, so why is it so hard to get out now? The word is heavy on my tongue, and when I look at Tripp, it *feels* heavier too. I can't say it. So I clear my throat and give him the realest answer I can. "It feels right. And if it feels this right and I'm not gay or straight, then I'm lost. How wouldn't I know it about myself? I'm dumb, but am I really *that* dumb? Does this mean I'm bi? I don't feel bi."

"I can't give you the answers, but from what you're saying ... maybe you can look up pansexuality."

I side-eye him. "Did you just make that up?"

He shoves me playfully. "Of course not. Seriously, look it up. And before you ask me, no, it has nothing to do with pots and pans."

That's exactly what I was going to ask.

"But before you look into it, we're going to meet the team. I want you to see what queer people being out really means. It's not trolls on social media who can spew hate and then walk away from their keyboard and forget it. It's people like them. Kids who see us living our lives, being happy, in successful careers, and it shows them they can be anything. It gives them hope. I would have killed to have that when I was younger, and I know you never experienced it, but maybe they can help you understand. No one has the same journey, Dex. It's okay if you haven't figured it out yet. That doesn't mean you're not valid."

It's that sentence that does it.

That doesn't mean you're not valid.

I'm hit with the weirdest prickling behind my nose like maybe I want to cry, but over what? It doesn't make sense. I cling tighter to Tripp's hand for a second before we let go and pull on our skates, me trying to swallow all the emotion down, but with those six words, something has relaxed inside me. Like maybe I can do this. Because maybe I'm not faking it at all.

We head down to the ice.

The coach of the kids' team spots us and skates over to the entrance.

"Tripp, it's been a while since I've seen you."

He gives his bashful grin. "I'm sure you've seen we've been under a bit of pressure lately."

"I have." He nods to me. "Nice to finally meet you, Dexter Mitchale."

"Just Dex, please." I shake his hand, and he introduces himself as William, but my attention strays back to Tripp. "You come here a lot?"

"Not as much as I did when I first moved here, but it's a good place to escape sometimes."

"You never told me."

"It's personal." He shrugs.

"Is that the Mitchell brothers?"

I look up to see a kid, maybe mid-teens, skating our way. I plaster the friendliest smile I can manage onto my face.

"In the flesh."

"*No way.* Guys, look!"

He gets the team's attention, and from there, Tripp and I don't get a chance to talk. We're surrounded by overenthusiastic kids, and for a couple of minutes, I'm in my element. We sign skates, and the entire time the nonstop *noise* comes at me from all directions. I love it.

"Thank you," someone says.

I look up into the pimply face of a kid so lanky he's almost my height. "What for?"

"You, umm … I always thought my best friend was straight, even when he'd be touchy and stuff like you two, and then after you guys got married, I got my shit together and asked him if he'd ever considered it."

My smile takes over my face. "Yeah? What did he say?"

The kid shakes his head. "Nah, it's not for him. But nothing changed. Just … I had an answer. You know?"

Well, thank fuck for that. The last thing I need is to be responsible for wrecking some kid's life. "I'm happy for you. Best friends are important."

His face reddens. "Yeah. Can you sign my skate?"

I take it that's it for the emotional stuff, then. Fair enough. I sign his skate, then a few others, and the whole time I can feel the sheer levels of enthusiasm.

When William finally gets everyone to calm down, Tripp and I help out with drills, and then we put on some pads and break into two teams for a practice game. I'm not sure if it's the absence of pressure or being in a supportive environment, but when we start to play, it's like I'm my old self.

We go easy on the kids. I let some strip the puck from me, and Tripp lets two easy goals past. But when I get close enough to take a shot, I have this brief flashback to how I used to feel playing him before he was traded. The nerves, the respect and admiration, the knowledge that if I get one past him, it's less about skill and more about luck.

Tripp's hands are ready, eyes sharp, and I don't hold back. I fire a bullet into the right corner, and for one wild second, I think Tripp's got it ...

Then it finds the net.

Satisfaction floods through me. The high I get from scoring never seems to go away, even in a game that means nothing, but also, somehow, everything.

Once we're finished, we follow the team back to the weights room, where we sit in a circle and the ones who are comfortable share their stories.

We're there for a few hours all up, and when it's time to leave, we pose for about a million selfies.

I feel lighter than I have in weeks.

It's not until I'm back out in the Vegas sun that I can breathe around the emotion again.

Before Tripp can take a step, I grab him and yank him into a hug.

I have no doubt this hasn't fixed my issues, but it's a start.

I belong.

My feelings for Tripp are bigger than nasty comments and Fensby's attitude. If something happens and it gets out that we made a dumb choice, it's not like that will change anything. Fake-real married or not, we're together now.

I can love Tripp the way my body always has because my brain has finally caught up.

The threat of a trade is still terrifying, but I have to believe we're stronger than that. We've had this connection from the start, and not even distance can get in the way of us.

I don't let him go for a really long time.
"You okay?" he asks.
I kiss the side of his head. "I really think I will be."

CHAPTER TWENTY-SIX

TRIPP

The whole way home, Dex doesn't stop touching me. He leans over and kisses my neck, runs his hand up my thigh until he's cupping me over my pants, and it takes all my strength to keep focus on the road.

We stop at a red light, and I relax into it. "Being a good role model really turns you on, huh?"

"Nope. But you showing me something that's important to you does. Taking me there just so I will feel better does. Everything you do turns me on."

"Fuck." I throw my head back.

Then a horn blasts behind us, and my eyes fly open to see the light is green.

"You're going to make me crash," I say.

"I can't help it."

"Pretty sure you can. You just need to remember kindergarten rules. We don't touch other people's private parts. In this case, at least until we get home. Then we can have grown-up rules again."

Dex pulls away and slumps in his seat. "Can you at least drive faster?"

Normally, a comment like that would make me drive slower, but my cock is straining against my pants, and horniness wins out over stubbornness.

"How long do we have until we need to be at the practice rink?" I ask.

"Can we call Coach and be like 'we just spent two hours on the ice with some kids, so can we not come in so we can have sex instead?'"

"Yes, Coach will love that."

Dex checks the time on his phone. "We have an hour and a half."

"Plenty of time to get off, get showered, and drive to Summerlin."

"Is it enough time for us to do something we haven't yet?"

I glance over at Dex to find him biting his lip nervously. "What were you wanting to do?"

"Well …" He swallows hard and looks away. "You said you were versatile, didn't you?"

My foot hits the accelerator so fast we get thrown back in our seats, and I almost rear-end the car in front of me.

"Okay, I'm getting the impression you'd rather die than let me top you. Is that what's happening here?" Dex smirks.

"I've been waiting for you to ask to top me forever."

Dex frowns. "Wait, why do I have to be the one to ask?"

"Because I don't know if you know this …" I lean in and whisper conspiratorially, "I've had sex with men before. You haven't."

"What's that got to do with anything?"

"I wanted to take this at your pace. Do what you're comfortable with. And you always seem to want me inside you, and I will never, ever say no to that."

Dex throws up his hands. "I've been waiting for you to ask because, I dunno … isn't it … gay etiquette?"

"For the last time, there is no gay etiquette. Do you think we go to a finishing school for gay sex—whoa. There's a sentence that changes the whole meaning of finishing school." I shudder.

I finally—finally—turn onto our street, and Dex can't remember the rules anymore. He goes back to touching me and driving me crazy.

"So we can do it? Do we have time? It takes a while to, you know, like prep."

"For you, maybe. Trust me, we have more than enough time." I reach over and pat his cheek.

The second I pull into our designated parking spot under the building and turn the car off, Dex is all over me.

His hands cup my face, his mouth presses against mine, and if there was room for him to climb over and straddle me, I'm sure he'd find it.

"Okay, we have time for sex. We don't have time to get injured in the car and then sex. Move your sexy ass upstairs now."

Still, he can't help himself. All the way through the parking lot to the elevators, his hands don't stop exploring. I back him up against the side of the elevator, and he grabs my ass in his big palms and squeezes.

"I can't wait to fuck you," he says. "Ooh, do we get to have hot goalie contortion sex?"

"Uh, what?" I'm in too much of a lust-filled daze to understand.

"The guys from the Collective are always joking about how bendy you are because you're a goalie."

I snort. "Want me to put my legs behind my head while we fuck?"

Dex's eyes widen. "You can do that?"

"Yup. Though it's not as sexy as you'd think. I gave myself a black eye once with a knee to my face. I can do the splits while bouncing on a dick, but I can't maintain it for long. Also doesn't feel all that great for me. It's more for show than anything."

"I want a show," Dex complains.

"Mm, maybe when we have the time. Not today."

"In the essence of saving time, then ... We've both had our medicals." He lets the implication hang in the air.

"You want to go bare?"

"I don't want anything between us," he rasps.

I go weak in the knees.

The thought of Dex rumbling that in my ear has been a mere fantasy, and now I'm getting my wish.

The elevator opens, and I struggle with my keys to the apartment because anticipation thrums through me like adrenaline on game night.

Once inside, clothes start coming off. Shoes first, socks—all the while, I stay attached to Dex's lips.

It's the kind of frantic need that could really do with a hard and fast orgasm from a hand or mouth, but I've wanted this moment for so long, I'm not going to give in to my desperation.

We get naked, but before Dex can get on the bed, I guide him toward the single armchair next to my bookshelf. I grip his shoulder and push him down.

"As much as I'd love to have sex on this chair, I don't think it will hold both of us." His mouth is right next to my hard cock, his breath hitting my skin with every word.

"We're not fucking on the chair." I grip my shaft and move the tip over his lips.

Dex hums and opens his mouth to let me in, but I force myself to step back.

"We're not doing that either."

"Then why am I sitting over here?"

I back up, moving away from him, and then I turn to my bedside drawer. "Because you're going to watch me as I prep myself."

"I don't get to do that part?"

"Not this time. But when we don't have to rush to get to practice, you can take your time doing whatever you want to me. This needs to be fast." I reach into my drawer and pull out lube and a toy I keep there for nights my hand isn't enough.

When I turn, Dex's eyes are locked on the dildo in my hand.

"I have to sit here and watch you use … that?"

"Yep."

"I'm not allowed to help?"

"Nope."

"Can I at least touch myself?"

"Hmm. I want to say no, just so by the time I'm ready, you're going to be aching for me."

He palms his cock. "I'm already there."

I watch as he strokes himself slowly, and I want to drop to my knees and worship his dick with my tongue, but I remind myself about the time constraint. I want him inside me for as long as possible before we need to clean up and head to practice.

"Save it for when I'm ready," I say, and his hand immediately stops.

I turn and kneel on the edge of the bed, spreading my thighs wide, but then I decide to give him a show after all.

A strangled groan comes from behind me when I widen my legs and shift so my feet are hanging off each side of the bed in a full split.

"That *is* sexy," Dex says, voice rough.

"Only about to get sexier."

I can't help smiling as I cover the dildo in lube. Leaning forward and resting one hand on the mattress, I reach behind me and place the head of the toy at my entrance.

"You're not even going to use your fingers first?" Dex asks.

"This will be faster." I've had more than enough anal to know how to relax and let it happen, but I go slow anyway. Mainly because of the sounds coming from Dex.

There's a sharp intake of breath, a groan that seems to get stuck in the back of his throat, and by the time the dildo fills me up, his breathing is harsh and panting.

"If I look over my shoulder, you better not be touching yourself," I warn. When I do turn my head, he quickly moves his hand away. "I'm going to have to keep my eye on you." Not that I can in this position.

I rest my free hand on the mattress in front of me while I begin to fuck myself with the dildo.

"Tripp," Dex whines, and I wish I could look at him and see the desperation in his eyes, but I can't like this. "Please let me touch myself."

"Wouldn't you rather touch me instead?"

"Are you ready?"

"Not yet, but come here."

Dex stands, and I can just picture his defined muscles all taut and mouthwatering. When he steps up behind me, I sit up and reach behind my head to grip him around the neck. His front pushes against my back, his hard cock digging into my spine, and I let out a breathy "Kiss me."

He leans over me, diving deep with his tongue, and then his hand wraps around my cock and gives me two hard pumps. The dildo brushes my prostate, and I can't help moaning into Dex's mouth.

"I'm ready." I blindly reach for the lube on the bed to pass back to him. "Use this, and then fuck me."

The sound of the lube cap opening echoes through the room. I keep pumping the toy in and out of me, making sure I'm stretched enough for him, and then his slick cock runs along my ass cheek while his hand closes over mine.

"Let me."

I let the toy go, and he moves it in and out of me a couple more times. When he pulls it out, I readjust myself so I'm back on my knees to give him easier access.

I lean forward to put my hands on the mattress, but his arm comes under mine and across my chest, holding me up.

Dex nips my ear. "I want you against me."

In one swift move, his cock fills me, sparking pain and pleasure inside me all at once. My head lolls back and rests against Dex's shoulder.

Every time Dex and I share anything that's more than platonic, I get this overwhelming sense that it's not really happening. Then a small part of me freaks out that it's all going to go away, which only makes me want to hold on tighter. Kiss him harder.

I cherish every move he makes, the way he's embracing me and supporting me while slowly waiting for me to adjust. His thrusts are small and languid even though his body is coiled tight.

I want him to unleash on me, but at the same time, right here, in the calm before the storm, we're just ... one. It doesn't take long for Dex to become impatient.

He moves faster, his grip becomes tighter, and when I tell him to let go, he doesn't hesitate to push me down face-first onto the bed.

My ass sticks up in the air, my legs still spread wide, and then Dex takes me in hard but long thrusts. He pulls out to the tip and slams back inside over and over again.

I'm vaguely aware of time ticking by, but I want to stay like this forever.

When it's only Dex and me, nothing else matters. Nothing except holding on to this thing between us for as long as I can have it.

"Tripp ..." Dex gasps.

Like that, best friend Dex and husband Dex collide in a way that makes my chest ache. I need more. Need him closer.

"Hold me," I beg.

His body blankets mine, one big arm wrapping around me while his other hand links with mine and pins it to the mattress above my head. Dex's lips work their way over my neck, his grunts loud in my ear as he pounds into my ass. Each thrust reverberates through my body, making me wish my cock was low enough to rub against the mattress, because the pressure is getting to be too much.

I need release.

I need to come.

But just as I go to reach for it, Dex anticipates me, and his hand is there first. I whine as his fist wraps around my shaft and jerks me in time with his thrusts. I'm so hard, so sensitive. Dex knows exactly how to work me over, and when he says, "Come for me," all I can do is obey.

My balls tighten right before my cock pulses with the first spurt of cum.

Dex groans, then slams back inside me once, twice, before he stills, hips pressed flush against my ass, as his release fills me. Neither of us talks while we catch our breaths.

Dex pulls out of me and collapses on his back by my side with a dopey grin filling his face. "At least we'll be nice and loose for practice."

I bolt upright. "Fuck, practice."

CHAPTER TWENTY-SEVEN

DEX

Yesterday went too fast for me to stop and think, let alone look into this sexuality stuff. After practice, we came home, ate dinner, and crashed from nearly a full day on the ice.

This morning, we flew into Denver early, dropped our things at the hotel, and then headed straight to Ball Arena for a practice skate.

Since yesterday, my mind has been on a roller coaster of ups and downs, and Tripp is right—the only thing that is going to help me is to get out of my head.

So after we're released from practice, we go back to the hotel, and I hold Tripp to me as I fuck him face-to-face. It's slow, and so sexy, plus being able to watch every expression cross his face adds a layer of intimacy I've never had before.

Not to mention the no-condom thing—*thank you*, preseason medical.

Sex has never been so good.

And after seeing Tripp naked, I'm then treated to the sight of him in a tailored suit. Black pants and blue jacket, he looks incredible. So incredible that when we arrive back at Ball Arena, I can't stop myself from taking his hand on the way through the parking lot.

I know there are people out there who would prefer we didn't "rub" our relationship in their faces, who would be more comfortable pretending we're still only friends, or who are okay with us as long as we let them forget we like dick, but I'm not going to play by their rules.

Maybe that means I attract more heat.

Maybe that means I put more of a target on my head than I already have.

But with Tripp's warm, large hand in mine, those people can all go and fuck themselves. Although, seeing the way Tripp took that dildo, I'm beginning to think that isn't the insult people think it is.

Next time someone tells me to go and fuck myself, I think I'll give it a try.

I send a grin Tripp's way, and he smiles back.

I'm not feeling confident, but I'm trying to squash the negativity down.

When we get to the locker room, I look around at the team, and it's clear I'm not the only one feeling the heaviness of all our losses. We strip out of our suits into our base layers, and a few guys head through to the weight room.

All I know is that if we go out there like this, we're going to lose. Guaranteed. And I know Tripp's been saying all along that we're not the problem, but we're literally the only change here. And if we're messing with team dynamics, I sure as hell want to fix it.

I pull a soccer ball out of the game-day bag Coach has, and Tripp jumps up to kick it around with me. Adler joins us, along with Keisky and McGillan, and the longer we're at it, the more people add to our circle.

For a short while, it takes me out of my head.

"Hey, Tripp, you going to keep them out of our goal tonight?" Keisky asks.

"Depends. Are you assholes going to actually defend our zone, or have you forgotten how that works?"

McGillan flips him off. "Maybe if our forwards could keep possession …" His gaze flicks to mine, but instead of encouraging the smack talk, I aim to shut it down.

"You're right. But I'm feeling good tonight, so let's all play our positions and show Colorado why we made it to the Stanley Cup final last season."

"We could really use some of that Mitchell Brothers magic, I'm not gonna lie," Adler says.

"Why are we the ones with the magic?" Tripp asks.

I wink at him. "It's all the gayness. Don't you know queer guys ride in on unicorns, shooting sparkles out of our asses?"

"That's not—" Adler shakes his head. "Come on, Dex, that's not what I meant."

"We know what you meant," Tripp says. "You thought we rode rainbows."

Adler laughs. "Fuck you guys."

I snigger and tap the ball to Keisky, who passes to McGillan.

In only a few minutes, it almost feels like the old team again.

Then Fensby walks into the room.

I'm not sure if I'm projecting, but that tension immediately snaps back around us, and our soccer game wraps up a few minutes later.

When we hit the ice for a warm-up skate, I do my best not to look out at the growing crowd.

With my fragile mindset, all it would take is the wrong sign to get me down, and I'm trying my hardest to get back to playing like the old Dex. I've taken a hit, but I'm still that same player. And at this point, the best thing I can do to shut up the speculation and people who are trying to push the idea that Tripp and I shouldn't be together is to prove them all wrong.

The assholes don't matter.

The Rainbow Raiders and others like them do.

And the whole time we were with that junior team, not one person mentioned how I was choking this season, which supports Tripp's assurance that it isn't only me.

I glance over at where Fensby is skating, lazy smile on his smug face, and realize I've never wanted to hit him more.

Which is surprising, because I've wanted to hit him a whole lot in the past.

That said, his negativity has only ever been directed at me because he's been after my position. And now, the entire team is having to deal with his ego—especially now he's playing first line.

Maybe it's not only me and Tripp. Maybe it's his attitude that's doing it. No one else in the team seems to have a problem with us, and the only time they're uncomfortable is when Fensby is running his mouth.

I skate over to Tripp. "I think it's Fensby."

"What is?"

"The reason the team is playing so bad. His attitude has never been as shitty as this season, and he's getting in everyone's head."

Tripp's hazel eyes stray to the other side of the rink where Fensby is. "Okay, but even if it is him, there's nothing we can do about it."

"I can get my position back."

"Of course you can, but that has nothing to do with him and everything to do with the fact you're a talented mofo."

I nod. "I'm gonna do it."

"That's my Dex. And now ... you know what we need to do." Tripp holds out his fist.

Yesss. We fist bump, chest bump, hug, fake-out high five, but where that's usually it, I step forward and add a kiss to the top of his helmet.

"Hey—"

"I figured mixing it up can't *hurt*." I slap his ass as I skate off.

That man is too damn good for me, but he's mine.

And it's the reminder of how I feel about Tripp and everything we do together that lets me pull my gaze from the ice and peek out at the crowd as we head off to make room for the preshow.

As expected, some of the signs are supportive, and others are ... well, assholes is what those people are.

I remind myself to block out the noise. If I don't, those people will get what they want and see one of us traded. We're going to make this work. We have to.

If I have to fight to stay with him, then that's what I'll do.

And fuck, the game is a fight.

There's no magic switch to get the team playing properly again, but our raw need is showing through. Every time I hit that ice, I go hard. I might feel slower and less instinctual than usual, but I put myself in front of the puck at every opportunity.

Colorado is fighting too though, and they make some good shots on goal, but Tripp shuts them out every time.

He fills the net, and I'm hit with awe again and again that someone that talented is who I go home to at night.

I spend more time on the bench than I'm used to in the game, but it means when I'm put back out there, I work harder than I ever have. When I get a penalty and Colorado scores on a power play, I force myself to shake it off, even while the disappointment and embarrassment threaten to take hold.

It doesn't help when our third line is rotated in and Fensby sneers at me over his shoulder. "Dumbass Dex. What's the bet you just lost the game for us after that sloppy move?"

"Shut your mouth, Fensby," Adler grits out. "If you're so good, get us back the point."

"Easy."

Apparently not, because he doesn't manage it, and we go into the third one point down. Instead of letting the despair in, I remind myself that if I can save us, no one will focus on the penalty. That doesn't help with the nerves or the way my body aches with wanting to be done with this, but I push through it all. I focus on the signs from people who support us, think of the kids back home, watching us play, feeling disappointed in our season so far, and when Mossier from Colorado passes to Tregary, I'm hit with a split second of past Dex and see the play before they make it.

I intercept the puck and take off down the ice.

Colorado is on me, and I don't see any of my team for support, so I pull up to the goal and shoot.

The goalie doesn't have Tripp's skill, but he's just fast enough to clip the puck and send it back into my blade.

Mossier shoves me from the side, blocking my attempt on goal, and I look up as Keisky appears as if from nowhere. I shoot the puck to him, and he fires it into the top right corner. The lamp lights up, and it's like I can finally breathe.

At the next face-off, I expect Coach to call my line back in, but he doesn't. I take up position, and after a sloppy start, we gain possession, but Colorado is everywhere. McGillan passes to Segoyer, who passes back to Keisky, to McGillan, to me.

We try to put another in the net but fail. Colorado intercepts the rebound and flies down the ice, but Tripp shuts out the goal and fires the puck straight back to McGillan.

We get it back into our offensive zone, but it's a scramble to keep possession. There are seconds left on the clock, and when Keisky gets close, both of Colorado's D-men close in. I lose track of who's who, and the mess of sticks and the fight for the puck draw their goalie out.

It's a mistake Tripp would never make.

Keisky gets off a pass to me, and there's nothing but an empty net in front of me.

I shoot, and for a split second, I think I've totally missed, but then the puck clips the side bar and ricochets into the goal.

Thank fuck.

Relief surges through me so fast, I barely notice when my team slams into me. Someone knocks my helmet, and gloves are patting my back, but I break away from them and head for Tripp.

He's grinning and holds up his mitt for a high five that I gladly accept.

"Feel good?" he asks.

"It'd feel better if it was on purpose."

"Why? None of your goals are ever on purpose."

I shove him, but we barely make it past the next face-off when the buzzer sounds.

"Shit, *yes*," I shout when the score of 2-1 flashes on the screen.

It was one of the hardest games I've played in a long time, and it was so far from perfect we're going to have to work hard to pull it off again, but for now, the win feels incredible.

It's the injection of hope the team needs.

The relief is obvious with us all.

Except Fensby.

The vein in the middle of his forehead is standing out against his reddened face, but even his bad attitude can't bring me down.

I ignore him and join the rest of the team, ready for a long-overdue celebration.

After pressers and showers, on our way out of the arena, Tripp leans into me. "You know what this means, don't you?"

"What?"

"You have to kiss my helmet before every game."

"If it helps us win, I'll suck your dick if I have to."

Tripp laces his fingers with mine. "Nah, that you can do for fun. *Whenever* you like. Whenever you're thinking about doing it. Just go for it. I won't stop you."

I really don't think he means every single time I think about it, because honestly, I think about it a lot. At the most inopportune times too. I don't see him saving a lot of goals if his cock is in my mouth during a game.

Shit. Maybe that's our problem on the ice. I'm too distracted thinking about my husband's cock to hockey properly.

Right. Okay. Time to switch my brain off when it comes to playing. It should be easy. I've had plenty of practice not using my head.

Our game turns around right now.

CHAPTER TWENTY-EIGHT

TRIPP

Our game doesn't turn around completely, but it also doesn't flatline again. We have to fight tooth and nail for every single win, but our losses aren't a complete slaughter.

After a packed week on the road to play Minnesota, Buffalo, Philly, Pittsburgh, and DC, we're finally home and have home games for the next two weeks.

We're barely into the season, and I'm already exhausted.

Last year, time flew so fast. Winning nearly every game does that though. It's still too early to tell, but I'm worried about our chances of even making the playoffs this season.

The schedule is always so busy with back-to-back games, road trips, and constant training that for the last three nights away, Dex and I haven't even wanted to make each other come, and when we got home last night, we went straight to bed and slept through until our alarms went off to tell us to get to the practice rink.

I don't have any insecurity about the lack of sex, because I've been more than happy to climb into bed next to him and fall asleep like we always did as friends.

That part of our relationship hasn't changed, and there's something promising in that. It gives me hope that when the year is up, we can go back to how it was between us. Maybe.

I will always love Dex and always want more from him, but it's not like I can force him to stay married to me. I can't chain him to my bed and not let him leave.

Although the image of Dex tied to my bed does have its appeal.

When we get home from this morning's practice skate, we drop our gear bags at the door, and Dex stalks toward the couch, but I chase after him and wrap my arm around his waist before he can throw himself down on it and stay there for the rest of the day.

"Let's go to bed," I murmur in his ear.

"And I'm suddenly not so exhausted."

We don't even bother undressing before collapsing on my bed.

We lie side by side, our legs intertwined, our mouths tasting and nipping at each other playfully.

While our hands wander, it's gentle and exploring. There's no need to hurry this up. It's only been a few days since we were intimate, but the need to cherish Dex is more powerful than the need to maul him just to get off.

I roll us over so I'm on top, my hardening cock grinding against him. He tries to lift his hips, but I'm in a torturous mood where I'm going to draw out every moan. I'm going to take my time and—

My phone starts ringing.

"Noooo," Dex complains.

"I'm turning it off." By the time I wrestle it out of my pocket, the call's gone to voicemail, but then Dex's starts. I climb off him so he can get his phone.

"That can't be good," I say as I see the team PR number on my missed calls list. "Is that Graham?"

"Yep." Dex hits Answer. "Hey, you're on speaker."

"We have a problem," Graham says. "You need to come in."

"What kind of problem?"

"There's an article. Somehow it's gotten out that you were married *before* officially breaking up with Jessica."

"What? How?" I ask.

Color drains from Dex's face.

"That's unclear," Graham says. "But we need to discuss our options."

"We'll be right there." Dex ends the call and stands.

I flop onto my back. "He couldn't have caught us while we were there?"

"It must've only been posted, or maybe he just missed us. We need to go." Dex turns. "Wait, where did I put my phone?" It's still in his hand, but he pats his pockets anyway. "Where's my wallet? We need to go. We need to—"

"Dex," I say and slowly get up. I approach him like he's a fretting animal. "It's going to be okay." I don't know if that's true or not, but I have to hold on to that.

"Nope." Dex paces halfway to the door and back again. "Everything I was worried about happening is happening, and if it was only my career on the line, I'd say fuck it because you're more important to me than hockey could ever be, but this involves you too, and I'll do whatever it takes to make sure you stay with the team. I'll ask for the trade, I'll—"

I wrap him in my arms. "We don't even know what it is yet. What site, what article. It could be *anything*. Graham might be overreacting. Let's go and figure it out. Okay?

No offering to be traded before we hear what our options are."

Dex lets out a long exhale. "Okay."

"I'll drive because you're in no state to be on the road."

We leave right away and go back down to the parking garage to get my car. The whole way, Dex is tense, his shoulders hunched, and I hate that the happiest person I know could be this stressed.

Dex doesn't stress about anything, not until this marriage fiasco anyway. He always goes with the flow, he's up for fun, and he doesn't have to think too hard. He's not a problem solver because he's never had any problems.

I hate seeing him go through this. As soon as we get on the road, I feel like I need to reassure him. But how? My brain can only come up with one solution, and I have to say, I'm not a fan of it.

"Maybe ..." Ugh. I can't believe I'm about to say this. "Maybe we should think about getting a divorce earlier than planned."

Dex turns in his seat, his eyes wide. I glance at him, hating that he looks so hurt and lost. I want to take that away.

"You want a *divorce*?"

"This marriage has done nothing but stress you out. The logical thing to do to stop it is to just ... end it."

"You don't want to be married to me anymore," Dex says. He turns away and looks out the window. "I didn't realize you were so unhappy."

"I'm not unhappy. You are. I didn't know one piece of paper could strip away my best friend."

"It's not just a piece of paper though, is it?"

"Isn't it? What's changed between us after getting married other than the physical stuff? Nothing. We're still best friends, we're still each other's number one priority. Nothing in our friendship has actually changed. The only difference apart from sex is how much stress it's put you under. Taking that out of the equation, what do we have left? The same best friends we always were."

Dex goes quiet for the rest of the drive, but we're only a couple of minutes away. When I pull into the parking lot at the rink, he goes to get out, but I grip his arm to stop him.

"Are you okay?"

He glares, catching me off guard. "Sure, why wouldn't I be okay? You have it all figured out."

"No, I don't have it figured out. That's why we're here. I'm trying to give us options."

"And your immediate thought is divorce. Good to know where your head is at, then." Dex pulls free of me and marches toward the building.

I can't catch up to him in time before Graham meets us at the entrance. It must be bad for him to be out here waiting for us.

"We have press and media turning up within the hour. We need to get our story straight to make a statement when they get here."

We follow him into his office, where Coach Roland and our GM, Walter Reid, are waiting.

I swallow hard. This is bigger than big.

The word trade flashes through my head over and over.

"What exactly did the article say?" I ask.

Graham looks at Dex. "When did you and Jessica break up exactly?"

"Like, what date?" Dex squeaks. "How am I supposed to remember?"

"Was it before or after you and Tripp got married?"

Dex looks at me, then back at Graham. His lips part, but no sound comes out.

"Was it the morning after you two tied the knot?"

Dex finds his voice. "Technically, it was the same day, but I texted her before we even planned to get married to check if it was over, and she didn't write back until the next morning."

Graham hangs his head. "That's what I was afraid of. There are claims you were cheating on her the whole time. We need you both to come clean over this whole thing and hope that the fans won't hate you for lying to them."

Cheating? *Dex*? There's no way. A surge of anger hits me that anyone could say that about him.

Coach leans forward. "I've been in talks with the LA team. We're trying to work out a trade." His gaze darts between both Dex and me. "If this goes the way we're predicting it to, we might have to—"

"I'll go," Dex blurts. "Trade me."

"Wait," I say. "We were talking on the way over here, and what would happen if we tell everyone that we're getting divorced? That Dex was feeling down about his breakup, so we got married because he didn't want to be alone—and there was *no* cheating. It was all a spur-of-the-moment, spontaneous thing that we tried to make work, but we've realized we're better off as friends. It's not a complete lie, but it shows that we have been taking our marriage seriously."

"Until now," Dex says so low I'm not sure the others hear him.

Graham, Coach, and the GM look at each other before nodding in agreement.

"We can try that," Graham says. "But we can't promise anything. We don't know how the public will react."

I glance at Dex, who's refusing to look at me.

"Just tell me what to do," Dex says.

Graham opens a laptop on the table. "Okay, let's get this statement ready."

CHAPTER TWENTY-NINE

DEX

How did the day go from everything feeling perfect to everything feeling so, so wrong? Between our agents, Graham, and Coach Roland talking us through our media release and how much to say, I'm numb. Their words wash over me, but Tripp asks all the right questions and keeps sending me these weird media-ready smiles instead of the crooked ones I'm in love with.

I can't stop watching him for a sign of hesitation, but there isn't one.

He wants a divorce. Those words shouldn't kill me like they do, because before we got married, I never wanted a wedding. Now I'm here dreading a divorce.

Meanwhile, my gut churns at the thought of going out there and doing this.

Not only am I standing up and lying *again*, staying on this team comes down to winning over public opinion, and I'm not in a very winning mood.

My heart is breaking.

I thought things were good. I thought what we had was real. But at the first opportunity to call this off and run, Tripp takes it.

"Dex?" Tripp's voice makes me blink back into the conversation. "You okay to do this?"

"Do I have a choice?" I don't mean to sound so bitter, but honestly? I don't think I *can* do this.

It's not the marriage that's been stressing me out; it's the lying. And now we're trying to cover a lie with an even bigger one. All because the team is worried about *image*?

This is my life.

And I never thought I'd say this, but being with him ... it's more important than hockey.

"I need some air." I shove away from the table but only make it as far as the hall outside before I fall back against the wall.

I'd say this sucks, but that's an understatement. I need to drop this mood. I know I do. If this is what Tripp wants, it's not like I can guilt him into keeping me. I've just been blindsided by it being his first thought.

This is what's best for him. A divorce. Then he can move on. Meanwhile, I'll remain pathetically in love with my best friend.

Holy shit ... I'm in love with Tripp.

The door beside me opens, and Graham steps into the hall.

"Are you sure you can do this?"

"Well, I'm due to get through one day without a fuckup, so surely the odds are with me."

Graham tilts his head. "Well, we're open to suggestions. What do you want us to do?"

My eyes prick with tears. "Does it make a difference what I want? Tripp wants a divorce. You think it's best for the team."

"Dex ..."

"Can we just get this over and done with?" Although, what happens then? My place is being leased for at least a few months, and even if it wasn't, the thought of going back there ... fuck. Maybe I can bully Phoebe into letting me stay with her? Tripp thinks we'll be best friends again after this, but it's going to take me time.

I can't go back to sleeping in his spare room.

Graham sticks his head back in the room and calls for the others, and when they join us, we make our way to the press room, where the media are waiting. Tripp's stare is burning into the side of my head, and when he tries to take my hand, I quickly scratch my face and step away.

Just before we enter, Tripp grabs a handful of my T-shirt and pulls me back.

"You look like you're going to pass out," he says. "It's okay. We can do this."

"Yep."

"Do you need me to do all the talking?" he asks.

"You're making all the decisions, so why not?"

His eyebrows come together, and what was that I said about not being bitter about this? Oops.

Tripp has always said I don't bother hiding my emotions, and I guess I'm proving him right, but how am I supposed to act okay when I'm breaking?

"What's that supposed to mean?" he asks.

"Nothing. It's fine. This is all fine."

"You don't seem fine."

"What do you want me to say?" I try to keep my voice low, but it comes out tight with exhaustion. "In the last hour, we've gone from being about to have sex to breaking up, and now we're announcing it to everyone. Sorry if my head is still spinning from whiplash."

"You're thinking about this too hard. We can't break up when we were never actually together."

Never ... *what*?

I gape at him. "W-We weren't?"

"I don't need to remind you the marriage was fake, right?" He's using his teasing tone, but it washes right off me.

"Maybe the marriage was, but we ... we were, I dunno, together ... *weren't we?*" Did I get this whole thing wrong?

"But ..." Tripp shakes his head like he's confused. "You were hooking up with me because we weren't allowed to hook up with anyone else. It wasn't real."

I yank my shirt from his grip. "It was real to me."

And maybe I shouldn't have said that, maybe I shouldn't have proven that I'm every bit as naive as people think I am, but it's the truth, and that's something I can never hide from Tripp.

I head for where the others are waiting.

"Wait, Dex—"

I ignore him.

"Dex—"

"We're ready," I tell Graham when I reach him.

"Actually, we need a minute," Tripp says, trying to steer me away again.

I pull my arm from his grip. "Nope, we're good to go."

Tripp lets out a noise of frustration, but it's too late. The door opens, we follow Graham into the room, and Coach Roland leads us up onto the media platform.

I take the first seat, but as Tripp passes, he leans down to whisper in my ear.

"If you think this is easy for me, you're wrong. I've wanted you since we first met."

Then he straightens and takes the chair on the other side of Coach, while I'm left there, shocked into silence.

Because he fucking *what*?

No matter how desperately I want everything to stop for a minute so I can process the influx of information that's being thrown at me from all sides, the press conference starts anyway.

I'm vaguely aware of Coach kicking things off by talking through the article, saying how he runs a tight team and wants to keep the drama low. He says Tripp and I deserve the opportunity to tell people what really happened.

The paper in front of me is all about how heartbroken I was over Jessica, but I don't think I've ever been heartbroken until this moment. I'm supposed to say I turned to him for comfort, the wedding was to help my pain, and then we tried to make it work, which I'd at least thought was half-true, but apparently that was only from my side.

And when Coach's hand lands on my shoulder and I realize it's my time to talk ... I can't. The words are all there in front of me, but all I can do is stare. The brain fuzz is kicking in.

There's a second of silence, when Tripp quickly jumps in. "The thing is, our marriage was fast. It was a spur-of-the-moment decision that needed more thought. Dex had broken up with his girlfriend, and he'd made a joke about the only relationship that has worked for him was our friendship and that he should just marry me." Tripp glances my way. "We've been best friends for three years, and after this, we'll continue to be inseparable. We've tried really hard to make this work, but—"

I know what's coming, and suddenly I can't hear it. "But this is all bullshit." My mouth is moving before I even realize what I've said.

A ripple goes through the waiting press, and Coach hurries to cover my microphone. "What are you doing?"

"Please let me do this." The brain fuzz is gone, and I'm thinking clearer than I ever have in my life.

Coach removes his hand.

I take a deep breath. "Tripp's right. It started out as a joke. We didn't even think the marriage would be legal. That might seem like we were making a joke out of marriage, but it wasn't out of disrespect. It came from a place of hurt, and friendship, and it felt right."

"Dex, I think we should—" Coach starts.

I cut him off. "I never cheated. I've always been scared of commitment and weddings, which is why Jessica and I broke up. It had nothing to do with Tripp. But because he's the greatest best friend in the history of ever, he agreed to my stupid idea of having a practice marriage so I'd know commitment wasn't so bad. Truthfully ... the only reason I could go through with it was because it's him." I tuck my trembling hands under the table. "I've spent the last few months married to my best friend, and it might have happened fast, but I've never experienced something so real. My stress this season wasn't about being married; it was about starting the rest of my life on a lie." I finally force myself to look at Tripp. His face is closed off, but I make myself get the words out. "I'm dumb a lot of the time, but the best dumb decision I ever made was marrying you. Because now I know why I could spend forever with you, and only you. I know we're supposed to stand up here and announce some bogus divorce, but I don't want that. I want us." My voice breaks. "Always. Forever. Because I am so fucking in love with you, I don't know myself without you."

"Swearing, Dex," Coach mutters.

Tripp stares at me with the cutest stunned look on his face.

Cameras go off.

Questions get yelled across the room.

Then my husband clears his throat and suddenly breaks eye contact and leans toward his mic to say, "This press conference is over."

I watch as he shoves out of his seat, then crosses to me and pulls me up with him. His hand closes over mine, and he doesn't stop walking until we're out into the hall, where he pushes me into the wall and kisses me.

I grunt into his mouth as my eyes fall closed and I ball my fists in his shirt. I cling to him so tight, I swear I'll never let him go again, and while he hasn't said the words, he doesn't need to. This kiss is everything. I can't believe how close I was to losing this.

"I want to keep you," I say between kisses.

"Did you mean it?" Tripp asks. "Or was it another lie to try to keep us both here?"

"That I'm in love with you? One hundred percent."

Tripp's eyes flutter closed. "You have no idea how long I've craved to hear you say that."

"I tell you I love you all the time."

"Yeah, that you love me like a brother."

"After all the orgasms we've given each other, I hope it's not brotherly."

Tripp shoves me. "I mean it. I never ..." He shakes his head and looks down at the ground. "I've been in love with you since the day I moved to Vegas."

"You have?"

"Why do you think the Collective guys always run interference when we're together? Why do you think Oskar lied and said he was my boyfriend? They've been trying to protect my feelings for years because I've been hopelessly and pathetically in love with you from the beginning."

I can't believe what I'm hearing. "You never said anything."

"I knew it would change things between us, and I would have rather had your friendship and suffered a little pining than not have you at all."

"I wish …" I wish I knew what to say to that. "I wish I'd known sooner. Maybe I would have woken up and realized how I really felt. Because I don't think this is a new thing."

Tripp hangs his head. "I didn't think it was a possibility. I've played that scenario over in my head a million times, and in each one, it ruined our friendship." He lets out a laugh. "The funniest part is probably that Anton knew before either of us."

"He what?"

"When we were away, he said that given the right circumstances, you could realize you're in love with me too. I didn't believe him, but—"

"He was right. He was so right. When you suggested getting a divorce, you ripped my heart out."

"I didn't mean to do that, but to me, outside of the legal crap, marriage is only a word. We could still get divorced, and I wouldn't care, so long as I have you in my life."

"Well, what I just did might have gotten one of us traded."

"If we—the two biggest commitment-phobes in the league—can make a *marriage* work, we can get through anything."

A throat clears beside us, and we both turn to see Graham standing there. Tripp's hold on me tightens.

"I'm sorry," I say. "I couldn't keep lying."

"Would have been nice to know that before you went out there."

"I don't know if you know this about me, but I don't exactly think things through." And even with the trade burning a hole in my gut, the lie is out. I have Tripp. And I've never felt so much relief.

Tripp tugs me closer. "What now?"

"Now, we wait and see what the blowback from this is."

CHAPTER THIRTY

TRIPP

With Dex's mouth on mine, his naked body under me while I straddle his lap, the press conference is all but forgotten. I rotate my hips, taking his cock deeper.

As soon as we got home, we knew we had to take advantage of the situation before everything blows up. None of that taking our time bullshit from earlier today.

Dex said he loves me—that he's in love with me.

I never thought this would happen. I never let myself think about it, because the possibility of my straight best friend falling for me was so minuscule, I didn't want to hurt myself by entertaining the idea. I'd fantasized about hooking up with him, sure. But even in my fantasies, he never actually fell in love with me.

I moan into his mouth before breaking away and trailing my lips down his neck. Dex's big arms surround me and hold me tight while I move up and down on his dick.

He buries his head in the crook of my shoulder and nips at my skin. "I could stay like this forever."

My breath is shaky as I say, "As much as I'd love that, you know our phones are going to start going off any minute."

As if on cue, one of them starts vibrating from the floor, where we dumped our clothes in a mad rush to get undressed.

"Don't answer it," Dex murmurs.

"Didn't plan to, but we'll need to stop at some point and deal with it."

"Not until we both come."

"Deal." I lean back slowly and plant one hand behind me on the mattress while my other hand wraps around the back of Dex's neck for leverage.

My cock stands tall between us, and Dex reaches for it, stroking me fast and hard. I throw my head back and ride him, the slow and intimate moves from before gone with the need to hurry up.

Dex trembles as he tries to hold out, but that encourages me to pick up the pace even more. I want him to fall apart and come inside me.

Own me.

"Tripp." Dex unleashes. He fills me up but never stops jerking me off even as his orgasm tears through him.

"Tell me again," I beg.

"Tell you what?" he breathes.

"That you're in love with me. I need to hear it. I need to make sure it's real."

With his free hand, Dex cups my cheek. "I've never loved anyone the way I love you. I thought our close bond was the best kind of friendship. I didn't ... I never knew it could be like this. I want to be with you forever. I want you to be my husband. In sickness and in health. Hockey or no hockey."

My muscles tighten, my balls draw up tight, and then I'm coming. I can barely hold myself up anymore as I shudder on top of my *husband*.

Dex wraps his arms around me and pulls me close while I come down from my orgasm and catch my breath. I'm Jell-O in his arms.

"I mean it," he says into my sweaty hair. "I love you. I'm *in* love with you. I want us forever."

I pull back and look into Dex's big warm brown eyes. "I've always been in love with you."

He touches his forehead to mine, and it grounds me in a way that the words don't. Dex is here. He's really saying these things. And this is real.

My accidental marriage turned out to be the catalyst that made every wish come true. This was my fantasy. My dream.

More buzzing comes from the floor.

And that's another reason I know this is actually happening. Because in my fantasies, we don't get interrupted by phone calls.

Dex kisses the tip of my nose and then eases me off his lap. "You recover. I'll deal with the phone calls."

Best. Husband. Ever.

I could fall asleep happy right now.

"Huh," Dex says.

That can't be good. "What is it?"

"I have two missed calls from Jessica."

"Way to kick off the drama. Are you going to call her back?"

"She left a voicemail the second time." He plays the message on speaker.

"Hey, Dex. Can you call me back? I think I know who leaked your story to the press."

I sit up. "She, what? You don't think it was her, do you?"

Dex stares at his phone hard. "Why would she call and say she thinks she knows? That would be weird."

"Call her," I say.

"You're okay with that?"

"You're allowed to talk to whoever you want. Let's not have that type of marriage where we police each other. That's not what a relationship should be."

Dex smiles and then leans over to kiss me. His tongue presses inside my mouth, but he pulls back way too soon. I try to follow him to keep kissing him, but he stands upright and hits Call on his phone.

"Dex," Jessica answers. Her voice seems chipper but with underlying ... sympathy?

"Hey, you're on speaker," Dex says. "Tripp's here too."

"I figured," she says softly. "I saw your press conference."

Dex shifts. "I'm assuming a lot of people have seen it by now."

"I feel really terrible about how everything went down between us."

Dex's brown eyes meet mine, expressing the same shocked question I'm thinking. Did she really just say that?

"When I found out you had married Tripp, my only thought was about how to save face," she continues. "It's why I turned to your teammate and posted that stupid Insta story. I knew how much you and he didn't get along, and ... I was in selfish mode. I was too blinded by that to realize you married him because you were upset over our breakup. I thought ... I thought maybe you guys went behind my back. And ... that's what I told Patrick. It's why we pretended to be together. But I can see that you and Tripp are the real deal. The way you looked at him during the press conference ... you never once looked at me like that."

"I don't understand why you're telling me this now," Dex says.

As usual, he missed what's being said because it's not being spelled out.

"She thinks Fensby is the one who told the press we cheated," I clarify for him.

"Right," she agrees.

"But what I don't get is why he'd do it now," I say.

"That's the other thing." Jessica lets out a loud breath. "He wanted more, and I didn't because you're so right about him. He's a jackass. So I ended it with him. Yesterday."

Dex's gaze snaps to mine.

It was fucking Fensby.

CHAPTER THIRTY-ONE

DEX

"I still think we should have gone straight to Fensby's house," I tell Tripp over the sound of the ringtone on speaker. I'd like nothing more than to knock out a few more of his teeth.

"Me too, but instead, we're taking Damon's advice. He hasn't steered me wrong yet."

Even I can't argue with that. The first person Tripp called when I hung up with Jessica was his agent, and while I might want to be reckless, Damon has been in our corner for this whole thing. He might not have been impressed with me going rogue at the press conference, but he's the only one who hasn't made me feel bad for it. I've got a string of angry texts from my agent, but I'm ignoring his calls.

"Tripp," Graham says when he answers.

"You're on speaker."

"Of course I am." He sighs. "This call had better not be that you've decided to break up after all. Or that you've cheated. Or accidentally adopted a kid."

"Definitely the last one," I say.

"You better be joking."

Tripp shoves me. "Jesus, Dex, you're going to give him a heart attack."

"Well, I am due a long vacation after this," Graham answers.

"This time, it's nothing bad," Tripp assures him. "At least not from us."

"That's a relief." There's the sound of traffic in the background, and I'd guess he's on his way home.

"It was Fensby," I say, not wanting to hold his day up any longer. "Jessica called me, and everything that the article said is what she told Fensby."

Instead of the immediate relief on the other end, there's silence. "Okay."

"That's it?"

There's a long pause. "The thing is, even if what you're saying is true, there's no way to prove it."

"But—"

"How do we know it wasn't her who told the press, and now she's trying to divert the attention away from her?"

I'm about to bite back that it's obvious, because Fensby is a douchey doucheface, but Tripp grabs my arm and squeezes.

"We get it," he says. "But isn't it worth looking into?"

The traffic dies down as it sounds like Graham stops driving. "We can. We can look into it and try to confirm sources, but it's likely he didn't give his real name. At this point, all management wants right now is silence. No more scandals, no more drama, no more media attention on anything but hockey. Their focus is on getting back their Stanley Cup finalist team."

"So they're still talking about a trade?" I ask. Logically, it makes sense. That doesn't mean I have to like it.

"They're ready to do whatever they have to. This is business. My recommendation? Focus on hockey. Get out there, play your game, and stop worrying about the noise. Whatever happens is going to happen whether you stress about it or not."

"There's nothing we can do?" I ask.

"Sure," he says. "Hope that there's a bigger scandal from another team. Until then, lie low."

And that's that.

We thank Graham and ... try to move on.

It takes a few games to hit my stride, but once I do, it's like I can breathe again. Things in the locker room are still tense with Fensby being openly hostile, but on the ice, I've got my shit together. And the better I play, the worse he gets, until a week into our home games when Coach tells me I'm back on first line.

It takes all of my energy not to turn to Fensby and gloat.

But I will be the bigger person.

Because I have Tripp, and I have hockey.

After a grueling game against Atlanta that we win by a point, Tripp and I stop to sign jerseys for some fans. I hand out two pucks, and we both pose for photos together.

I've largely been avoiding social media and the backlash from our press conference, but Graham tells us it's been mixed. The majority of the fans are supportive of us, but that doesn't mean I'm not affected by the few who aren't, even if I'm not seeing what's actually being said online.

I'll never understand why people care where I put my dick, but I know what I signed up for.

They can pry my husband away from my cold, dead, pansexual ass, because I'm not giving him up for all the haters in the world.

I smile to myself, like I always do, when the words *my husband* flit through my brain and catch me off guard.

For the first time since this whole thing happened, they finally feel real.

I lean over and kiss his cheek, well aware of all the phones pointed in our direction.

Tripp laughs as he pulls me down the chute. "You're such an attention whore."

"It's not my fault you're irresistible. In fact, it's *your* fault I can never stop touching you, and you should take pity on me."

"Why? I'm the one being smothered with attention."

"Oh, no," I mock. "My husband loves me."

"I swear, any excuse for you to use the *H* word."

"I know how much you like hearing it."

"I prefer the *L* word myself."

"Loser?"

"Fuck you."

"Naw." I ruffle his sweaty red hair. "Look at you being all affectionate."

Tripp bats my hand away. "You're bad for my image."

"Sure, because it's my fault you're known as the sweetheart of the league."

"I don't even know where that reputation came from."

"It's your big, pretty eyes."

Tripp scowls. "My eyes aren't pretty."

"They're very pretty. The rest of you ..." My gaze tracks over his sweat-soaked jersey. He might be wearing too much padding to make out his body, but I've seen it enough now that my mind can fill in the blanks.

"Keep looking at me like that and we're not going to make it to celebration drinks," Tripp sings.

"You really think that's going to stop me?"

"If you don't want me mauling you in public, it is."

And as hot as that sounds, I'm happy to leave the public sex up to Oskar. "Fine," I relent. "I will stop eye-fucking you."

"Good."

"As long as you fuck me later."

Tripp answers by squirting his water bottle at me. I snatch it from him and spray him back, and by the time we stumble into the locker room, we're both wrestling and roughhousing. Exactly like we've always been, but better.

Most of the team have already started their cooldown, but there are a few still hanging around.

I let Tripp go and cop another shot of water to my face. "Cheater."

"You were open."

I grin as I swipe at my cheeks. "I don't think this is what people mean when they talk about water sports."

Tripp cringes dramatically, but a loud scoff comes from behind him.

"Do you two ever stop? The rest of us don't want to hear that." Fensby has already stripped out of his pads, and he's glowering at us from in front of his cubby.

"How dare we have fun. Stop, Tripp, it's disgusting!"

Tripp pretends to sniff. "Smells like homophobic dick-weeds in here."

I snap my fingers. "*That's* what that smell is. I thought it was sweaty ball sacs."

"Easy mistake to make."

"Fuck you both." Fensby sneers. "Won't be so cocky when one of you is traded." And he must see the worry cross my face because he stands. "Rumor has it Coach has been shopping around for a new goalie. You really think you could screw with team dynamics and get away with it?"

"Did you?" I lean forward. "You think we don't know what you did?"

He eyes me, clearly confused, but I'm done with not saying anything, and if the trade rumors are true, I have nothing to lose.

"Jessica told us everything. Including how she was using you." I pretend to cringe. "How embarrassing for you to go for my ex-girlfriend and my position on this team and then fail at both."

"Dumbass Dex at it again. No one will believe that shit."

"They don't need to." I wink at him, not letting his taunt get to me. "We know what's up, big guy."

"You say that like it matters. As far as anyone is concerned, you two are trouble. Good luck with your"—he uses air quotes—"marriage."

I slap Tripp's ass. "Come on, hubby. Let's cool down and shower. We've got drinks with our names on them."

And before he can respond, someone clears their throat behind us.

I jerk around to see Coach standing there. He doesn't say anything, just cocks an eyebrow, gives us all a pointed stare, and then turns on his heel and heads for his office.

Fuck.

We were told no more drama, and here we are bringing it to the locker room.

Tripp and I share the same concerned glance.

We might have just sealed our fate.

One of us is getting traded.

CHAPTER THIRTY-TWO

TRIPP

Dex has been freaking out since Coach witnessed us in the locker room having it out with Fensby. He's convinced one of us is about to get a call that could tear us apart, and so he keeps staring at his phone as if willing it to ring—like if he looks away from it, they might call me instead.

He's also had the sports channel on the TV nonstop in case news breaks there first. Most teams are good at telling the players they're traded before announcing it but not always.

Fensby said the rumor was about me, but I don't believe a word that comes out of that douche's mouth.

The only reprieve we've had was when my parents flew in for a few days and took us out for a "really married" celebration dinner.

I take the spot next to Dex on the couch and squeeze his leg in reassurance. We had a light day today, weight training this morning but no practice skate until tomorrow, so he's had all the time in the world to obsess over this trade.

"Hey, whichever one of us it is, LA could be a fun place to live. They have the beach, Hollywood ... Ooh, actually, I hope it's me. I could use my free celebrity pass if I were to ever run into Zachary Quinto."

Dex frowns. "Zachary Quinto? I thought you were obsessed with Ryan Reynolds."

"Yeah, but Zachary Quinto is gay. I have to go with the odds."

"That's cheating."

"No, it's not. He's my free pass."

"I mean picking someone you only kind of like as your pass just because he happens to be queer and therefore you have a bigger chance of getting some. And also, stop talking like it's going to be you. I told them to trade me." He lowers his voice and murmurs, "It has to be me."

I grip his hand and hold tight. "Like I said, whoever it is, LA won't be too bad. It's a forty-minute flight. Four hours in the car. Ooh, maybe Anaheim could want one of us too. We could both move to the beach and have sex with Zachary Quinto."

Dex screws up his face. "You can have sex with him. I'll have sex with Jennifer Lawrence."

I shake my head. "Dude, go with the odds. Pick someone single."

"It's Hollywood. She'll be single again eventually."

"My husband." I touch my heart. "Believer in forever and true love."

Dex gets me in a headlock. "I believe it when it's you and me."

I push him off me. "Which is why, no matter what happens, you and I will get through anything. We can make LA work. And if it doesn't, how long have you got left on your contract? I've only got one more signed year, though Damon started negotiations after we made it to the Stanley Cup final last season. Maybe I retire or—"

"If it comes down to that, I won't re-sign. My contract's up for renewal this season."

I lean back against the couch. "Wow. Retirement. That's scary. What would you do instead?"

"Well, if we're in LA, I'm obviously going to stalk Jennifer Lawrence."

"Obviously."

"I'll go to the beach every day while you're skating and paying my way. Being my sugar daddy."

"Shit. Can we take it back? I'll retire first."

"Nope. Too late." Dex grins, but it quickly falls. "You know what would be better than all of that?"

"Not being traded at all," I say.

"Exactly. I love it here. There might not be a beach, but there's, you know ... gambling and debauchery."

"Always fun things to have."

"I like the home crowd here."

"Me too." They've mostly supported us through this whole thing.

"I don't like change."

"I know."

And as if hearing our conversation, the people on the TV announce a trade for Vegas. My attention snaps to the screen so fast my neck protests.

"Oh, fuck." I thought that maybe, possibly, it wasn't going to happen—that the threats would eventuate to nothing. I guess I was wrong.

"They haven't called," Dex says, lifting his phone to his face again.

"*Vegas will be losing a center forward to Winnipeg.*"

Center forward. *Dex*.

Winnipeg. What?

LA to Vegas long-distance is doable. Vegas to Nowhere Canada?

Zen and peace. Zen and fucking peace.

Then a photo of the last person I was expecting pops up on the screen next to the news anchor, and I've never known such relief.

"It's not you," I say.

"What?" Dex lifts his head.

"They didn't trade you. They traded Fensby." I would celebrate and cheer, but I'm still trying to process it.

Dex doesn't have that problem. He jumps out of his seat. "Yes! Holy shit, this is amazing."

"I don't think it means we're in the clear," I point out. "Though our fans have been loyal and more supportive than ever, so maybe we are?"

Apparently, the public thinks the way we got married as best friends and then found more is adorable.

Dex dances around the coffee table while I laugh.

He pumps his fists in the air, singing, "We don't have to move to LA. I don't have to hunt down Zachary Quinto and commit first-degree murder."

"Hey! Now *that* would be cheating. You can't kill my free pass to prevent me from sleeping with him."

"What can I say? I don't want anyone to touch my husband but me."

Is it possible to melt into a pile of goo? Because I think that's what I'm doing. "No one touches me, huh?"

He approaches and pulls me up off the couch. "No one."

"Mm," I hum. "I like possessive Dex."

"You like belonging to me?"

"I mean, in a non-codependent, healthy kind of way, yes. I like the way you worship my body like I'm a prized possession and not a toy to play with. I like that you respect me and love me, and you've always been yourself around me. I love who we are together. I love our bond. Most of all, I love you."

"I love you too."

"With Fensby gone, just watch our season take off. This is our year. I can feel it."

—

Yeah, this is our year to choke so hard there's no chance of us making the playoffs.

We're playing Buffalo, a team notorious for finishing near the bottom of the damn leaderboard every year, and yet, here they are, up by three in the third period, and there's no way we can turn this game around.

Our morale is down, we're losing way more games than we should, but I can't put my finger on why. I thought maybe the team was off because of Dex and me, but everything on that front is good now certain dickweeds aren't on the team.

It's not that we're a total disaster on the ice or not playing well. We're all just a little ... off. We can't seem to get it together.

I see everything from where I am. Every mistake. Every missed opportunity. We're not losing because we keep fucking up. We don't fuck up that much.

I'm beginning to think with where we're sitting on the leaderboard, it has to be the mind games. We're losing our faith in the team and our ability to do well, and the further into the season we get, the more that heavy cloud sits above us.

We scramble in the last minutes, the play staying firmly in our offensive zone, but we only manage to narrow the margin by one. When the clock runs out, we march into the locker room with our heads held low.

"What happened to the team from last year?" Coach yells at us.

I'd like to know the same thing.

This could possibly be the first year we don't make the playoffs since the expansion team was created. And that sucks.

I glance over at Dex as he shucks off his skates. He has a huge smile on his face, but I have no idea why. I nudge him. "You seem happy considering we got our asses kicked."

Dex shrugs. "What can I say? I *am* happy."

"You're ... happy that we lost?"

"Nope. I'm happy that I get to go out on that ice every day with the love of my life and get to play the game I was born to play. Yeah, we're losing, and chances are we're not going all the way this year, but look around this locker room." He gestures to where our teammates are in various states of undress. "We have the best job in the world."

"Mm, the constant stench of man sweat."

"Come on, if you think about it, would you rather be doing anything else with your life?"

The quick answer to that is no, I wouldn't. The longer answer is I'd give all of this up if it meant being able to be with Dex. For right now, we get to have it all, but a hockey player's career can be short. This amazing time that Dex is talking about is fleeting. I can't help it; I smile too. One day, it will all be over for both of us, and while I'm as grateful for this possibility as he is, I know that life extends beyond hockey.

I will accept retirement when my time comes, but one thing I won't be able to live without is him.

Hockey is my present.

Dex is my future.

CHAPTER THIRTY-THREE

DEX

"I still don't understand why I'm paying for this shit," I say to Phoebe, looking around at the balls-to-the-wall birthday party going on around us.

"Thirty is the new twenty-one," she declares. "You'll understand when you get there in two years."

The club is loud, pulsing, the perfect place to get blackout drunk and dance until you drop, and when it gets late enough, Tripp and I will leave the VIP section and do exactly that since we don't have a game for another two days.

"That still doesn't explain why *I'm* the one paying though."

Phoebe turns with her most patronizing big-sister expression and pats my chest. "Because after these last few months, you owe me."

"Fair point." I tip back my drink. "You seen my husband?"

"Yeah, he was flirting with some guy from Sienna's work."

Even though I know she's joking, my pulse spikes. "Fuck you. He would never."

"You two are so disgustingly in love. But … thank you for that."

"What do you mean?"

"Well, after Mom and Dad ... you know ..."

I screw up my face, not wanting our parents' marriage even in the same sentence as mine. "What about it?"

"You've made me realize true love does exist, and I've decided if you can have that, so can I."

My sister, the woman allergic to relationships. I'm gaping at her when Tripp appears.

"What's up with you?" he asks.

I point at Phoebe. "Apparently we're an inspiration." I don't even know what to think about that.

Phoebe waves someone over. "Yep, and we actually have something to tell you guys."

"Who ..."

Sienna joins her side, and I watch as they link hands. What—and I cannot stress this enough—the fuck?

Phoebe and *Sienna*?

"Nope. No." Tripp shakes his head. "Decline."

Our sisters are both smiling manically. "We got married!"

My eyes shoot wide. There is no way this is happening. They're ... they're like sisters. Neither of them has ever, *ever*—

Tripp cracks up laughing. "I think you broke Dex."

"What's wrong, little brother?" Phoebe asks, and I finally note her teasing tone. "Aren't you happy for us?"

"Bullshit."

Sienna relents. "Okay, we're totally kidding. We did sleep together though."

"And we're buying a house together."

"And having each other's babies."

"And I'm giving Sienna my left kidney."

I roll my eyes. "You guys are so funny."

"And *so* in love." Phoebe leans closer to Sienna. "You're right, this was fun."

"If you're done teasing us now …" I take Tripp's hand and pull him away from Tweedle-Dee and Tweedle-Dick.

"Where are we going?"

"Dancing."

"Ooh, dangerous. Remember what happened last time?"

I tilt a grin back at him as I pull him along. "Bold of you to assume that isn't my plan."

"You're turning into Oskar. Am I going to have to get you help for this public sex obsession?"

When we get far enough onto the dance floor, I pull him against me. His hard body molds to mine, like we were made for each other.

And every day we spend together makes it harder to believe we weren't.

"No public sex obsession," I say by his ear. "Just a standard, run-of-the-mill Tripp obsession."

Tripp pulls back and rests his forehead against mine. His crooked smile is in place, doing weird things deep in my gut, and even though our hockey playing has seen better days and is a constant source of annoyance, I've never seen him so happy. It's all there, in his big eyes, in the way he looks at me, so much happiness radiating from him that he could light up a whole damn hockey stadium.

My throat clogs with emotion as I realize I almost missed this.

That we might have made it our whole lives totally in love but not together. I shudder even imagining that future.

Thank fuck for being a dumbass.

Thank fuck for my harebrained idea and Tripp reluctantly going along with my plans.

I frown at that thought. It *was* reluctant. And even though neither of us regrets what happened, I maybe regret one thing.

I duck my lips to his ear and utter the two words I should have said to begin with. "Marry me?"

Tripp jerks back, obviously trying not to laugh. "Ah ... are you having an episode? Quick, what day is it?"

I pinch his side. "I'm serious, you dick."

"What do you mean? We're already married. You have been following the last few months, haven't you?"

"Okay, even *I'm* not that dumb."

"You sure? Because you're not being convincing right now."

I shake my head. "No, it's just ... you never got that. You never had the actual proper proposal. You had me rambling at you about being freaked-out and needing you all so I could marry someone else and I—" I shake my head again. I can't seem to stop.

Fuck it.

I sink to one knee.

And almost cop a hip to the head for my efforts.

Okay, so maybe the middle of the dance floor wasn't the smartest place for this, but I'm all in now. And then I glance up and find Tripp looking at me with an expression that steals my breath. I slide the titanium band off his finger that we bought when we decided we were staying together and hold it up.

"You deserve to bring a man to his knees," I shout over the music. "And you do with me. Every day. You're amazing, and I can't believe I'm the one you chose, even when you thought that meant choosing nothing."

Tripp steps closer and cups my face.

"But I'm going to give you everything now. Because that's what you do for me." I reach up and grab his shirt, tugging him down so I don't have to shout anymore. "Will you marry me?"

His face explodes with a smile. "You dopey, romantic man. Of course I will." He hauls me to my feet to avoid us getting trampled and takes my mouth in a kiss that leaves me weak. I cling to him, not wanting him to get too far, and when he pulls back and holds out his hand, it takes me a second to remember I'm still holding his ring.

I slip it on and pull out my phone.

"One other thing we never got to do."

"Take a selfie? Because we've got a thousand."

"The obligatory announcement photo."

"Geez, you're weird."

I pull him against me. "Says more about you than it says about me."

Then he holds up his hand as I press a kiss to his cheek. My flash goes off, and even with the photo done, we still don't break apart.

Together is where we're meant to be.

I open my private social media page and upload the photo along with a three-word caption.

He said yes.

EPILOGUE

ALL-STARS WEEK

TRIPP

I raise my hand to knock on Ezra's apartment door, and he answers with a, "Hey, losers."

"Why are we friends with you again?" I ask.

"Because since being with Anton, I have simmered into a mature human being, and you love me."

Dex cocks his head. "That doesn't sound right."

"So why are we losers?"

"Because you didn't get picked for All-Stars. Duh."

"Neither did you," I point out.

"No, but Anton did, so therefore, I'm not a loser by association. Also, Boston's not sitting below Buffalo on the leaderboard for points this season."

"Hey, Buffalo are having a surprisingly good season," I argue. I don't add on the *for them* part. "They might actually make a playoffs one of these days."

"Mm, maybe. Rumor has it Little Dalton will be joining them next season."

"Westly's brother?" I ask. West was part of the Collective before he retired.

"Yep. Someone else is going to have to invite him to join the queer collective though. For some weird reason, he doesn't like me?"

"Someone not liking you? Shocking! Let us in." I push past him. "So just how much has Anton been rubbing All-Stars in your face?"

"He's been unbearable since he found out."

That sounds about right.

Inside the apartment, some of the other Collective are already there. Ollie Strömberg, Oskar, who's talking to someone vaguely familiar but I can't place. And retired Caleb Sorensen.

"Well, if it isn't the happy couple," Ollie says.

"Here we are. In the flesh." It's the first time we've all been in the one place for a while, though we are missing a few. Foster is playing with Anton at All-Stars, and West is at home in Vermont with his family. Still, I wait for the inevitable questions to come.

Instead, Ollie turns to Ezra. "Got any Macallan? I think it's time we officially welcome Dex into the fold. That is, if the marriage is actually legit?" He gives us a pointed look. "It's hard to tell with the conflicting stories in the media."

Some people have bought the truth—that it started as a joke, but now we're in love. Others are skeptical.

"It's legit," Dex says and throws himself on the couch next to Ollie. "All I'm saying is why couldn't any of you have pointed out to me that I was in love with Tripp all this time?"

Ezra curses. "No. Do not tell Anton he was right. He loves being right."

Oskar nods. "We didn't know. We thought you were his big affectionate puppy."

"Oh, he's that too," I say and squeeze in on the end of the couch next to my husband. "But what can I say? My winning personality is clearly what won him over.

Because unlike some people in this room"—I cover the word *everyone* with a cough—"I am humble and nice."

Dex wraps his arm around me. "Oh, pumpkin. I know you think you're joking, but that's actually true."

"True in comparison to all of you, maybe."

"Hey, Lane might beat you out," Oskar says, gesturing to the guy next to him, who has a scowl on his face. "Mr. Goody Two-shoes over here is always nice. Except when it comes to me. Then he can be as naughty as he wants."

"Lane ..." I say. "As in your team's PR dude who you like to torment?"

Lane huffs. "Oh, great. So you've told them about me."

I have to say, I get what Oskar means. With his dark hair and silver-flecked beard, Lane is the kind of guy you *want* to punish you.

"We're dating." Oskar places his arm around Lane's shoulder.

Lane takes Oskar's hand and places it back in Oskar's lap. "You can dream, but we both know I'm making sure you don't get yourself into trouble because apparently, babysitting you is a full-time job, and you've already run off my interns with your shit."

"See? He's falling in love with me," Oskar gloats.

Dex looks at Lane. "Hate to say it, man, but sleeping with him might be easier than following him around everywhere."

I agree. "He'll give up after he's had you. He has the attention span of a walnut."

Lane glowers. "Sex with me isn't the problem."

"See, we're totally dating."

Lane shoves Oskar. "That's not what I meant, and you know it." Lane turns to us. "We haven't had sex. We will *never* have sex. I value my job. The problem is when he goes out and has *public sex* with guys in alleyways where there are security cameras."

"Guys?" I ask. "Plural? How many?"

Everyone turns to me with disapproving stares.

"Oh. Right. Damn it, Oskar ... that's so naughty." I lean over Dex and whisper to Oskar, "Tell me all the details later."

"No details," Lane says. "That's how stuff gets out."

Oskar grins. "Hmm, no, I'd say having sex in front of security cameras is how things get out."

Lane throws his head back. "I quit. When we get back to San Jose, I'm quitting."

"So you can be with me? Aww, honey, I didn't realize we were picking each other over our careers so soon in our relationship."

Ezra takes a glass of dark liquid over to Lane. "It sounds like you might need this."

"Thank you." Lane throws it back.

"Only way to deal with me," Oskar points out.

Lane sets his glass down and says so low I almost miss it, "We both know I can deal with you."

"It's starting," Ollie says.

Ezra turns up the TV to where the skills portion starts. When Anton's introduced, Ezra yells at the TV, "Kick ass, baby!"

"Why didn't you go with him for support and cheer him on from the stands?" I ask.

"I love him, but I love having All-Stars week off more."

"Ooh," Soren says from across the room where he's sitting with Ollie. "It's all downhill from here. When you'd rather rest instead of being invited to All-Stars, there's only a few years left before the dreaded retirement word starts floating around."

Ezra's face falls. "Why would you say such a mean thing?"

Soren laughs.

"There's nothing wrong with retirement," Ollie says. "I'm going to welcome it come July."

I snort. "You think New York is making it to the Stanley Cup game this season? *Really*?"

"Hey, we have more of a chance than Vegas."

Everyone snickers, so Dex and I flip them all off.

Foster and Anton compete in the shootout competition, and seeing two queer guys out there is amazing.

"Idea!" Ezra yells out of nowhere.

We all groan. This could be anything from *let's start a drinking game for every goal scored* to *let's have an orgy*.

"No, hear me out. We have the goal of getting a queer dude on every team. What if we buy our own expansion team and have an all-queer team?"

"You got that kind of money?" Dex asks.

"No, but we could all pool and own our own team."

"No," we all say at the same time.

"You guys are no fun. I'm just saying, look at those two out there. All of us together, we'd be unstoppable."

"Except with Ollie and Soren retired, we have like six players. Great team," I say dryly.

"More would come out," Ezra says. "I happen to know someone itching to come out."

"Oh, seven," I deadpan. "That changes everything."

"Fine. No queer team."

"It's not a bad idea," Lane says. "Maybe not going as far as having an expansion team, but all of you getting together in the off-season and doing events for queer kids. Exhibition games or a one-week training camp ... that kind of thing."

"Exhibition," Oskar mutters, pumping his eyebrows at Lane.

Lane ignores him.

"Anton would be all over that," Ezra says.

"So would I," Dex adds.

"Really?" I cock my head at him.

"Could you imagine the look on the kids' faces from the Rainbow Raiders if we all walked in and told them we're playing hockey with them?"

I grip Dex's hand. "We're up for that."

"I think it's a great idea," Soren says. "I know you all think Ollie and I are the reason you have careers because we were the first to come out, but the next generation are going to look up to you guys. You're the future of queer players in the NHL, and you need to do everything you can to make sure your voices are heard and that other queer people out there feel represented."

There are murmurs of agreement, but then Anton wins the shootout, and Ezra's out of his seat cheering.

Dex leans in closer to me and says, "What you've got here is really special, isn't it? I don't think I've understood it until now. You're not just a bunch of guys who have something in common to bond over. It's a brotherhood."

"They're my hockey family. No, they're *our* hockey family. You're one of us now too."

His smile is blinding. "Yeah, I am."

Read on for a preview of

Shameless Puckboy ...

Lane

I stare at my screen, watching the CCTV footage that's gone viral. The back door of a club opens and spits Oskar Voyjik and two others into the alley. They're a tangle of groping limbs, hot mouths, and clear intent.

The PR manager in me is fucking pissed this has happened *again*, but the red-blooded gay man in me is struggling to pull my eyes away. If this was a random clip online instead of our star player, it'd be perfect jerk-off material.

Which probably explains why it's the center of most news stories this morning.

"I'm sorry," Keerson says, burying his face in his hands. "He's out of control."

Well, I can't disagree there, but this isn't a simple *oopsie* that we can talk our way out of. Oskar's becoming a real problem for San Jose, which means he's a real problem for me.

"You had one job," I remind Keerson. "And I'm sure I was clear in my expectations."

"What was I supposed to do? Chain him to me? I've been available at his beck and call, and the things he's been calling me with ..." Keerson stops to take a level breath. "I'm sorry. I'm out of ideas. I dropped him off at his place at nine so I could go home to bed, and he said he was going to do the same. I remember specifically because he said, 'You can tell your boss I'm being a good little hockey player.' What else could I do? Short of sleepovers, I just ..." He mouths wordlessly, and even though I try not to be softhearted when it comes to work, I do feel for him. He has a family he's barely seen for the last month, thanks to being solely assigned to Oskar.

The PR department is supposed to look after the entire team, but it's true what they say about twenty percent of the people taking up eighty percent of the time. In this case, Oskar is the complete twenty percent all to himself.

I'd thought giving him a direct PR liaison would help him make better choices, but Keerson is the third person I've assigned to him, and the third person to completely fail at keeping up. At this rate, San Jose is going to fire my ass and find someone better equipped to deal with the situation.

Oskar should be the one getting fired, but he's too damn good at what he does. Team management has made it clear that it's our job to put an end to the scandals. It's kind of hard to do that when he has threesomes in seedy alleys.

I rub my jaw, gaze straying back to the screen and where Oskar has his hand down one of the guys' pants while the other drops to his knees. It might be my imagination, but I swear Oskar's eyes keep flicking to the surveillance camera, and if that bastard knew it was there, he won't need to worry about being fired—I'll kill him myself.

"This is my fault," I say, finally tapping my keyboard to pause the video. "I've put too much on the rest of you when you have lives outside of work. Unluckily for Oskar Voyjik, that won't be a problem for me. I'm a thirty-nine-year-old, single workaholic who will do anything for this team."

Keerson cracks a smile. "Are you ... do you mean ..."

"It's my turn. If I can't sort him out, they might as well fire me now."

He cringes because we both know that while my words are light, it's a very real possibility. "He's, ah, waiting in the hall."

Oskar Voyjik showing patience? I wouldn't have guessed that.

"Good. At least he can follow *some* directions." Still, I need a minute before I can face him. A minute to gather my weak professionalism and remind myself that his flirting is all bullshit. He might be my exact type, but I absolutely cannot look at him that way unless I want to kiss my career goodbye.

"Are you sure you can manage?" Keerson asks. "He's a handful, and you already have a busy schedule."

"I know how to delegate. If this is where my focus needs to be, then so be it." I compulsively straighten my desk. "Send him in on your way out."

Keerson jumps up, clearly relieved to be free, and I watch him all the way to the door, refusing to let my focus slip back to the monitor beside me. Murmured voices sound from the hall, and it's easy to pick Oskar's low, scratchy tone.

A second later, he walks in and closes the door, and my resolve about being professional flies out the window.

All the air in the room suctions his way, like there's this great gravitational pull toward the man who is literally sex on legs. From his just-been-fucked dark blond hair to the scruff on his jaw, his intense eyes, and those sexy tattoos all over his body, every day is a mission to be good.

Especially when he opens his mouth.

"*Mr.* Pierce." His confidence takes all the air in the room as he stalks closer and takes the seat opposite mine.

I lean back in my chair, holding his gaze and doing everything in my power to show he has no effect on me. He might be hot, but my willpower always holds. "Look at that, you do know how to be respectful."

His lips quirk. "When it gets me what I want, I do."

"Is what you want to continue playing for this team? Because if so, your professionalism could use some work."

I tilt my screen toward him and hit Play, right at the moment things start to heat up. Oskar doesn't react at all to the footage—not that I thought he would.

"Interesting …" he says.

"Not the first word that comes to my mind."

He sniggers. "It's interesting that you've watched so much of it. Like what you see?"

"Personally, of course, we both know how good-looking you are." And for the first time since he walked in, he looks like I've said something unexpected. I never should have admitted that, but I'm an openly gay man with eyes. He'd know I was lying if I said otherwise. Good-looking might not be an apt description, or enough of one, because when it comes to Oskar Voyjik, I don't think there're enough words in the dictionary to describe how sexy he really is. "Professionally, this makes me want to hit you over the head with a hockey stick."

"You're not the first person to say that to me."

"Not surprising at all."

Oskar threads his hands through his hair and leans back, lifting the front two legs of the chair from the ground, and mimicking my relaxed posture. "You know, if you're into corporal punishment, I hear spanking is more effective."

"I have something better in mind."

He eyes me. "I'm not a fan of paddling, but I suppose I could give it a try."

And damn that asshole, a laugh slips from me. "I'll keep that information in my back pocket. But no. Congratulations, *Mr.* Voyjik, you've been upgraded. You're looking at your new PR minder."

"You?" He doesn't look anywhere near as worried as he should. "Aren't I below your pay grade?"

"If you're calling yourself cheap, I'm not going to argue, but don't worry, I like getting my hands dirty."

"Cheap and dirty. If I didn't know better, I'd say you were coming on to me."

"Do you talk to all your PR managers this way? Because it would explain why you've been through so many in the last few years."

"Only the hot ones." He winks, and he has no right to make it look so smooth. "Cute of you to assume this club revolves around me though."

I don't point out that it basically does. It was a fast lesson I learned when I was first accepted for this position and moved to San Jose. It's why I'm bothering with trying to control him in the first place. The reasons given for the high turnover of my position have been bogus things like *scheduling conflicts* and *culture fits* when I know that the actual reason is sitting right in front of me. If San Jose had any other players with even an ounce of Oskar's talent, I can guarantee he'd be out on his ass already. So the way I see it is I either need to step in and help the coaches find a D-man with Oskar's talent or keep him under the thumb. And if I can pull Oskar Voyjik in line, I'll have teams lining up to work with me.

I give him a benign smile. "Feel free to drop off a key whenever you get a chance."

His calculating eyes narrow. "Key?"

"I know we'll be together a lot of the time, but I'd like to have the freedom to come and go as I please."

His chair *thunks* back to the ground. "Back up. I'm not following."

"You want to act like a child? Fine. We're playing by kindergarten rules now, and from today, the buddy system is officially in place."

"I don't think I like where this is going."

"Probably a good thing since this *is* a punishment." I tuck my hands behind my head this time because while this isn't an official dick-measuring contest, I'm sure as hell going to show Oskar who's in charge. "The buddy system is simple. I know where you are at all times. At *all* times. You won't need to call us to clear if you can go out or not, because when you do, I'll be right there beside you. And the only way for me to monitor you that closely is to move into your spare room."

The worry I'm expecting doesn't come. "Technically, if you want twenty-four seven supervision, you really should share my bed. You know, to be safe."

"We both know sharing a bed would be the furthest thing from safe. And like I said, this is a punishment."

He sneers. "There's no way management is agreeing to that."

"I think you're underestimating how far management is willing to go for these antics"—I point to the screen, where Oskar and his guys are finishing up—"to go away."

"So … what? Sleepovers at home, sharing a room at away games?" He pumps his eyebrows. "I hear Ezra and Anton made great use of their shared rooms while they were on the road."

"And you will make great use of ours too. By not sneaking out and going right to sleep."

"I don't know whether it's adorable or naive that you think following me around will stop me."

"I don't know whether it's adorable or naive that you think I'm not up to the challenge."

We hold each other's stare for a moment, and I know Oskar is puzzling out how to play this. On one hand, the whole situation isn't ideal—for me as well as him—but on the other, I know that backing down isn't in his nature.

He'll agree, if for no other reason than his need to prove he can outsmart me.

"Fine." The smile he gives me is dangerous. "I've always wanted a roomie."

"Oh, Mr. Voyjik. You should be careful what you wish for."